LEARNING BY DOING...

"Well, Jimmy, I think I'm just going to have to take this Dralthi for a test drive. Better stand clear."

Even through the helmet faceplate, Hunter could see the tech's eyes widen. "But, sir — " he protested.

Hunter ignored him, popped the bottom hatch and crawled up into the alien fighter. *This's a peculiar way to do things,* he thought, climbing up into the cockpit and sliding over into the pilot's chair. He latched the hatch, listening as it automatically sealed to become airtight. His spacesuit readings said that the cockpit was slowly pressurizing with breathable air. *Good.* He wriggled in the seat, trying to make it feel more comfortable. The seat was made of plant fibers woven into a chair, with a large empty spot at the back of the chair ... *for the cat's tail,* he decided. The seat was too large for him, but he strapped himself in anyhow. As his suit readouts switched to green, indicating that the cockpit was fully pressurized, he popped his faceplate; the suit had twenty minutes on the emergency tank, but there was no reason to use it now.

"Hunter, are you authorized for this?" Jimmy's voice said anxiously through the speakers in Hunter's helmet.

"Not a problem, mate!" Hunter replied, looking in perplexity at the control panel. All of the controls were labelled in the odd vertical letters of the Kilrathi language, which Hunter had never learned to read. *But that looks like a joystick, and that's for air pressure ... I don't know what that is but I'm sure I won't need it, and that looks like an engine power gauge ... I wonder what that switch is next to it?*

He pressed it ....

WING COMMANDER™

FREEDOM FLIGHT

MERCEDES LACKEY
ELLEN GUON

BAEN
BOOKS

FREEDOM FLIGHT

This is a work of fiction. All the characters and events portrayed in this book are fictional, and any resemblance to real people or incidents is purely coincidental.

A Baen Books Original

Wing Commander is a registered trademark of ORIGIN Systems, Inc. All rights reserved. Used herein under license from ORIGIN Systems, Inc.

Baen Publishing Enterprises
P.O. Box 1403
Riverdale, NY 10471

ISBN: 0-671-72145-3

Cover art by Paul Alexander

First Printing, December 1992

Printed in the United States of America

Distributed by Simon & Schuster
1230 Avenue of the Americas
New York, NY 10020

• CHAPTER ONE

The interrogator's lip curled in a contemptuous snarl. "The traitor is silent. He cannot even speak in his own defense! This is not a highborn lord of Kilrah; this is a carrion-eater!"

Standing before the interrogator, Lord Ralgha *nar* Hhallas stared bleakly at his enemy. A green haze fogged Ralgha's eyes, the mist of rage. He fought to contain it, forcing his fur to lie flat, his ears to remain erect, his eyes to remain wide open and without visible guile. He won the battle with his instincts and emotions, as he had won the eight eights of similar battles during the past few hours. His vision came clear again, and the urge to tear out the throats of his enemies — any enemies — subsided. He knew from the posture of the burly guards watching him that he had not betrayed himself by so much as a tail-twitch.

He could not falter, could not show fear, even for an instant. In this test of loyalties, any sign of weakness would be instant proof of treason . . . a true Kilrathi would be upheld and strengthened by his Honor, impervious to pain or fear. No torture would break him, no threats would touch his spirit. If Ralgha showed no fear, if he remained calm and steadfast throughout this ordeal, then he could not be a traitor.

So does age and experience deceive youth and vigor.

Had he been in charge of this interrogation, *he* would have had his captive wired and monitored. Perhaps he should be glad that someone like him was not in charge. But blood would tell, and breeding; that was a truism. Breeding would carry him through this. He had to believe that.

A whisper of sound from the shadow-shrouded figure seated at the end of the room. "Can he be trusted, Kalrahr?"

Ralgha *nar* Hhallas stiffened to attention, the hair of his ruff and spine rising despite his efforts to make it lie flat, uncertain whether he was going to survive the next few moments. He had seen this shadowy room before, and had walked through the carved stone corridors of Imperial Intelligence Headquarters on Ghorah Khar many times, but always as Lord Ralgha *nar* Hhallas, commanding officer of the *Ras Nik'hra,* a Fralthi-class cruiser that had fought in many battles for the glory of the Emperor of Kilrah.

Now, for the first time, he saw these walls through other eyes . . . as a prisoner. An interesting experience — if he lived through it.

Ralgha had stood in the center of this room for over five hours now, answering every question placed to him, patiently managing to keep his temper despite the taunts of the interrogators. That was their job, after all; to make him lose his temper, to prove that he was a traitor by angry word or action. They dared not lay paw to him; he was too high of rank for *lerkrath,* interrogation by drugs, or *kalkrath,* interrogation by torture. Only the Emperor himself could decree questioning a *Thrak'hra* lord by needle or knife. But they could deliberately try to provoke him, to invoke the killing-rage that lay close to the surface of every Kilrathi's mind — and if he lost control even for an instant, if he neglected to remain in the military-submissive posture, if he forgot that he was, temporarily, the lowest-ranked Kilrathi in the room, he would prove that he was a traitor. Even now, the two burly Imperial guards watched him carefully, in case he should try to make any kind of movement — either to escape or harm Jahkai, the Kalrahr of Imperial Security, or to make an attempt on the life of the other, even more important Kilrathi in this room, the one seated in the shadows.

Jahkai was watching him with eyes narrowed to slits with his concentration. As well he might. There was more to this than the questioning of a possible traitor; more than a conflict between two male Kilrathi. Ralgha had hated Jahkai since they had first met years ago.

The lowborn brute had pretended to noble airs at a troop review, bringing shame on the highborn present, that he had *dared* to imitate his betters. And there was no hiding the fact that Jahkai was lowborn; one merely had to look at him, and see the mottled, mingled colors of his coarse fur marking him as *Kilra'hra*, a commoner. So very unlike Ralgha's own sleek pelt, bright with the colours and sharply distinct patterns of one of the highest-born families in the Empire. Even the blunt shape of Jahkai's muzzle, the flatness of his head, and the blunted teeth of one who was not a hunter showed his lowborn breeding.

Ralgha had repaid that shame by shaming Jahkai in his turn, making a mockery of him, then laughing in his face, not realizing then that Jahkai was Kalrahr of Imperial Security for the entire planetary system of Ghorah Khar. . . .

Now the situation was very different. A word from Jahkai could condemn Ralgha to death, low-born or not. If the other Kilrathi in this room decided that the word was justified. It had all come down to this; the word of an enemy, the record of his achievements, and the judgment of a superior.

This was the most dangerous moment of his life. Nothing else had ever put him into such peril, not even during the battle against the humans for the Vega Sector.

He remembered that conflict with a small warmth of pride, pride he cherished against the anger that sought to consume him. He concentrated on his memories of the hours of maneuvering against the Terran ship, waves of fighter assaults, culminating in the glorious explosion of the Waterloo-class ship, the blossoming fireball and drifting debris. The ship had been named the *Leningrad,* he had learned later, and over five hundred humans had died when it had been destroyed. Five hundred enemies. Five hundred gifts to Sivar, the War God.

He remembered one moment of fear in that battle, seeing a tiny Terran fighter diving toward his ship, knowing that half of their forward cannons were disabled and there was nothing he or his crew could do to stop it. . . .

. . . then the wing of Imperial Jalthi fighters had banked in sharply and destroyed the human ship with a well-aimed volley.

Now Ralgha felt that same paralyzing fear, watching

his fate being decided before him, and knowing that there was nothing he could do about it at all.

Again, the purring whisper. "I am waiting for your answer, Jahkai."

Kalrahr Jahkai turned and spoke to the shadowed figure seated in the corner of the room. "My lord, I cannot say. In five hours, we have neither seen nor heard a single hint of treason from Lord Ralgha. But...."

Ralgha stood silently, muscles locked in the rigidity of submissive fear, and wished with all his heart that he was back in the battle for the Vega Sector, commanding the crew of the *Ras Nik'hra* against the Terran fleet. At least then, he had an obvious opponent to fight. Not this shadow-war of loyalties and treason, where a single gesture could result in his immediate death. They would not even grant him the honor of death in combat... he could die in this room, shot like a coward or a prisoner of war, and no one would ever know....

"Enough." The tall Kilrathi rose from his chair in the corner of the room, striding forward to face Ralgha. Prince Thrakhath, Heir to the Throne of Kilrah, stared into his eyes, thoughtful and calculating. Gold rings glistened in Thrakhath's ears, bright against his red-brown fur and his red cloak. The spicy musk of one who dallied often with females wafted to Ralgha's nostrils, but Ralgha refused to be distracted by it. "Tell me, Ralgha... who do you serve?"

"The glory of the Emperor and the Empire of Kilrah," Ralgha said, stiffly. "I am yours to command, my Prince."

"Yes." The Prince spoke quietly, his voice low and

resonant in the small room. "I believe you are, Ralgha. You will do well." The Prince turned to the intelligence officer. "Enough of this farce, Jahkai. I had suspected a personal animosity when you brought me your suspicions; now I am certain of it. We are finished here. I will return to K'Tithrak Mang tonight. *You* will give up this grudge of yours. And to ensure that there will be no repetition of this — scene — I require that you bring me concrete proof of deceit before you make any further accusations."

Jahkai flattened his ears and lowered his muzzle submissively; his tail dragged on the ground, completely limp. Though his eyes were still full of hate when he looked at Ralgha, the *Thrak'hra* lord was certain that he would not dare disobey the Prince's orders. He held his rank on sufferance alone, and many hated him. They would be glad to see him fall.

The Prince glared down at Jahkai. "The Lord Ralgha may return to his usual duties." The Prince glanced at Ralgha. "What are your standing orders, Lord Ralgha?"

Ralgha brought his head up, at full attention. "My ship leaves for the N'Tanya System tonight, my lord," Ralgha said. "We are to join the strike force departing for the Terran frontier."

The Prince nodded. "You will bring honor to your *hrai*, I am certain of it. Fight well, Ralgha."

"My lord." Ralgha bowed his head, his tail curled down in a gesture of respect and submission; careful not to spoil his show of appropriate behavior by displaying the shock the Prince's last statement had given him. *He cannot know,* Ralgha thought. *All of my* hrai, *down to my littlest sibling . . . dead now, these last five years. I have no family now, no way to share the honors I have won in combat. No one, nothing worth living for. . . .*

My only joy has been fighting the humans. Killing as many of them as I can, for the glory of the Empire. Taunting them in battle, ignoring them as they call us "kitten" or "cat" . . . I wonder what a cat is? . . . and then rejoicing in my victory, hearing their death-screams. Winning honor for my hrai, for my family name.

Now that is meaningless. Without my hrai. . . .

Prince Thrakhath nodded once to Jahkai, and left the room. Ralgha began to follow him, but was stopped by a guard's claws on shoulder.

"You may not leave yet, Ralgha," Jahkai hissed in a low voice.

Had the lowborn learned *nothing*? If Ralgha had been younger, more given to impulse, Jahkai would have been dead at that moment. The chemicals of anger and fear still sang in his blood, and made his ears ring. "I am not one of your hirelings, Jahkai, or a human slave. Do not presume to give me orders. I am a lord of the Empire. Hinder me, and . . ." Ralgha smiled, showing teeth. "And I will rip out your throat, *Kilra'hra* scum."

"Fine words from a suspected traitor," Jahkai spat.

"Dangerous words from a low-born Kilrathi. Now that the Prince has cleared me of suspicion, you might wish to remember that I outrank you, fool." He narrowed his eyes, and allowed his neck-ruff to rise. "You are too unworthy to challenge. Would you like to spend some time in your own stockade? It is not very comfortable, as I have learned in these last days."

Jahkai gestured sharply, and the guards stepped

back. Ralgha smiled again, the full smile of the victor, all fangs exposed, and walked into the hallway. A few moments later, he was out in the street, breathing deeply of the clean air. He had been locked in a dark, damp cell for ten days, and in that time had not seen the warm sunlight on the leaves of the *birha* trees. They were blossoming now, large red flowers filling the air with a sweet scent. This street was lined with the trees, a sharp contrast to the stone buildings and grey-paved streets, the white-capped mountains overlooking the Old City. It reminded him of home, of his native planet of Hhallas, where he had lived his childhood, before spending his years in officer's training on Kilrah. Many Kilrathi said they admired the metallic splendor of Kilrah, the silver walls and tall towers of the Imperial planet. Not Ralgha . . . even after all these years he still yearned for the wild mountains and untamed wilderness of his home planet.

The sun was setting behind the icy peaks, bright against the snow. Ralgha began to walk quickly. There was not much time left, before he had to board his ship and order his crew for their departure.

He walked through the winding streets, stepping over an unconscious Kilra'hra that was thoroughly intoxicated on *arakh* leaves, walking past a group of slaves laboring in the street. At the next street, he turned into the open market, smelling the rich scents of fresh meat and fish displayed on carts and tables. The market was not too crowded at this hour, as the shopkeepers and carters had already sold most of their wares.

A young female human, with very short dark

head-fur and dressed in a plain brown shift decorated with the sigil of Sivar, looked up at Ralgha for a long moment as he strode past. A slave of the Priestesses of the Warrior-God, he guessed. He glanced back at the next corner, to see her only a few feet behind him. Following him, yes. He walked down the street, pausing in a doorway to let the female catch up with him. "What do you want, girl?" he asked gruffly.

"Eight eights of pardons, my lord," the girl said in heavily-accented Kilrathi. "Lady Hassa would speak with you, my lord. If you would please to follow me, I will take you to her now."

He nodded and followed her down the shadowed street. She moved with surprising grace, for a human. Ralgha had not had much experience with humans, except for a few slaves and, of course, captured enemy pilots, and those only for a few moments before they were taken away by Imperial Intelligence. He had heard many strange things about humans. The oddest was that the Terrans actually *chose* their leaders, like one would choose a fine cut of meat in the market. Just the thought of a leader chosen by his followers made Ralgha's tail twitch. Though what he did now, that was perilously close to what the humans did . . . selecting a leader.

As he had expected, the girl was leading him to the local Temple of Sivar, an ampitheatre set into the side of the mountain. He followed her down the stone steps, to where a tall Kilrathi woman, wearing the ceremonial cloak of a Priestess of Sivar, awaited him.

"Ralgha." Hassa moved toward him. In a gesture

that he remembered from their childhood on Hhallas, she ran her claws through his mane, smoothing down the thick fur. "You are well?"

He twitched his shoulders, deprecatingly. "As well as can be expected. They questioned me for days, Hassa."

Hassa nodded and turned to the slavegirl. "Esther, go fetch drink and *arakh* leaves for Lord Ralgha. Go now, quickly."

The human girl bowed and ran up the steps.

"You may speak freely now, my lord." Hassa sat on a stone bench. "What happened in there?"

Ralgha sat beside her, looking down at the plain grey stone. Too like the plain gray stone of his cell. "It was difficult, but not as bad as I thought it might be. Questions, day and night. They often would not allow me to sleep, but otherwise did not harm me."

"I was very worried, when I heard that you had been arrested." Hassa's eyes were dark and unreadable, all pupil. "We were afraid that you would reveal what you know of the rebellion."

He bristled at the implication of weakness. "Never! Even if they had tortured me, I would have revealed nothing!"

"So they set you free." Hassa's claws extended and retracted nervously. "They set you free . . . why?"

In a way, that puzzled him too. "I assume, because they could not find anything, nor trick me into giving them information. Because they believe that I am loyal to the Emperor. Because I am *Thrak'hra*, and a decorated ship's captain. Prince Thrakhath himself attended my final interrogation, and ordered them to release me."

"I see." Hassa was silent for a long moment, and

then spoke. "The Council met last night, Ralgha, while we were still uncertain as to your fate. They decided that if you survived the interrogation, they would have a task for you."

He flushed with the heat of excitement; his fur itched. After all this time — they had something they wanted him to do.

"We must gain help for this rebellion against the Emperor, if it is to succeed," she continued. "You will be our envoy, our ambassador . . . you will go to the humans and demand their assistance for us. We will be their allies, but they must send us troops, weapons, starships. You will surrender your ship, the *Ras Nik'hra*, to them as a gesture of good faith."

"Surrender . . . my ship?" Ralgha stared at her, so stunned with shock, he felt like a tiny *merdha* must, when the teeth of the hunter met in its neck. "Give it to the humans? My *ship*? How can you ask this of me?"

Hassa's face was fiercely adamant; he knew there would be no moving her. Though she cared for him as an old friend and beloved, the rebellion was something like an offspring to her. As a mother would abandon mate to fight for the life of a cub, she would give all to her cause. "You must! If you do not, Ralgha *nar* Hhallas, you are an oathbreaker. You swore an oath to the Council that you would aid us in overthrowing the Emperor . . . can you be forsworn now?"

He shook his head. "But the humans would destroy us on sight — "

She cut him off with a gesture. "We have communicated with the Terrans . . . there will be a ship waiting for you in the Firekka System, the *Tiger's*

Claw. You will give the *Ras Nik'hra* to them, and tell them of our rebellion."

Silence hung between them for a long time, as Ralgha fought his emotions again, and considered what she had said in as dispassionate a light as he could manage under the circumstances. "I will do this," Ralgha said slowly. "I must. I will not be forsworn. But I know what it means . . . I will never be able to return. I will never see you, or my home of Hhallas again." He looked up at the mountain above them, the first stars beginning to appear in the night sky. "Sometimes I wonder if we should ever have left our planet, Hassa. We were so happy there as children, we could have stayed there . . . perhaps I should have claimed you as my mate and bearer of my children when I had the chance. Years ago, before politics and soldiering claimed my life, and the Lord Sivar claimed yours."

Hassa touched his face hesitantly. "Do you think we would have been happy, Ralgha? Living out our lives in the mountains of Hhallas? A life without honor, without a future? I think not. Better to burn brightly, if only for a short time, than never to have truly lived at all. I have no regrets." She glanced up at the entrance of the ampitheatre. "Where is that human child? She only had to cross the street to the house, not run across the entire city!"

Hassa climbed the steps, looking out into the street. She turned back to Ralgha, too slowly to be casual, and walked down to where he waited.

"There are Imperial soldiers outside my house," she said quietly. "Ralgha, you must go. They will doubtless search here next, when they realize I am not in my home. Something must have gone wrong."

Fear for her, and anger, made his voice into a growl; his claws extended, and his neck-ruff rose. "But what of you, Hassa?"

She raised head and tail proudly. "I am a priestess of Sivar, sworn to his glory. I will not run away or hide, there is no honor or courage in that." She touched the ritual knife sheathed at her belt. "If they come for me, I will be ready."

He could say nothing; his instinct urged him to stay and fight at her side; his duty told him to go.

She gave him a long, searching look, as if trying to memorize his face. "Go now, and quickly. Deliver our message and your ship to the humans, Ralgha." She pointed to the other exit of the ampitheatre, a small doorway that led into the twisting warren of the streets of the Old City. A moment more, as conflicting urges warred within him, then duty won. He turned to go.

The door opened on silent hinges, and Ralgha slipped through. Beyond the vine-covered alcove, the street was deserted. Ralgha strode away from the ampitheatre as a squad of soldiers, dressed in uniforms with the black sigil of Imperial Security, marched past him toward the main entrance to the Temple of Sivar.

Ralgha walked quickly through the darkened streets, never once looking back.

On the bridge of the *Ras Nik'hra*, Kirha checked the weapons list one more time. "More heat-seeking missiles," he said, tapping his claw on the offending item. "At least twice as many heat-seeking missiles. Do you want our pilots to run out of missiles when they're flying against the humans?"

Did you think I was so young and inexperienced *that I would overlook that mistake?* Kirha thought with contempt. *No, I have studied with the finest officer in the Emperor's service, and Lord Ralgha nar Hhallas would never let his pilots go into combat with less than the ordnance they require.* "Attend to this immediately," Kirha said aloud.

The Ordnance Officer bowed to him, walking away. "And do it quickly, we are supposed to depart within the hour!" Kirha called after him, putting an edge of anger into his voice. The officer doubled his pace as he hurried off the bridge.

Kirha subvocalized a growl, and prowled the bridge. "Has anyone seen Lord Ralgha?" Kirha asked the under-officers taking their places and making their pre-flight checks. "He should have been here by now."

The Pilot Officer bared his teeth as Kirha moved past him. "Perhaps they haven't let him out of prison yet," he said, a hint of something Kirha could not read in his voice.

Kirha spun, his claws at the Pilot Officer's throat before the other officer could react. He could feel the other's pulse beneath his pad-tips, beating very quickly. "Do not speak so of Lord Ralgha, if you expect to survive this expedition," Kirha hissed. "He has been mistakenly accused; he will be acquitted of this false stain upon his honor. He will be here in time. I know he will." He released the officer's throat, leaving several welling points of bright red blood on the other Kilrathi's brown fur. "Attend to your duties, officer."

"Of course, sir." The Pilot Officer bowed, rather

unsteadily, and turned back to his computer console for his pre-flight checks.

Where is Lord Ralgha? Kirha asked himself, his stomach stretched tight and hard with tension, looking around at the flurry of activity aboard the crowded bridge. *He must be here soon, he must. . . .*

The lift doors opened, and Lord Ralgha nar Hhallas strode onto the bridge, his cloak fluttering behind him. Immediately, Kirha felt his stomach relax. The commanding officer was here; all was well. The world was now proceeding as it should.

"Khantahr on the bridge!" Kirha called, and immediately knelt before his superior officer. The other officers knelt as well, as Ralgha surveyed the bridge. "Who is the new Pilot Officer?" Lord Ralgha asked Kirha.

"Drakj'khai nar Ghorah Khar, my lord," Kirha said quietly. The other officers stood and returned to their duties, but the Pilot Officer still knelt before the *Khantahr.* "He replaces Rakti, who still has not recovered completely from his honorable wounds received when fighting the humans in the Vega Sector."

"Are you oathsworn to another *Khantahr,* Drakj'khai?" Lord Ralgha inquired mildly.

The Pilot Officer looked up at Lord Ralgha, and there was mingled fear and respect in his expression and posture. Kirha was pleased. The *Thrak'hra* lord was an imposing enough Kilrathi to demand anyone's respect. "My previous kalrahr released me from my oath when I was transferred to the *Ras Nik'hra,* my lord."

"Swear fealty to me now," the lord said, pointedly

ignoring the spots of blood on the Pilot Officer's throat.

Kirha stood at attention as the Ghorah Kharran spoke the ceremonial words, binding his life to that of his lord. A small thread of blood trickled down Drakj'khai's neck as he recited the ritual speech and completed it by baring his throat to the *Thrak'hra's* claws. Ralgha's claw-tips rested lightly on the blood-spots where Kirha's claws had been; then he let the Pilot Officer rise.

"I accept your oath," Ralgha said, and turned to Kirha. "Your report, Kirha?"

"The seventh engine has failed its preliminary testing. The technicians are working on that now," Kirha recited. "We are awaiting a complete shipment of heat-seeking missiles; the shipment we received is only half of what we need. Two of the crew are not yet aboard the ship and Security has been unable to find them in the Old City."

Lord Ralgha nodded. "Send a message to Security that if our missing crewmen do not appear by our departure time, they are to be housed in detention until our return. Also, tell the Navigation Officer to make certain that we have the most current starmaps for the Firekka System before we depart."

Firekka?

"But, sir — " Kirha began, as Lord Ralgha walked to the lift.

Ralgha spoke over his shoulder. "I will be inspecting the ship for the next hour. You have my comlink number if you need to consult with me about anything, Kirha."

We are not supposed to go to Firekka!

"Sir — "

Ralgha did not even slow his steps.

Kirha glanced around the crowded bridge, knowing that he still had tasks to complete here, but . . . he had to know. He ducked around two technicians working on the weapons control console, leaping into the lift with Lord Ralgha just before the doors closed. The lift silently descended toward the Launch Bays.

"What is it, little cub?" Ralgha asked, a hint of amusement in his voice. "Do you wish to inspect the ship as well?"

"My lord." Kirha bowed before him, his hands raised with claws retracted. "I would not question your orders, but . . . are we not to depart for the N'Tanya System, not Firekka? I saw our orders as they came in from K'Tithrak Mang . . . why do we need starmaps for the Firekka System?"

Ralgha leaned against the wall of the lift. He looked very tired, Kirha thought. "Kirha, our . . . our orders have been changed. Tonight we leave for Firekka."

"But those orders did not arrive with the Imperial courier, my lord. How did we receive these new orders?" Kirha asked hesitantly.

Lord Ralgha reached out and pulled the switch that locked the lift in mid-transit. Kirha froze as it hissed to a halt. "Kirha . . . I must have one person that I can speak freely with aboard this ship. I have always trusted you. Can I trust you now?"

Kirha looked at him, completely bewildered by the strange words, then knelt before him, raising his chin to present his throat. "I am oathsworn to you, my lord. My life is yours. Do you not remember the day that my father delivered me to your service? I was only a tiny cub, but that day will always burn brightly in my memory. My family has served your *hrai* for over ten generations; I serve you now, as my offspring will serve as well. You can trust me with your life and your honor, my lord." He rose to his feet, standing at attention before his lord.

Lord Ralgha considered that for a moment before speaking. "You are correct, Kirha, our orders are to report to the Fleet Kalrahr in the N'Tanya System, to join with a strike force departing for Deneb Sector. But my honor requires that we go to the Firekka System."

Kirha tried not to look like a lowborn country-cub, with his jaw gaping in shock at everything he saw. But it was hard not to gape, with mingled surprise and confusion. "But why, sir?"

Ralgha huffed out a sigh. It sounded melancholy. Kirha had never heard his lord sound melancholy before. "What do you know of my *hrai*, Kirha?"

Kirha looked at him uncertainly. "All of your *hrai* were killed on that ship on Hhallas, several years ago. Most of my family, their retainers, died that day as well. Only you survived, as you were fighting the humans at the time. I would have died as well, if I had been aboard that ship rather than defending the estates from the humans."

But he knows all this —

"Why did they die?" Ralgha continued, inexorably, although Kirha thought that he detected pain in his lord's voice now, a pain that he shared. He did not want to think of this. He did not want to remember it.

But his lord demanded it of him.

"It was . . . it was an accident." he said with difficulty,

his voice low and hoarse. "The local kalrahr thought it was one of the human ships, and fired on the ship before confirming the indentification code. But you know this, my lord!" he said, with growing desperation. "Why do you ask me of it now?"

But Ralgha was not through. "And what did you feel, cubling," he asked, in a voice flat and dull, "when you learned of the accident?"

Kirha clenched his fists, remembering the rage he had felt that day, the rage that still chilled him inside. "I wanted to kill humans. It was because of the humans that everyone of your *hrai* died, that my parents and siblings were killed as well. That was when I asked you to take me with you, to serve you here aboard the *Ras Nik'hra,* to let me fight against the humans."

"And was there any honor in my *hrai*'s deaths?" his lord said quietly.

Kirha stared at him, as if he had suddenly turned into an alien creature. *No honor? But —*

"I will tell you what you do not know," Ralgha continued. "The humans attacked Hhallas in retaliation for *our* destruction of several of *their* colonies, which we attacked after some failed battle, trying to capture more human territory. . . ." His voice trailed off, and he shook his shoulders, sadly. "Can you not see it, Kirha? The futility of it all? There was no honor in the deaths of my *hrai,* or your family. They were nothing more than game pieces, and they meant nothing to the players of either side. Their deaths served *no purpose,* Kirha."

Kirha felt as if he was balancing on the edge of a void, his lord's words battering against all that he had believed in. His claws extended, as if to keep him from falling into the lightless depths.

"The humans are the first alien race we have encountered that we have not conquered outright," Ralgha continued. "We have fought against them for many years now, and there is no end to this war in sight. And all that we do — *all* — is to trade conquered territories. We are no closer to winning this war than we were when we began it."

Kirha shook his head, trying to understand, and feeling his stomach tense again with unhappiness. "But the humans are inferior to us, a prey-species! We have not won this war yet, but Kilrah will be triumphant! You know that we will conquer them eventually!"

"Will we?" Ralgha bared his teeth, and Kirha drew back at the burning look in his Khantahr's eyes. "What if we cannot? How many lives have we spent in this war, with no true victory? We win a system, and lose another. What do we gain by this? And what does it cost us, this exercise in futility?"

"But we must fight them!" Kirha protested. "That is our destiny! What are we if we are not warriors?"

Lord Ralgha nodded grimly. "I do not know. But it would be interesting to find out, eh?"

"I — I don't understand, my lord." He felt very small, smaller than a cub, and as helpless as a prey-beast in a corner.

"I doubt it will happen in your lifetime, Kirha." He paced the short width of the lift. "Only a few among our people have seen the truth, that this war is a pointless exchange of territories. There is no honor in it, or victory, because both sides will lose more than they can gain. If we could truly conquer the humans . . . then, perhaps, there would be glory for us. But without any hope of victory, what is the purpose of this war? There is only death. Meaningless death, with no honor or glory in it. And for what? The glory of the Emperor? That useless fool whose backside warms the Throne of Kilrah, who has not fought for decades, who does not realize the price of this war?"

"My lord, you speak . . . you speak treason," Kirha said slowly, the shock of his master's words reverberating through him. "Treason against the Emperor. . . ."

Ralgha glanced at him. "Yes, cubling. Now you know the truth. For two years now, I have been working with the rebels on Ghorah Khar, attempting to overthrow the Empire. That is why I was arrested, though they could not prove my connection to the rebels, and that is why we now must go to the Firekka System. Where I will contact the humans and . . . and surrender this ship to them."

The void had opened beneath Kirha's feet, and he fell into it. Shock held him rigid. "S-surrender the ship? My lord, you cannot! What of yourself, and the crew?"

"We will become prisoners of war." Ralgha's mouth tightened so that the tips of his fangs showed against the taut skin. "If they do not kill us outright. So, Kirha? Do you still obey me, cubling?"

"You are my liege lord, and I am yours to kill or command," Kirha said automatically, finding some comfort in the ritual words. "I will always obey your orders, my lord. But I do not wish to be a prisoner of war. Let me kill myself instead." Here was a way out of his confusion, and he raised his head in hope.

"Can you allow me this, Lord Ralgha?"

Ralgha's lips curled back in something like a smile. "Perhaps I can find some alternative for you, Kirha. Trust me in this, I will not compromise your honor if I can. You have served me too loyally for that." He pushed the lever of the lift, which lurched back into motion, descending to the Launch Bay. "Now, you have duties to attend to, cubling. I will return shortly to the Bridge for a complete report."

Kirha went numb, taking refuge in duty. "As you wish, my lord," he said automatically.

The lord stepped out of the lift as the doors opened to the huge Launch Bay, the Jalthi and Dralthi fighters assembled in neat rows like soldiers for his review.

Kirha closed his eyes and leaned against the curved wall of the lift as the doors closed again. *How can my lord do this?* he asked himself. *How can he ask me to follow him into dishonor, and surrender to the humans?*

I am sworn to him, the last of his hrai, *as he is the last of mine. I will not disobey him. He is my liege lord, and my Lord Ralgha, and I will not fail him.*

But I do not wish to surrender to the humans. I would rather die . . . I would rather die. . . .

● CHAPTER TWO

"I'll raise you ten," Hunter said, propping his feet up on the table and fanning himself with his hand of cards. The temperature controls in the pilots' barracks were on the fritz again, and it was just a little too warm in the room.

Though it ought to feel just like home, he reminded himself. *Hot and muggy, not a breeze in sight, with just that cozy little hint in the air of mildew and old tennis shoes. And they wonder why I smoke cigars. Home on the bilabong, mates.*

Like the rest of the systems in the Confederation carrier *Tiger's Claw,* the cooling system was over eleven years old, and starting to show its age.

Like all the rest of us, I guess. "How 'bout it, mate?" he asked the the only remaining player.

"Too rich for my blood," the young redheaded lieutenant said. "Folding." Lieutenant Peter "Puma" Youngblood looked like he'd bitten into something sour as he tossed his cards onto the table.

Hunter grinned around the fat cigar in his mouth and reached for the small pile of chips. "Thank you, thank you. You're all too kind, financin' my leave." He picked up a small blue plastic chit out of the pile, a voucher for the planetary shuttle, and smiled at the young Japanese woman next to him. "Thanks for the shuttle ticket,

Mariko," he said. "That'll be real useful for my trip downside to the planet tonight."

Mariko sighed, and shook her shoulder-length black hair away from her neck again. "You are welcome to my seat on that shuttlecraft, Hunter. I will be on duty for the next week, now that Colonel Halcyon has changed the duty roster. I hope you have a pleasant stay on Firekka."

"Thank you, m'dear," he said, dropping the voucher into his pocket. "I'm looking forward to it." He picked up the rest of the cards and began shuffling them with deft motions. "Anyone up for another hand of seven-card stud, or maybe five card draw?"

Iceman shook his head and gathered up his few remaining chips. "You've already won enough of my pay for this week, Hunter."

Lieutenant Youngblood, one of the new pilots who was visiting from the TCS *Austin*, the sister ship to the TCS *Tiger's Claw* for this mission, looked like he'd rather spit. "No thank you, Captain St. John," he said tersely, in an obvious effort to be polite, and left the room.

My, my. Them Yanks surely can be sore losers.

"Prickly little runt, isn't he?" Hunter observed after Youngblood slammed the barracks hatchway shut behind him.

"He's young and doesn't like to lose," Iceman said, and came about as close to a grin as he ever did. "He reminds me of you, Hunter, when you first transferred aboard the *Tiger's Claw*."

"Surprised you remember that far back, Iceman," Hunter drawled.

"Remember?" Iceman's eyebrows rose toward

his hairline. "None of us are likely to forget Lieutenant Ian St. John, callsign 'Hunter'. . . ." He shook his head, in mock mourning. "Oh yes, I remember when you came back from your first combat mission, swearing that the Kilrathi had never even managed to get close to you, and then all of us saw all the burn marks on the side of your ship. Looked like half your engines were fried!"

Hunter laughed. "And I've learned a lot since then . . . like when and how to lie!"

"You've learned, but you haven't changed," Mariko said in her gentle way. "You are my friend, but many times I feel that I do not know you. You are always so cheerful, always looking for the next 'good time.' Sometimes I wonder if any of this really matters to you, whether anything or anyone really touches you at all."

"What do you mean?" Hunter protested. "I risk my ass flying missions every week against the cats! That's not enough?"

"You fly missions for the adrenaline, not because of the enemy," Iceman said quietly. "I've seen it. That's how you are, Ian, whether you admit it or not."

"Well, enough pickin' on poor Hunter already! Let's play some cards!" Hunter put the cards, neatly shuffled, in the center of the table so that anyone could examine them if they chose. Old tradition, and no one felt the need to check for cheating. *Tiger's Claw* pilots didn't cheat, and with luck like Hunter had, he wouldn't have needed to anyway.

"Not me, Ian. I'm flying patrol at oh-six-hundred tomorrow, so I need to hit the sack," Iceman said, shoving his chair away from the table, and rising to his feet. "Good night, Ian, Mariko."

"G'night, Ice." Hunter grinned. "Thanks for the credit chips."

"I'll even the score next week, you'll see," Ice said from the hatchway.

"In your dreams, mate!" Hunter laughed. In the sudden quiet of the barracks, he glanced at Mariko. "So they're not lettin' you take any leave, lady? I'm surprised the Old Man is doing that to you, considerin' how well you flew in our last campaign."

Mariko Tanaka, callsign "Spirit," smiled and shook her head. "It is my choice and by my request, Hunter. I am too distracted now to enjoy a downside leave."

He knew why, unfortunately. *Those bastard cats. First her man gets transferred away from her, and now the buggers are trying to capture the installation he was sent to,* Hunter thought, wishing there was something he could do or say that would make any difference at all. Poor little Spirit, with her calm, remotely sad eyes and gentle ways . . . *Ah, Mariko, life hasn't been fair to you at all. First your dad's death, and now this. You're like a little sister to all of us here in the fighter squadron, and a damn fine pilot . . . I hate to see you hurtin' like this, girl.*

"Still no word from Epsilon Station?" Hunter asked gently. He thought he saw tears forming in the beautiful young woman's eyes as she looked away for a moment; but no, those dark eyes were calm and clear, as always. She would never show her pain; that was her strength and her weakness, both.

"The last report said that the station was still under assault, but that reinforcements were on the way," Spirit said, her voice as dispasssionate as if Philip was nothing more than a casual acquaintance. "My last communication from Philip was before the Kilrathi invaded the system. I have not heard from him since."

"Hell, your fiance is a tough guy, he'll do all right," Hunter said. "I remember arm-wrestling with him last time he visited the *Claw,* the bloke nearly sprained my wrist. He'll give the cats a good fight for their money, I'd wager on it. Next time you see 'im, he'll probably have a half dozen kills stenciled on his fighter!"

"I know, but it is so difficult, not knowing what is happening there. . . ." The dark-haired young woman managed a smile. "Better to stay here, and on duty, where I have other things to think of."

"But some downside leave might do you good," Hunter argued. "You could go see the sights; something new, something to think about! Go see one of them Firekkan Fire-Temples or something!"

"Maybe some of the squadron could all take leave together," Mariko suggested shyly. "Like a family. Go somewhere together. . . ."

"There's an idea," Hunter agreed heartily. "When we've finished playing babysitters to the Diplomatic Corps here in the Firekka System, and our Confed boys have chased those damn cats away from Epsilon Station, the entire squadron could take their leave together. Maybe we could go to Earth. Has your fiance ever seen Earth?"

"Only once, before I was stationed here on the *Tiger's Claw.* I have not been home in several years now," she said hesitantly. "Sometimes — I wonder if it has changed too much. Or I have — "

He clapped her on the shoulder, and turned it into a brotherly hug. "Then we'll do that, Mariko.

Tell you what, we'll go visit my old homestead. I'll treat you, Phil, and the squadron to some genuine Australian hospitality . . . I'm sure Grandma would love to have company out on the ranch, and we could do a little scuba-diving off the Barrier Reef. Hit a concert in Sydney. Get a friend of mine to show us the Rock, when 'is tribe isn't havin' a Dreamtime shindig. And then we can catch a low-orbital flight up to Tokyo and see your family. Just so long as I don't have to eat any of that raw fish, okay?"

"Sushi is very good food, Ian," Mariko began. "Very healthy for you, low in fat, high in minerals . . ."

He shook his head and laughed. "Not for me, sweetheart! I'll take you to the best steakhouse in Sydney. Costs a week's pay, but it's worth it!"

"Thank you, Hunter," Spirit said seriously.

"For what?" he asked.

"For making me think of something else. Anything else. It's been so difficult." She shook her head, as if to chase away whatever thought followed that. "So, tell me . . . when are you going down to the planet tonight?"

"The nineteen-hundred flight. Should be interesting. I'm curious to see the place," he said, keeping his tone light and bantering. "Great chance, actually, seeing the newest planet to join the Terran Confederation before it gets to look like everyplace else. Shotglass was telling me about them . . . the natives look kinda like parakeets. Big, six-foot-tall parakeets. But I've never met any of them." *Except for K'Kai, and I never really saw her, she was just a voice over the comlink . . . a vague kind of blur on the viewscreen.*

"I have seen vids of them," Spirit said. "They look like friendly people. Do you like birds, Hunter?"

He nodded. "I used to raise pigeons and doves back on my Grandma's ranch outside Sydney. It should be interestin'. A little excitement to liven things up." He sighed. "What a boring assignment. Honor Guard to the Diplomatic Corps . . . who'd have guessed they'd farm us out to *this,* after the Vega Campaign!"

Mariko sighed, and played with her remaining chips. "I think they gave us this assignment so that we would have some time to recuperate from Vega and Operation Thor's Hammer. I'm sure they were concerned about the effects of that many combat missions on our crew."

"Hey, we've all held up just fine under the stress!" he laughed.

"All?" she asked gently.

"Well. . . Except for Todd Marshall, who's completely slipped his leash, if you ask me." He shook his head unhappily. Marshall worried him. It was something that he and the other pilots in the squadron didn't talk about, their fears of being assigned the kid as a wingman. He was totally unpredictable now, possibly suicidal.

You don't want a guy like that on your wing, not if you were plannin' to come back from your mission.

"That boy never had his brains screwed in tight enough to start with, and with the stress of that last campaign . . . too much for him, I think. He sure picked his callsign right, Maniac fits him just fine now." He tried not to think of how Marshall might have "called" his own fate by picking that callsign in the first place. That's what some of the others were saying. Any more thoughts like that, and he'd start wondering what fate Spirit was calling with her chosen callsign. . . .

You're too damn superstitious, he scolded himself. *Don't get like the others, lookin' for omens and hangin' onto good-luck trinkets! Mariko is no more callin' her fate than Maniac called his!*

He picked up his flight jacket. "Well, I'd better start packing for the trip. See you when I get back, eh?"

"Enjoy your leave, Hunter," she said, smiling a little.

He just wished her smile hadn't looked so . . . faded.

Ten minutes later, Hunter was walking down the corridor to the flight deck, his haversack slung over his shoulder. He figured he had everything he'd need for the trip . . . a couple of sets of clothing, a carefully-folded Confed Navy Dress uniform for impressing the ladies, a pair of hiking boots for exploring the native turf, and several bottles of good Scotch. Couldn't go on shore leave without the Scotch . . . no telling what the Firekkan natives drank, but he figured the odds were against twelve-year single malts. He wondered if he should bring some rations with him, just in case they tried to feed him birdseed, too. *No, there are plenty of humans down there now, they've probably opened a bar and grill for all of us.*

There was already a line outside the flight deck for the downside shuttle. He nodded a greeting at the two flight deck technicians who were directly ahead of him in line, and one of the Bridge officers, who was wearing a brightly-coloured Hawaiian shirt and skirt instead of her usual crisp blue uniform.

Looks good, too, he thought, admiring her legs. *Hmm. Didn't realize quite how good. Have to look her up when we get downside. We're both Captains, even . . . that's a good opening line I can use, maybe. . . .*

No one from his squadron, though. In a way, Hunter wished that there was. Going downside with some of his closest friends, the people who flew combat missions with him every day, would've made this trip better. There was something about partying with the people who watched your back and had saved your life a few times — not to mention the fact that you'd done the same for them — that made downside leave more enjoyable. Mariko was right, they should try to organize a squadron trip someday. Someday when the Confederation didn't need them. . . .

Someday when they weren't spending watch after watch in the thick of battle, taking on the Kilrathi at impossible odds in one dogfight after another.

This was probably the closest to peace and quiet that they'd ever see. *I shouldn't bitch about this assignment, we could be getting our tails shot at by the cats. . . .*

"Captain, did you hear about the patrol that ran into a Kilrathi transport convoy?" It was one of the techs, a blond boy with a serious expression on his face. The kid looked maybe in his late teens. And scared as hell under the bravado.

God, we're robbing the cradle now to get our combat techs! Hunter thought. *How old is this kid? Eighteen? Nineteen?*

"Impossible," Hunter said. "There aren't any Kilrathi in this system. We're completely off their trade routes, and several jumps away from the battle front. That convoy must've gotten lost, jumped into the wrong system by mistake. Happens sometimes; even the cats get bad navigators once in a while."

The kid persisted, his blue eyes nervous. "But, Captain, what if the Kilrathi try to invade this system? We don't have any real forces, just us and the *Austin....*"

Hunter sighed. "Kid, don't let your imagination run away with you!" He took a closer look; noted the new look to the uniform, the spit-and-polish and regulation haircut. *Lord love a duck. Kid hasn't even got the shiny rubbed off him yet.* "Let me guess . . . you were assigned to the *Claw* after we came back from Goddard, right?"

The kid looked puzzled. "Yes, sir, but . . ."

Hunter interrupted him with a wave. "Don't go chasin' cats before you have to. And don't go seein' ghost-cats where there aren't any. You'll see real action soon enough, when we're reassigned to the battle front. In the meantime, you've got a whole planet to explore! Have you ever met an alien before, kid?"

"No, sir," the young man said earnestly.

Oh Lord. I can't stand it. Never could resist temptation. "Well, you're in for an interesting experience," Hunter said with a straight face. "The Firekkans are kind of like wasps, huge six-foot bugs with deadly stingers. You've heard that they catch mammals and tie them up in their nests to use as breeders for their young, right?" He paused, and the kid nodded vigorously, his eyes big and round.

Of course, he hadn't heard anything of the sort, but he wouldn't admit that to Hunter. Not to the Big Bad Fighter Pilot. . . . Hunter dropped his voice, and spoke in a confidential tone. "That's what happened to the exploration team that discovered Firekka, you know. They were trapped in one of the nests . . . we didn't know what happened to them for months, and by then, of course — " he paused again, for effect. " — it was too late."

The kid swallowed, visibly pale. "How — ah — interesting, sir."

Hunter shrugged. "Once they realized we were fellow sapients, they took us off the hunting list. Or — well, they were supposed to, anyway. Of course, some of the Firekkans don't want their planet to join the Confederation. So I'd be careful if someone invites you on a tour of a nest, if I were you. You might never make it back."

"Thank you for the advice, sir," the kid said, looking like he was going to be sick, right there on the flight deck.

The hatchway opened in front of them, and the shuttlecraft pilot stepped through. "Drop your duffles in the forward hatch, take a seat and buckle in," he droned, holding out his hand for the plastic vouchers.

"I don't . . . I don't think I want to go down to the planet after all," the young tech said faintly.

"Oh, come on, Jimmy!" his friend protested. "You can't back out on me now!"

The pilot watched this exchange with a bored expression, finally reaching out to yank the flight voucher from the kid's nerveless hand and shoving him forcefully toward the shuttle hatch. "Drop your duffle in the forward hatch, take a seat and buckle in," he muttered to Hunter, who smiled as he presented his shuttle voucher.

Hunter slid into one of the forward seats, closer to one of the clear ports that would give him a good view of the planet as they approached. A few minutes later, he heard the rumble of the shuttle's engines igniting, then the shuttle accelerated out of the launch bay and into open space. He tightened his seat straps again as they left the artificial gravity of the carrier. Someone's flight cap drifted upward to float near the ceiling as the shuttle banked away from the carrier, heading down toward the planet.

It's a very pretty world, Hunter thought, watching the planet through the port, growing larger and larger as the shuttle approached it. *Blue and white. . . Looks a little like Earth, with all those oceans. I've spent too much time in ship corridors and space stations, I'd forgotten how beautiful a planet can be.*

The ride down to the planet was bumpy with atmospheric turbulence, but no worse than some of the planetary combat missions Hunter had flown. The technician, he noticed, looked more and more nervous the closer they came to the planet's surface. The touchdown was gentle, considering that there wasn't an Automated Landing System yet for this planet. Hunter's opinion of the pilot's skills went up several points . . . he wasn't certain if *he* could've brought the shuttle down that smoothly. Through the viewport, he could see the barren rock of the landing strip, with red-brown mountains visible in the distance.

The pilot popped open the shuttle hatch almost as soon as the ship had stopped moving. Hunter picked up his haversack as he climbed down the ladder, looking around at this strange new world.

They were parked on a tall mesa of dark brown rock. Off to one side, Hunter could see a Firekkan nest tucked into another cliff face, the tall towers fashioned of what looked like tan reeds sewn together. It was larger than he'd expected, several dozen towers silhouetted against the sunrise.

And he saw his first Firekkan, as several of the alien creatures flew over the shuttlecraft, obviously curious about the new human arrivals. *Shotglass wasn't entirely right,* he thought, *They don't look exactly like parakeets. More like some kind of predatory bird, with that sharp beak and the brown and yellow feathers. Like a hawk, kind of.*

He wondered how they'd get across to the nest, when he saw the improvised rope bridge that had been slung over the gap. He started for the bridge, and heard an outraged yell from behind him. The technician, Jimmy. "Hey, they're not bugs at all! They're birds! They're six-foot birds!"

Hunter grinned, and pulled out a cigar. Maybe this shore leave wasn't going to be as boring as he'd thought. . . .

He was sweating by the time he got across the bridge; not from fear, like the tech, but from sheer exertion. He'd forgotten what it was like to balance your way across one of those things — basic training had been a long time ago.

"Anything to declare, Kep-tain?" asked a strange voice in his ear, as he paused to take a breath and ease the ache in his side.

He jumped, and turned. A tall Firekkan stood

beside him, half-hidden by the shelter of woven reeds.

"Like what?" he asked. *Customs! Son of a — brand new world, and already they're setting up Customs agents!*

The Firekkan cocked his head to one side. "Anything to sell," he said. "Anything to trade."

Hunter heaved a sigh of relief. He'd gotten off easily —

"Anything to drink," the Firekkan concluded. "Al-co-hol."

Aw, hell. Resigned, he unloaded his precious Scotch from his bag, and lined up the bottles on the Customs' table. The Firekkan watched impassively.

"Ten credits' duty," he said. And as Hunter started to object, added, "each."

"What?" Hunter yelped. "This is personal consumption only! This is highway robbery! This is — "

"Ten credits each," the Firekkan replied impassively. "You have choice. Pay duty, or — " He pulled a box from beneath the table, containing padding, a roll of tape, and a marker. " — or you send back to ship on shuttle."

Well, there *was* no choice. Paying the duty would seriously cut into his funds. Grumbling, he packed up the bottles with careful, loving hands, sealed the box, and wrote name and ID on it. The Firekkan added it to a stack of similar boxes behind him, and even as Hunter watched, one of the loading crew came to take it back to the shuttle he had just left. He sighed, watching his lovely Scotch going back home . . . leaving him behind.

"Have you an escort, Kep-tain?" the Firekkan asked as he watched.

"I'm supposed to meet Captain K'Kai here," he

muttered, wondering what he was supposed to drink now. Water? It would be a damn poor shore-leave. . .

"Ah. Kep-tain K'Kai is waiting for pilot-Kep-tain. There." The Firekkan pointed with his beak, towards the right. "Look for sign of Red Flower."

"Thanks," Hunter replied, trying very hard not to sound as sour as he felt. He started off in the indicated direction.

"And Kep-tain?" called the Firekkan.

He turned to look back over his shoulder. The bird had its beak gaped in what looked an awful lot like a grin.

"Try drink called 'Firekka's Finest.' Miss your bottles, you will not."

Species didn't seem to matter; wherever there were fliers, there seemed to be a bar. This bar was certainly different from any he'd seen before, though. For one thing, it didn't have much of a floor, or chairs. Firekkans were perched every few feet on branches woven into the tower, extending up into the shadows a hundred feet above him. Only the bartenders were on the ground level, flying up to carry drinks to the customers. They *had* made some concessions for the human guests, though . . . there were several dozen hammock-like seats slung at various intervals up the tower, where humans were drinking and chatting with the Firek-kans.

He craned his neck a little, wondering how he was going to recognize K'Kai; he'd never seen any more of her than rather blurry face-shots on the vid, and had heard her voice only via comlink. And at the moment, every Firekkan looked like every other Firekkan to him. With a sigh, he walked to the closest ladder — doubtless also installed for the convenience of the humans — and began climbing.

Though they'd never actually been physically present in the same place, he'd "met" the Captain on patrol; she was flying a freighter. That had been something of a surprise. He'd been assigned as her fighter escort, and over the course of the trip, he'd found out quite a bit about her and her "flock." And though they'd never met face-to-face . . . or face-to-beak, in this situation, they'd talked for hours over the comlink.

Firekkan social groups were fairly large as a rule, consisting of a matriarch and all her immediate relatives. But K'Kai was something of a maverick — which so far as Hunter was concerned, gave her a lot in common with *him*. She'd no sooner been introduced to the concept of spaceflight than she had broken away from her own family flock — much to their horror, he had no doubt — and presented herself at the spaceport, demanding to be trained.

She'd proven to be quite a pilot; she'd made that old freighter move in ways he'd never suspected it could — and in ways that would have had a human pilot looking for the air-sick bag. Hunter suspected that being a flyer by birth probably helped her there, since she'd been born with a natural aptitude for it. Before very long, she'd been joined by other misfit, oddball Firekkans, all of them looking for a way off-planet and out into space. Pretty soon she had her "flock" — and she was a matriarch of a freighter crew. She trained them herself, and

Hunter knew for a fact that the other birds were just as good as she was, if a little on the strange side.

But that still wasn't going to help him pick her out of this crowd —

A piercing whistle made him grab his ears, and then grab again for the safety of the ladder — and a whirlwind of feathers and clattering beaks descended on him as he dropped his haversack.

Not that it mattered — one of the birds grabbed it before it hit the ground; the rest started *pawing* him — roughing him up —

No, he realized, after a moment of panic. *No, it's okay. I remember now* — He tried to relax under their questing claw-tips, running through his hair, poking into crevices in his clothing —

This was the Firekkan greeting of affection — like getting hugged by a bunch of friends, or so he'd been told. It was really ritualized grooming — a search for bugs and lice so that an honored friend would not be plagued by pests during a visit.

Oh yeah? What about the feathered pests? He tried not to wince as those sharp claws poked his scalp, and came awfully close to his eyes —

One of them was starting to groom his *eyelashes* when another sharp whistle, this one not nearly so loud, made them finally break it off. Another Firekkan pushed her way into the flock — she was clearly female, both by virtue of her drab coloring and her larger size. And he realized then that he could never have mistaken *this* bird for any other; by the grin-gape on her beak, and a certain rakish good humor in her eyes, this could only be K'Kai herself.

"G'day, K'Kai," Hunter said, holding onto the ladder with one hand and reaching out to ruffle her feathers in what he hoped was a similar greeting to what he'd just endured.

"Kep-tain Sain' Dzon! Hun-ter!" She leaned in very close to study his face from three inches away. Hunter fought the impulse to pull away, remembering that he was hanging off a ladder roughly twenty feet in the air, and fast movement was definitely not a good idea. *I wouldn't wager that one of these bird-beasties could catch me if I took a nose-dive off this ladder. . . .*

"Come come, sit with me!" K'Kai pulled one of the hanging hammock-seats closer to the ladder for him. Hunter grabbed it and hauled himself into it. K'Kai let go of the chair and it swung out over the open floor, nearly slamming into a Firekkan carrying several drinks. The Firekkan shrieked something shrilly in their own language and neatly ducked out of the way, continuing to fly toward the top of the tower. K'Kai shrieked something right back, and the Firekkans nearest them bent over backwards, beaks clattering. At first, Hunter thought they had been hit with some kind of fit . . . then he realized they were laughing.

Hunter held onto the chair with both hands until it slowed to a stop, hanging out over the floor twenty feet below. He hoped that she couldn't see his whitened knuckles. *Hell, she saw you take on four Jalthi single-handedly,* he thought. *Don't let her think that you're afraid of heights now!*

It's not the heights I'm afraid of, or even falling. It's just that sudden stop at the bottom. . . .

K'Kai opened her wings and soared to the closest perch, several other Firekkans following her a moment later, all taking perches slightly lower than hers. She canted her head, looking at him closely. "So, Hun-ter, you are very diff'rent than I expected. Not so tall."

No great surprise, that . . . every Firekkan in the bar was at least a foot taller than himself. *Seven*-foot parakeets, not six-foot like Shotglass had said. "You're not quite what I expected, either. But it's good to be here, to meet you. I was wondering if I'd ever see you again, after we left Vega."

"It is . . . it is. . . ." K'Kai struggled for a word. "I do not know how to say it in your language. Something that was meant to happen?"

"Fate," Hunter said, searching his jacket pocket for a cigar. "Destiny, maybe. You believe in destiny?"

K'Kai ducked her head down between her shoulders in something that looked like embarrassment. "I should, but I am not very religious."

Hunter nodded. "Yeah, me either. The only thing I really believe in is my own flying skills, and my ship, and the fact that the Kilrathi will always try to shoot it out from under me. Speaking of combat flying . . . have you ever thought about training to be a combat pilot?" It was something he'd been thinking about since they'd met back in the Vega Sector, after he'd seen her fly that damned freighter in a series of tighter turns than he'd ever thought was possible, boxing in the Jalthi to force it directly in front of Hunter's guns. *With a wingman like this lady, I could take on the entire Kilrathi fleet,* he thought. "You ever think of going for Confed pilot training?"

K'Kai tilted her head, as if considering it for the first time. "I have never thought of it, no. But the idea is pleasing. Do you think I could be good at it, Hun-ter?"

He laughed, a short, sharp bark. "You'd be amazing at it, lady. I'd take you as my wingman any day of the week." He fished in his pocket for his lighter, and lit the cigar.

"What is that thing in your mouth?" K'Kai was staring at it with unfeigned curiosity. Some of the other Firekkans also leaned in close to look, as Hunter exhaled a large cloud of aromatic smoke.

"A cigar," he explained. "Uh . . . dried tobacco leaves. You burn it and inhale the smoke. It's relaxing, like drinking alcoholic beverages. It isn't good for you, though . . . I'd say that smoking will kill me eventually, but I'm sure the Kilrathi will get me first."

"Al-co-hol does not affect us," K'Kai said. "We drink *kika'li*. It is made from the *kika* seeds, mixed with al-co-hol to bring out the natural flavor of the seeds. Firekkans like to eat *kika* seeds, which are very tasty and draw away any stresses or pain from us. And the human diplomats like *kika'li* too, because of the al-co-hol in it. So now the Red Flower serves it to the humans. They call it Firekka's Finest. Would you like some?"

"Sure," Hunter said. *Anything would be better than drinking water . . . considering what fish do in it.*

K'Kai whistled again, sharp and loud. There was an answering whistle from below. She gave Hunter another curious look, and scratched herself on the back of her neck with an extended claw. "How long will you be on Firekka, Hun-ter?"

"I have leave for the next three days," he said. "Then I'm back on patrol duty."

"Good. So I can show you my home. This is the first time I have been home in several rotations. My crew and I . . ." She gestured at the hovering flock of wide-eyed Firekkans. "We have been too busy to travel home, too many important cargoes to deliver for the Confederation. But for the treaty-signing, I knew I had to be here. I saw the first Terran ship land on our planet many rotations ago, and now I will see our planet join the Confederation. It is a great moment for us, a good time to be alive."

"Your family is important in local politics, aren't they?" Hunter asked. "I remember you mentioning something about that back in Vega, and later I saw a newsvid about Firekka on the *Tiger's Claw*. They talked about you and your crew, and that your family are major local honchos."

K'Kai blinked. "Hon-chos?"

"VIPs. Politicos. Ah. . ." He searched for the right word. "Flock-leaders?"

K'Kai's beak opened wide, the same gesture that Hunter recognized from the customs officer. "Yes. My sister leads the largest flock on Firekka. She is the *Teehyn Ree*, the leader of flock-leaders. It is she, with the other flock-leaders, who agreed to the treaty with the Confederation diplomats. She will sign it tomorrow for all of Firekka."

"Your sister, eh? Does this mean that you'll inherit the family flock someday?" Hunter asked.

The Firekkan was silent for a moment before answering. "No, her daughter Rikik will claim the flock. I am too . . . too different for them to choose me as flock-leader. Better for me to pilot a freighter for the humans than try to lead a flock here."

There's more to this than she's willing to talk about, Hunter guessed. *I'd wager that K'Kai's leavetaking of her home planet was a little more spectacular than what she's said so far. She was one of the first of her people to leave her planet, she and Larrhi . . . the newsvid people always talk about them as great heroes, as brave adventurers, but no one ever asks the question, "Why?"*

And something else occurred to him. How would a species whose entire culture was based on flock-behavior regard someone who left the flock? As a kind of trail-blazer — or a traitor?

Another Firekkan with a brightly-coloured head-crest flew close to them, slowing enough that K'Kai could take the tall tubes from his hands. She handed one to Hunter, who looked at it curiously. The tube was made of a plant of some kind, hollowed out to hold liquid. Whatever was inside the tube smelled spicy, a little like jalapeno peppers.

K'Kai raised her "glass" in a silent toast to him, and drank.

He took a careful swallow, and gasped for breath as the fiery liquid burned a path down his throat and into his gut. It was hotter than hell, like drinking the juice of a cayenne pepper. A moment later, the alcohol hit his system like a brick.

"I can . . . I can see why humans like this stuff," Hunter said, trying to remember how to breathe. *The stuff is at least a hundred proof. And I think it just burned out my taste buds,* he thought wryly. *But good, damn good.* He drained the last of the drink, feeling like he'd drunk several stiff shots of whiskey mixed with a gallon of Tabasco sauce.

K'Kai had already finished her drink, and was now chewing on the empty tube. Her beak was open in what he now knew had to be a Firekkan grin.

"Another round of drinks for K'Kai and her

crew!" Hunter called down to the Firekkans below, following it with a shrill wolf whistle.

K'Kai's eyes widened. "That whistle-sound . . . do you know what it means in Firekkan?"

"Probably the same thing it means back on Earth. More drinks, mates! This round's on me!"

Hunter vaguely remembered ordering more drinks after that, as the rest of the evening blurred into too many sights and sounds and rounds of Firekka's Finest. K'Kai's flock helped them down from their perches in the bar so they could continue the evening elsewhere, watching the midnight ceremonies in the Fire-Temple as Firekkans flew in intricate patterns around the roiling flames, graceful and delicate as any Earth ballet.

Then back to the Red Flower for refills. "Another round of drinks for my mates, bartender!"

Over more tubes of Firekka's Finest . . . Hunter had lost count of how many drinks at this point . . . K'Kai told him about the night races through the nearby canyons. They had to see it, of course. The intricate obstacle course was lit by spluttering torches, and the racers had to touch the wooden poles of the course with a dab of paint as they passed. Occasionally they'd miss the mark and paint would fly up onto the ledge where the spectators watched.

Speckled with bright blue and red paint, K'Kai finally gave in to the urgings of her crew and flew down to the beginning of the course. Hunter cheered with the rest as K'Kai flew a perfect race, easily beating the rest of the competitors. She accepted a leather thong with some kind of winner's token with an embarrassed ducking of her head, her victory marred only by the fact that she was wobbling on her feet from too much Firekka's Finest.

The only solution to that, Hunter said, was to drink more!

The sun was rising over the Firekkan towers by the time he and K'Kai staggered out of the Red Flower again. Her crew had long since wandered off, flying unsteadily to their nests. Hunter blinked at the bright sunlight. "Is it always so bright here in the morning?" he grumbled.

K'Kai leaned against the tower wall for support. "Time for sleep, Hun-ter. I will take you to the Visitor's Nest, where there is a hammock-bed waiting for you, and a solid perch for me."

"Sounds great. Heavenly. Do we have to walk far to get there?"

There was no answer from K'Kai. He turned to look for her, and realized that she'd vanished. No, not vanished . . . only slid down to a sitting position against the wall.

"Come on, my feathered friend," he said, hauling her up to stand wobbly on her clawed feet. "Let's find a place to crash."

Somehow they managed to walk to the Visitor's Nest, and Hunter fell through the large doorway with a sigh of relief. Some thoughtful individual had set out dozens of large pillows for the humans on the floor, with a few perches for Firekkans above. With another sigh, Hunter stretched out on a couple of pillows, and was asleep . . . or unconscious . . . a few seconds later.

There was a pair of boots in front of him. With a woman's body above the boots, neatly garbed in a uniform. A hand shook his shoulder — gently — but the room tumbled around him as if he was going through a stress-test. "Captain St. John?"

He blinked, trying to focus on the young woman's insignia. For some reason, his eyes weren't quite working right. The insignia came into focus after another moment of staring at it. *Military Police, Shore Patrol. Oh, hell. Now what've I done?*

"Captain St. John?" the woman asked again.

"Thas — that's me," he said. "Wha' is it?" He tried to get up on one elbow, felt his stomach heave, and gave it up as a bad idea.

"Your leave has been revoked by Colonel Halcyon," she said, slapping a piece of paper into his hand. "You are to report to the planetary shuttle immediately and return to the *Tiger's Claw* for further instructions." She surveyed him, not bothering to hide her amusement. "Do you need assistance in walking to the shuttlecraft, sir?"

"No, I can walk . . . I think." He managed to get up into a sitting position as the room decided to do a spin; he waited for it to steady, then looked around the nest for K'Kai, and spotted her perched on a branch a few feet away. The Firekkan was listing slightly to starboard on her perch, he saw, but otherwise she looked in better shape than he was. "K'Kai, it's — it's been great," he said. "Sorry about this, but duty calls. I'll try to come back downside, though."

"We will meet again, Hun-ter," K'Kai said gravely, looking down at him from her unsteady perch. "I know we will."

"The shuttle, sir," the MP said impatiently.

"Later, K'Kai," he said, waving at her. His

stomach lurched; he closed his eyes and concentrated on controlling it.

*Her Highness is just gonna have to wait. Can't rush
these things. . . .*

With his eyes still closed, he felt his way up the
wall, pulling himself slowly to his feet. Every time he
moved his stomach lurched again, but finally he
stood erect and opened his eyes triumphantly.

The MP caught him as he overbalanced and
started to fall.

He clutched his stomach as it heaved again, and
felt the blood draining out of his face. The MP
sighed, picked up his haversack, and slung his arm
around her shoulder, half-carrying him in the
direction of the shuttlecraft.

• CHAPTER THREE

"Did you have a nice shore leave, Captain?" said an unfamiliar voice.

Hunter, slumped on the ground in the line for the shuttle, looked up blearily. By now he was almost used to the way that his surroundings started to spin every time he moved his head. Now if only his stomach would get used to it. . . .

It was the young blond tech, of course, looking like *he'd* had plenty of sleep the night before. Hunter squinted at him through the waves of pain emanating from both temples and meeting just over his nose. He wanted to growl. No one should look that alert and — and — healthy. It just wasn't right.

"You look a little under the weather, sir," the tech said, his eyes sparkling, but his expression sober. "Are you all right?"

The kid's voice seemed awfully sharp. And it sounded like he was projecting, or something. "Don' talk so loud, kid," Hunter muttered, searching his jacket for a cigar. A good smoke, that's what he needed right now. His head felt like someone had stuffed it with cotton and then started playing bongo drums on it, and his stomach . . . he didn't want to think about his stomach at all. Definitely not.

The kid grinned and took a breakfast sandwich out of his backpack. It was still steaming in its clear wrapper. Hunter watched in nauseous shock as the kid bit into the sandwich, and bacon grease dripped down the side of the sandwich. The spicy smell of jalapeno peppers and bacon hit Hunter's nose an instant later.

Oh no oh no oh no . . .

Hunter pressed his hand to his mouth as he realized he was losing the battle with his stomach. He managed to stagger to the edge of the landing field before losing it all over the bare rock. By the time his stomach stopped fighting, he was down to dry heaves; his head was splitting so badly he'd have welcomed an axe-murderer with open arms, and his legs were shaking so hard he wondered if they'd hold him.

The kid was already aboard the shuttlecraft when Hunter could stand again, which was probably good for the kid's health, he reflected. *I think I'll kill him if he eats any more of that sandwich in front of me.* He tried to walk onto the shuttle with something like dignity, but settled for slumping into the closest seat.

The same laconic shuttle pilot walked into the cabin, looking over his passengers. He took one look at Hunter and handed him a spacesick sack. "Try not to heave all over the cabin," he advised. "It took us three days to clean out the shuttle after the last guy who did that."

Hunter nodded, not trusting his guts enough to open his mouth to speak.

The shuttle engines roared into life a few minutes later, sounding and feeling so loud to Hunter's ears that he might have been strapped to them. The rumbling didn't help his head at all. He could hear the techie kid several rows back, talking and laughing. He sat back in the seat, closed his eyes, and wished he was anywhere but on a shuttle about to lift at several gees and then go weightless for their trip beyond the planet's gravity well to the *Claw*. The shuttle lifted with a sudden pull of acceleration, too loud and too fast, and Hunter was suddenly very glad that the pilot had given him a spacesick sack.

And to think he'd assumed there wasn't anything more in his stomach.

Unless, of course, he was tossing up his socks. He might well be, by now. . . .

By the time they were out of the atmosphere and floating free in zero gee, Hunter was beyond caring. He lay back in his seat and thought about dying. *Anything but this!* His head *had* been split open by an axe-murderer, every muscle ached, he shook with chills one moment, and sweated with fever the next. He had to keep his eyes closed, or he'd have seen the shuttle doing a litte spin around him.

Finally the shuttle slowed for its approach to the *Tiger's Claw*, and Hunter felt the craft lurch slightly as the Automated Carrier Landing System engaged. Then the ACLS brought them into the flight deck, as smooth as sliding a fried egg onto a plate . . . Hunter felt his stomach lurch again. *No, don't think about food, just don't think about it!*

Another minute as the shuttle's engines powered down, and then the hatchway slid open. Two crewmen in the bright green of Medical peered through the hatch, then saw Hunter.

Who was close to panicking. *No, not them again!*

"Captain St. John?" the taller medico asked politely, as his partner unstrapped Hunter from his chair and pulled him to his feet. From the back of the bus, Hunter could hear the tech kid snickering. "You have an appointment in Medical, sir."

"Can't we talk about this, mates?" Hunter pleaded as they hauled him in the direction of Sickbay. "Maybe you could pretend that I missed the shuttle, eh? Just let me go back to the barracks and sleep this off, I'll be fine in another few hours, I swear . . ."

"You're scheduled for a briefing in fifteen minutes, sir," the first medico said, opening the door to Sickbay. "I'm afraid we don't have any choice." He spoke over Hunter's head to his partner. "You get the hypo set, I'll get the — "

No, not the green goop! "Come on, boys, let's not be too hasty!" Hunter said, trying to stagger in the direction of the doorway. "Hey, I'm almost sober now! I can make the briefing! Can't we — " He tripped and landed on the floor in a sprawl, as the medicos closed in on him from either side. " — talk 'bout this?"

The first injection was just north of his left thigh, followed by a second even further north of that. Hunter yelped and tried to protect that delicate area of his anatomy with his hands. "Gents, please! I'll have to sit in a cockpit in another hour!" Hunter choked as they prepped the third injection. As a small gesture of kindness, they gave him the third shot in his trapezius muscle instead. Then it was time to drink the "green goop," which hit Hunter's stomach like an exploding firecracker, and reactivated the lurching that he thought he'd gotten under control. He barely managed to run to the Sickbay bathroom in time, and heard them turning on the shower behind him. He was beyond resistance as they stripped him down and shoved him into the icy cold spray.

Five minutes later, he thought that maybe he would survive this after all. His stomach had settled; his headache was slowly receding. The only chills he had now were the ones caused by the frigid water needling him. He stood away from it, plastering himself against the wall. "Can I please have my clothes back, boys?" he pleaded from inside the shower.

A hand reached in and cut off the water. They handed him a towel, and laid out a clean flight suit uniform for him on the counter.

The taller medico chuckled as Hunter stepped from the shower, toweling himself gently. He still felt as if someone had scraped the first layer of his skin off, and one of the effects of the second shot was to make everything a little *too* sharp and clear. "How many times has this been, Hunter? Four? Five?"

Hunter glared at him. "It's the last time, that's what it is," he said, drying off quickly and wrapping the towel around his midriff. "I'll never give you professional sadists an excuse to work me over again."

"That's what you said last time," the other medico observed. Hunter saw the man's grin and considered punching him just to wipe that smile off his face, but decided that being taken to the brig by Security would be an even worse ending to what had started as a thoroughly wretched day.

And now that they'd hit him with that third shot, there wasn't even a chance he'd be able to sleep what was left of the hangover off. He felt like his eyelids had been glued to his eyebrows, and he knew from past experience that he'd be buzzing like a hummingbird for the next twenty-four hours.

"Well, so long and thanks for nothin', gents," he said as cheerfully as he could (not very), starting for the Sickbay door.

"Ah, Hunter . . . your uniform?" the tall medico said, holding up the jumpsuit and grinning.

"Son of a — " Hunter grabbed the uniform from his hand and stalked off to the bathroom to dress, still grumbling obscenities under his breath.

"As you can see, the probable flight paths begin at Jump Point 1 and Jump Point 2 . . ." Colonel Halcyon glanced at the door of the Briefing Room as Hunter took a seat at the back of the room. "Good morning, Hunter. Glad you could join us." Hunter winced at the sarcasm in the Colonel's voice.

"As I was saying, we think the enemy cruiser . . . if there even is an enemy cruiser . . . is approaching from one of these jump points. Of course, there's a peculiarity in the Firekka System, which some of you may know of, that will make it a little more difficult to track down this Kilrathi convoy. The Firekka System is like the famous Enigma Sector, but on a much smaller scale. Where the Enigma Sector is affected by a singularity that allows you to cross the entire sector in a single jump, Firekka is crisscrossed with different Jump Points that allow you to mini-jump within the system. Depending on whether the Kilrathi know of that peculiarity, we could have a difficult hunt ahead of us." He frowned. "If there's even anything out there at all. Tactical thinks that what they detected was a ship jumping in-system, but they've been recalibrating their detection equipment, so God knows what could be out there.

"Pilots, even if there isn't anything out there, we have to make certain. We can't afford for the cats to disrupt the treaty signing.

"We'll send out patrols staggered at fifteen minute intervals, following the probable flight paths of that ship," he continued. "I'm pairing our experienced pilots with some of the newer flyers from the TCS *Austin*. Iceman, you're partnered with Doomsday. Hunter, you'll fly with Jazz. Spirit, take Puma under your wing. All of you, get down to the flight deck for immediate launch. On the next patrol, Paladin will fly with . . ."

Hunter followed the other pilots of the first patrol out of the briefing room, feeling as though his heart was beating double-time. *It's those damn drugs, they make me feel like I'm a live electric wire.*

If I can just live through the next couple hours, I'll be fine. . . .

In the lift down to the flight deck, Hunter leaned against the wall, trying to calm his racing heartbeat. Spirit, looking too alert and ready in her flight suit, watched him with a small smile. "You look as though you had a good shore leave, Hunter."

He grimaced. "It was a great shore leave, until that MP dragged me out of bed. And for what? This sounds like a wild goose chase to me."

"We need every pilot to cover the flight paths," Spirit said seriously. "The Colonel is right, the treaty between Firekka and the Confederation is too important to risk the Kilrathi disrupting it."

"Yeah, but why me?"

She gave him a smile that was as warm as a touch, as the lift doors opened to the flight deck, noisy and filled with technicians readying the starfighters for their pilots. "Fly well, my friend, and return safely," Spirit said quietly.

"Thanks, lady," he said, and grabbed his helmet from the rack next to the lift doors.

He started for his fighter, and realized that someone was following him. A young man in a flight suit, maybe twenty years old, with a shock of unruly brown hair and dark, serious eyes. His helmet was tucked under his arm, marked with the callsign "Jazz" and several musical notes.

Oh, right. My wingman.

Colson, that was his name. One of the younger pilots from the *Austin*. Hunter vaguely remembered hearing him playing piano in the rec room a week before. The boy assumed an at-attention stance.

"Oh, God, stand at ease, kid." Hunter rubbed his temples. His head still hurt, despite all the drugs. "You're Jazz, right? Jazz Colson?"

"Lieutenant Zachary 'Jazz' Colson, ready for duty, sir!" Jazz saluted sharply.

"Right, right. You're the piano player, aren't you? I heard you play last week. You're good. Damn good. Let's see if you can fly that well. How many combat missions have you flown, Jazz?"

"Two. I iced a Salthi and a Dralthi." There was pride on the young man's face.

"Not bad, mate. Okay, listen up. We're supposed

to fly a simple patrol, but I've learned that nothing is ever simple, not in this war. You'll stick to me like glue, understand? We probably won't run into any cats, but if we do . . . no heroics, nothing fancy, just good flying. Follow my lead, stay close on my wing, and you'll do fine." Hunter leaned against the closest fighter for support during this small speech, wishing more than anything that all he could do was go lie down for a while. His brain might've been on overdrive from the stimulants, but his legs still weren't working quite right.

"Are you feeling all right, Captain?" Jazz asked solicitously. "You don't look so great, sir."

"I'm fine, I'm fine. Go on, get started with your pre-flight checks. We're supposed to launch in another few minutes. Once you've launched, get out of the landing pattern area and wait for me, 'bout five thousand kilometres to starboard."

Hunter continued across the flight deck to his fighter, which was still being serviced by the ground crew.

Next to his Rapier fighter, Paladin was talking quietly with a strange-looking young man, his dark face marked with an intricate tattooed pattern. Spirit was having a similar talk with her wingman, Puma, AKA Lieutenant Youngblood. *Sorry you got saddled with that boy, Mariko,* Hunter thought, climbing up the ladder into his fighter cockpit. *Nobody deserves that one.*

The blond boy from the shuttlecraft was crawling out from under the Rapier's left engine as Hunter walked up. Like everyone else this morning, he looked too alert and cheerful. "Ready for flight, sir!" he said, saluting.

And I'm seeing too damn many salutes this morning, Hunter thought grumpily. "Thanks, Ensign, ah . . ." He squinted to see the name on the kid's jumpsuit. "Ensign Cafrelli. Thank you."

"My pleasure. And you can call me Jimmy if you'd like, sir." The kid was obviously trying hard to keep a straight face. "By the way, sir, you look much better now than you did on the shuttle this morning. Sir."

"Don't remind me," Hunter muttered, then called louder. "All personnel, clear for takeoff!" He clipped the comlink wires to his helmet, and pressed the button to close the cockpit.

"Hey, Hunter, how's it hangin'?" The wry Southerner voice said into his ear, as the flight control officer's face appeared, green and fuzzy, on the vid.

Hunter grinned. Of all of the flight control officers, "Mississippi Steve" was the most entertaining. "Just fine, Steve. How soon can I launch?"

"You're first in the pattern, Captain, with immediate clearance. Your flight plan is uploading to your Nav computer right now. Have a good flight and a safe return, sir."

"Thanks, Steve." Hunter finished his pre-flight checklist and strapped himself in, then double-checked to make sure that all the ground personnel were clear of the engines. Then he flipped the switches and thumbed the engines into life.

Even through the closed cockpit, the roar of the engines drowned out all the other noise of the flight deck. Hunter clicked up the volume on his comlink as the entire fighter vibrated, straining against the braking system. Carefully, he pushed the throttle up slightly, moving the huge fighter toward the brightly-marked launch strip.

As he maneuvered into position for the launch, the Deck Officer held up one hand, his other hand cupping his headset to listen more closely. Hunter eased up on the throttle, feeling the fighter quivering around him. The Deck Officer brought his hand down sharply, and Hunter punched the engines to full throttle, accelerating forward through the launch tube. A moment later the fighter broke through the magnetic airshield with a bare instant of resistance, and then he was free of the ship and its artificial gravity.

Hunter banked the ship sharply to starboard, easily clearing the landing pattern traffic and heading into open space. A few seconds later he was five thousand klicks out and killed his engines, after reversing the engines briefly to bring his speed down to zero. He drifted there, weightless, waiting for his wingman. It was peaceful, even with the noise of the open com channel chattering in his ear.

This is worth it all, he thought, looking back at the *Tiger's Claw,* the sphere of the blue-green planet Firekka beyond it. *Just to be out here in space flying a fighter, this is worth all of the military crap, everything I have to deal with in the Navy.*

He watched as another Rapier launched from the carrier, veering sharply toward him. *There's the boy,* Hunter thought. *He's looking good, has a light hand on the controls. Not overcorrecting, or turning too tightly. I think this one's going to do just fine.*

The second Rapier slowed as it approached his position. The vid flickered to life, Jazz's helmeted face smiling at him. "Lieutenant Colson reporting for duty, sir."

"Let's check out our Nav points in sequence,

Jazz. Set the nav computer for Nav 1, and AutoNav on my mark. Three . . . two . . . one . . . mark!"

Hunter punched in the buttons in sequence, and felt the fighter accelerate as the autopilot engaged. He sat back in his chair to enjoy the ride, glancing at the Nav map occasionally to check their position.

Three thousand klicks out from the Nav Point, the AutoNav dropped out and Hunter took the joystick to resume manual control of the spacecraft.

"No Kilrathi on the sensors, Captain," Jazz reported over the vidlink.

"Looks like this point is clear," Hunter said. "Reset AutoNav for Nav 2 . . ."

Jazz's image broke up on the monitor, to be replaced by Colonel Halcyon on vid override. Hunter stopped in mid-word, knowing that the Colonel never contacted pilots during a patrol unless it was an absolute emergency.

"Hunter, your orders have changed. Set course for your Nav 3 and then keep going another five thousand klicks. Spirit and Youngblood are in serious trouble. Two heavy cruisers with full fighter complement. Get moving, man!"

"Affirmative, Colonel. On my way. I'm sending Jazz back to the carrier."

Jazz's voice burst over the comlink, though the Colonel was still overriding the vid circuits. "Captain, you can't!"

"Listen to me, mate. You've flown two missions . . . I've flown dozens. What do you think your odds are of surviving this? I'm saving your life, kid. Obey my orders and go back to the *Claw*."

"Affirmative, Captain." Hunter glanced out the side cockpit view, to see Jazz's fighter peeling off in the correct direction. *At least the kid obeys orders.* He punched up the new navigation coordinates, and checked his afterburner fuel reserve. He had enough to get himself there on partial burn, with enough to use in reserve for the fight. Fortunately, the main engines on this fighter ran on nuclear cells, so he wasn't in danger of being stranded. He kicked in the 'burners and felt the engines vibrating as they soared up to full power. *Let's go, let's go!*

He keyed through the comm channels until he heard Spirit's voice, faint and crackling with static. "Youngblood, where . . . you . . . form . . . my wing . . . NOW!"

Spirit rolled her Raptor fighter hard right to stay close behind the Kilrathi, glancing desperately at the power readings on her ship's neutron guns, slowly building up to full power again. The small fighter's powerplant was straining to recharge the weapons . . . she waited until the last moment, when the Kilrathi fighter was veering sharply away, to pull the trigger and let loose the volley of deadly red fire. The aft engine of the enemy fighter peeled away and exploded, taking the rest of the fighter with it. Spirit veered again to avoid the debris, scanning her aft view for Youngblood.

She couldn't see him, either aft or to either side. What she could see were the two Kilrathi heavy cruisers, and the enemy fighters launching from those cruisers, one by one. As soon as they had a full complement of fighters launched, they'd be after her.

She and Youngblood had come out of the asteroid field and into this ambush without warning. Only one more enemy fighter was attacking them now, but in another few seconds a dozen more would join in the fight. "Youngblood, where are you? Form on my wing, right now!"

There was still no sign of the Lieutenant, but his image formed on her vidscreen. "Spirit, I'm on one guy's tail! Can't break now!"

"Youngblood, there are too many of them! Form on my wing, we have to get out of here!" She had a clear run now that the fighter attacking her was destroyed, an open path back to the asteroids. No fighters would be able to intercept her before she was in the dubious safety of the asteroid field. At least if she was in the rocks they wouldn't be able to use their superior numbers against her. In the asteroid field they'd have at least a small chance of surviving this ambush. "Youngblood, do it now!"

"Spirit, I nearly have missile lock . . . I've almost got tone . . ."

"Damn it, Youngblood!" Spirit yanked the joystick hard to bring her fighter around in a tight turn. She couldn't leave him behind, even though she knew she was probably committing suicide by trying to save him.

She lined up for a missile lock on the fighter that he was pursuing, listening for the tone before firing. The shrill lock signal wailed in her ear, and she punched the missile a moment later, already turning to head back toward the asteroid field. "He's history, Youngblood! Now get on my wing!" she shouted over the com.

"Damn it, that was my kill, Spirit!"

"Get on my wing, Youngblood, or we're both dead! Can't you see that they're launching more fighters, you idiot!"

Looking aft, Spirit saw the heat-seeking missile following the lone Kilrathi as he twisted and dove, trying to break the lock. A moment later, there was a bright flash as the enemy fighter exploded. Youngblood steered into position on her left wing as they ran for the asteroids.

Too late, Spirit saw, looking back. There were at least a dozen enemy fighters moving toward them. They'd be overtaken before they were in the asteroid field. Spirit tried to breathe slowly and calmly, watching the enemy ships approaching in her aft view. The Kilrathi were only a few hundred meters behind the two Terran ships when they blossomed into an attack formation, banking in from all sides to target them.

She felt the vibration of the engines straining at the base of her spine as she flew at top speed, willing her Raptor to leap across the remaining distance and into the rocks . . .

The first two Kilrathi ships tilted down into position behind them, angling for cannon targeting. She saw the burst of cannon fire a moment later, and rolled her fighter to avoid it. "Roll left, Youngblood!" she shouted into the com, knowing that he probably wouldn't have time to react.

The laserfire caught his fighter on the edge of one engine, which exploded in a hail of sparks. Youngblood's fighter spun helplessly out of control, back toward the Kilrathi fighters closely pursuing them. Two of the Kilrathi rolled sharply to avoid the damaged Terran fighter; the third crashed head-long into it. The explosion burned white-hot in her eyes, blinding her for a moment to everything else. The shockwave hit her fighter a split-second later, and she punched the afterburners, fighting hard to keep control of her craft.

Youngblood's image was still on the monitor, frozen in mid-word. His eyes were wide with surprise and horror as the image fizzled out a moment later.

Damn them! Spirit kept her thumb on the afterburners, knowing that her only chance now was in speed. *If I can get into the cover of the asteroids, there still might be a chance to get out of this alive. . . .*

"Hey, sweetheart, what's up?" Hunter's voice came through the com a moment before his face appeared on the screen.

"Hunter! Where are you?" She glanced at the radar, and saw the blue blip that was his ship on the edge of the screen. *Too far away to help. . . .*

"I'm in the asteroids, heading toward your last known position. If you can get into the rocks, lady, we can take on these bastards. I'm readin' five tailing you, with some more coming in from those cruisers."

"Hunter, don't do this! Head back to the *Claw,* you can't help me now."

"Hey, you're not giving up on me, lady! What, y'think you can have a cat-chasin' party without me? Just get into those rocks, I'll be there in another minute. . . ."

She hit the edge of the asteroid field at full burn, flying on pure instinct and luck. The rocks were going past her at a blur . . . she dodged and weaved a path through the rocks, yanked the 'stick down to duck under one asteroid. There was an alien scream over her headset and another explosion as one of the Kilrathi impacted against rock she had just avoided.

Cannon fire scorched past her right wing; she swung left into the thickest of the asteroids, slowing her speed just enough so she could dodge the rocks.

She glanced down at her 'scope, and saw Hunter's blip, moving toward her at top speed. *Just a little further . . . a little further . . .*

The wail of a missile lock warning ripped through her ears. She looked back to see the missile closing in on her, homing in on her engines. No time to dodge, no time to do anything, even scream. . . .

She slammed on the brakes, reversing the engine to come to a hard stop and then killing the engine at the last second. The sudden stop shoved her forward, then back into the pilot's chair so hard that she thought she was going to black out, but the heat-seeking missile sailed past to explode harmlessly against an asteroid. Behind her, the Kilrathi banked to avoid a collision . . . *they're learning,* she thought grimly . . . then the three enemy fighters swerved to come in for an attack run.

Spirit punched on the Raptor's engines . . . for an awful second, all she could hear was the splutter of her ship's engines as they failed to ignite. Then they roared back into life and she hit the afterburners. She was beyond the diving Kilrathi a moment later, using the asteroids to block their weapons' fire. But she knew she couldn't play this game forever . . . soon they'd maneuver to box her in, to force her in front of their guns, and it would be over.

She banked up and over one asteroid, down and around another spinning rock. The Kilrathi tried to flank her, then one of them broke formation to close on her tail. She swerved left, but not before she heard the warning wail of a missile lock. In another split-second the Kilrathi pilot would fire.

Another Terran fighter soared past her, barely five feet away from her cockpit, the Rapier firing all guns directly at the enemy craft on her tail. Through the cockpit, she caught a glimpse of Hunter's wide grin. Then her fighter shook with the explosion of the Kilrathi that had been tailing her. Glancing aft, she saw the fragments of the enemy fighter drifting in all directions.

The other two Kilrathi panicked, realizing that what had been an obvious and easy kill was now even odds again. Spirit yanked the 'stick in a hard turn and let fly a friend-or-foe missile at one of the Kilrathi at point-blank range, braking right to avoid the resulting explosion. The last Kilrathi shrieked something in his alien language on her vidscreen as he crashed into an asteroid in his attempts to avoid Hunter's deadly aim.

"You all right, sweetheart?" Hunter's helmeted face appeared in her vid. "Are there any other cats after you?"

She nodded. "Yes, but we have time to get out of here, if we move fast. The other pilots will have to find us in these asteroids."

"Top speed back to the *Claw,* Mariko. What about Youngblood?"

"He did not survive."

"Damn." Hunter sighed. "Let's get moving, lady. We have a report to file at home base. Any idea why two cat cruisers decided to take a ride through this system in the middle of nowhere?"

She knew what he was thinking. *What in the hell are*

they doing here? She only wished she had an answer.

"No idea. But I am sure we will find out soon, Hunter-san."

The Briefing Room on the *Tiger's Claw* was filled to overflowing with pilots and other officers. Hunter and Spirit had to fight to get into the room and find a place to stand. *And all I want to do right now is go get a cold brew,* Hunter thought. *Damn, but Spirit is still pale and shaky. That was too close.*

And Youngblood. The kid didn't have a chance, from what Mariko was saying. I'm glad I sent Jazz Colson back to base . . . with our luck, he would've tried to be a hero too and we'd have two dead kids on our hands instead of just one.

Colonel Halcyon, looking more harried and grey-haired than usual, worked his way to the front of the room to stand behind the podium.

"As most of you have heard, every single patrol ran into a serious Kilrathi presence in this system," he began with preamble. "Tactical has no idea why the Kilrathi are arriving in this system in these numbers.

"Until we have some answers, we'll need to fly constant patrols to make certain that there are no surprises moving in on the *Claw* and the *Austin*. That means twenty-four hour on-call duty for all pilots, with no more shore leaves."

A muted groan went through the assembled crowd. *I hope I at least have a chance to talk to K'Kai again before we leave this place,* Hunter thought. *But why in the hell are the Kilrathi moving in on this system? What could they want with Firekka?*

* * *

To descend upon the family nest with her own flock in tow — or to go alone, proud and unashamed of her own individuality. That was the choice that faced K'Kai now. The invitation had been issued this afternoon, the first since her break with WhiteFlower flock to go to space. Now, she had to answer it.

It was a choice she would have to make within the hour. The humans said that the Kilrathi were on the threshold; how soon until they pushed their way into the system? When that happened, her freighter would be in constant use, ferrying supplies for their human allies. She would have to make her peace with her family now, for the freighter would be a prime target for the Kilrathi. She might not get another chance.

K'Kai did not want to think about the possibility that the Kilrathi might actually invade the nestworld. It was easier to do as her people had always done; deal with the current troubles, and leave the future to tend to itself. The doctrine of the Flame Winds taught that the universe was in a constant state of change, and any one of those changes could completely negate anything that had been planned. So there was no point in planning things in too great a detail; it was better to ride the winds as they came.

The current trouble she faced now — reconciling with her family. That could not be left undone, in the face of what was coming.

The flock was more important than any individual; that was what she had always believed. And yet, there was another, lesser-known tenet of Firekkan belief — not of the Flame Winds, but of the Living Spark.

The acts of a leader shape the flocks. The acts of a leader shape the future. And the brilliant leader was more important than the wishes of the flocks, who might be mired in the past. The rebel might be the only one in the flock with vision, a vision that could bring the flocks to new feeding grounds — metaphorical, or actual.

K'Kai's idol Larrhi, the first Firekkan to leave her planet, he who now flew fighters for the Confederation forces — had he been a brilliant leader, or an aberrant rebel? And she, who followed in his wake, followed his flight to the stars, what was she?

She *had* gained a flock. Enough to fully crew a freighter.

Was she a leader? Or was she simply a rallying-point for more unnatural rebels?

She thought she was a leader — for that matter, she was certain that Larrhi was. But what did others think of her?

That was what she needed to determine. And if she could, change their minds.

She decided to go without her flock; as herself. After all, it was no secret that her flock existed — and if she went with them, it might be perceived as a power-play, bringing in her adherents to tip the balance of power in the family flock.

So she contacted the WhiteFlower messenger and told him she would be coming for a short visit at mainmeal time, then ordered a complete shakedown of the freighter; it would need such a thing soon anyway, and if the conflicts within the system increased, there would be no time for one. That would keep her fledglings busy; busy enough that they would not miss her for a few hours.

She waited in her command chair on the bridge, one specially adapted to an avian form, and as much supporting perch as chair, watching her energetic flock through the monitors as they stripped and polished, checked and replaced, repaired and repainted. When they seemed to be completely wrapped up in their work, she left the bridge as if she were going somewhere else within the ship — but instead, she left the ship altogether, still in her adopted uniform, and headed for the WhiteFlower family tower.

She was met by her father, which was a good omen, and conducted to the family roost by not only her father, but by most of the younger members of the flock. And from the conversation over mainmeal, her "defection" from WhiteFlower might never have happened.

So — they had chosen to ignore her strange behavior rather than deal with it. In a way, that was heartening. At least it meant that the flock had not chosen to consider her as being cast out.

K'Kai was patient, as patient as anyone who had to deal with the humans must be. If it took time for them to come to terms with what she had done, so be it.

But after mainmeal, she was fair game for the entire flock. The flock-dance that followed gave any of them ample opportunity to accost her when the patterns of the dance left her roosting until her turn came around again.

There was always the same question: "Everything we need is here — why go out there? Where there are no winds to carry you, and you do not fly on your own two wings but inside a steel egg?"

She tried to answer them; tried to convey her dream, which had begun when she learned that Larrhi, a Firekkan male, had left their planet for the stars. Tried to explain her own excitement with sailing the invisible winds between the stars, the power and delight in trusting herself to something larger and infinitely stronger than she was, and making it do her will. Tried to show them the thrill of seeing what no Firekkan had ever seen with her own eyes before. But she knew it was hopeless; even her own crew had trouble grasping some of what she felt. They were often as completely Firekkan in their outlook as the most orthodox of WhiteFlower flock. Sometimes she thought that the only difference between her flock and WhiteFlower was that her collection of misfits had responded to something she could not calculate — her charisma, or her enthusiasm, perhaps — and had chosen her as their leader instead of someone with less of a presence.

Finally, she dropped out of the dance and took a perch a little out of the way of the rest. She watched her relatives swirling in the decorous patterns, lost in something that was older than anyone had been able to trace. Perhaps it even went back to their days of pre-sentience.

Perhaps that was why she was unable to lose herself in those patterns. She was one who made patterns, not one who followed them.

"Aunt?" came a small, soft chirp from below her. "May I come up, Aunt?"

She looked down, her thoughts disrupted. It was her young niece, Rikik, still in her juvenile plumage. K'Kai whistled her approval, and Rikik flapped awkwardly to a perch beside her.

"What can I do for you, brancher?" she asked, fondly, giving her niece the title of one about to leave the nest.

Rikik roused her feathers with pleasure, and preened to cover it. "Tell me about flying the spaceship," she said, eagerly. "Tell me about the stars."

Well, that was a new request, and one that K'Kai was quite willing to grant. She did her best to give her niece the answers to every question, describing the thrill of spaceflight and likening it to creating a new dance; recounting some of her experiences among the humans and others. Rikik drew closer, prompting her aunt to groom her affectionately as she continued her stories.

Finally Rikik sighed and drooped on her perch. "I would like to fly off into space as you are," she said wistfully. "I would like to see these metal nests that the humans make — to look out and see the stars so bright in all that night-dark. I would like to be like Larrhi . . ." She sighed again. "It cannot happen, though."

K'Kai nodded sympathetically. Already Rikik's mother had chosen this fledgling to succeed her as WhiteFlower leader, and presumably as leader of the massed flocks as well. K'Kai knew her sister only too well; if it had been Kree'Kai that had been the leader when K'Kai had made her bid for freedom and space, there would be no Firekkan-crewed freighter now. It was impossible to get Kree'Kai to change her mind once it was made up, and she was the most orthodox of any Firekkan in K'Kai's aquaintance. There was no spaceflight in Rikik's future — not unless politics required her to make a flight as a passenger. And even then, it would be as brief a journey as could be arranged.

K'Kai saw the disappointment in her niece's eyes, and preened her carefully as a wordless expression of sympathy. But before she could say anything, Kree'Kai spotted her niece conversing with her renegade aunt, and called her back to the dance with an irritated squawk.

And a look that could have left scorched feathers, if K'Kai were not impervious to her sister's looks already. But the encounter left her feeling very depressed, and before long she took her formal leave and returned to her ship.

As she mounted the ramp to her ship, she realized that she felt more eagerness to return there than she had been to return to the WhiteFlower nest. The ship felt more like home than the nest did.

And that only left her wondering, as she took her perch in the command chair with real relief, and saw that her flock was still hard at work at their tasks. Was this what Larrhi felt?

And would she ever be truly accepted — or feel comfortable among her own people — again?

● CHAPTER FOUR

"We are ready for final jump into the Firekka System, my lord," the Pilot Officer reported. "Your orders?"

Ralgha *nar* Hhallas spoke quietly. "Engage jump engines, Officer. As soon as we appear in the Firekka System, do *not* launch fighters for reconnaissance, but perform a full sensory scan of the immediate area."

"My lord? You are certain that you do not wish us to launch fighters?" Kirha asked politely from his station.

Ralgha wanted to laugh, but kept his face set in a serious expression. That was Kirha's way, of course, always the one to delicately point out his lord's mistakes, without ever inferring that they were actual mistakes. Ralgha felt a small glow of pride, as though Kirha was one of his own cubs. It was unfortunate what he must do; Kirha could have had an excellent future as a warrior in the Emperor's service.

He cuffed Kirha across the ear, the only part of the cub he could reach from where he sat. "Do you question my orders, cubling?"

Kirha's eyes dropped. Ralgha noticed the young Kilrathi's belly quivering; probably from the tension. "Of course not, my lord," he said submissively.

"Good. Communications Officer, I require all

control of external communications to be transferred to my cabin immediately, for a closed-channel discussion. Kirha, I require your assistance now."

The Communications Officer bowed to him, and turned to his console to begin programming the change. Ralgha strode to the lift, Kirha a few steps behind him.

In his cabin, Ralgha allowed himself a moment of relaxation, stretching out on the woven fibers of his suspended chair to chew some *arakh* leaves. He felt the vibration of the jump engines as he chewed the sour leaves, the juice running down his throat to calm his belly. A few eights of minutes later, he felt relaxed enough to begin the task before him.

Kirha, of course, still stood at attention near the hatchway.

For the first time in his life, Ralgha wished that he had bothered to learn one of the Terran languages. Now everything would depend on Kirha's loyalty. Ralgha could not risk transmitting his message in Kilrathi, both for fear that one of his own crew would detect and understand it and also for the risk that the humans would not. The only Kilrathi other than Kirha aboard the ship who spoke Terran, according to the ship's roster, was the new Pilot Officer, but he would be too busy with his duties to hear this message. Or so Ralgha hoped.

He keyed in the monitor in his cabin to the outside communications channel, quickly running a scan of the channel to make certain that it was not being tapped, and that no other communication systems on the ship were in use.

Ralgha *nar* Hhallas, Lord of the Empire, was furious to realize that he was nervous, angry at himself, and appalled at the situation that forced him to this pass. Small wonder his stomach was in a turmoil. What he did now was his first true betrayal of the Emperor. He had sworn an oath to the rebels on Ghorah Khar, that he would aid them in any way he could to overthrow the Empire, but had never actually taken part in any of their plans. What he did could not be called honorable by any, to surrender his ship without a fight to the alien enemy. But he was oathsworn to the rebel council. To fail them now was the worst dishonor of all. It was no choice at all, save among bad and worse. For a split moment wonderment at finding himself in such a dishonorable dilemma rose to the surface of his mind, but as ever there was no time to think about *that*.

He took a deep breath, and began. "Kirha, you will translate and transmit this message."

"Of course, my lord," the young officer said.

"To the lord captain of the Terran carrier, *Tiger's Claw*," Ralgha dictated. "I am Ralgha *nar* Hhallas, lord of the Kilrathi Empire, and captain of the Fralthi cruiser *Ras Nik'hra*. In the names of the rebel lords of Ghorah Khar, I bid you welcome in all honor. At their request, I bring you messages suing for alliance with your Confederation against the Imperial Kilrathi, and my own Imperial ship as a gift. The *Ras Nik'hra* will continue toward the planet Firekka from this jump point, so that you may rendezvous with us at any time." Ralgha listed the ship's coordinates in the Kilrathi reckoning, which he hoped the humans could translate into their own system.

He saw that Kirha was trembling as the young Kilrathi finished translating his speech. Kirha pressed the button to transmit the message and turned to Ralgha. "May I be excused, my lord?"

Ralgha nodded, and Kirha quickly left the cabin, his tail curled low around his legs. This was, perhaps, the worst moment of Kirha's life. Well, and it was no great occasion for joy for Ralgha, either. *I know, cubling. Now we have truly travelled into unknown space. To the humans, to surrender my ship to them. No Kilrathi has ever walked this path before.*

He thought about calling Kirha back, then decided against it. This was no time for a show of weakness. Kirha was only one small piece in this game of Empires. Soon the cubling would be a prisoner of war, and not a game piece at all. There was no way to know what would become of them. Ralgha leaned back in his chair, feeling the tension in his muscles and belly.

Soon, he thought. *Soon I will face the humans in a battle that I cannot win . . .*

"We are gathered here today to honor the memory of a young pilot who died in the line of duty. Lieutenant Peter Youngblood fought bravely. . . ."

Hunter stood stiffly at attention on the Outside Deck, the magnetic shoes of his spacesuit holding him tightly to the metal deck. As always, he felt very cold inside, standing out in open space. He knew it was only in his mind, that if his suit was ever breached enough to let in the cold, he'd be dead a half-second later. But still, he felt the chill.

Maybe it's because the only time I ever go "outside" is for these damned funerals, he thought. *Bloody depressing, all of this. I hate the thought of Colonel Halcyon standing out here and eulogizing me if I should get blown away on a mission . . . I'd rather they just chuck my body out an air-lock and have a serious party. A good rousing wake, that's what I'd like. All of my friends getting drunk as my bod floats off into space. . . .*

". . . against overwhelming odds, he reached for victory despite the dangers . . ."

He tried for glory and caught ordnance, is what he did. . . .

Kien Chen stood on Hunter's right, the fighter pilot obviously intent on the Colonel's speech. Mariko Tanaka was standing on his other side, motionless. Beneath the pale glow of her helmet light, Hunter saw the tears trickling down her face, bright in her eyes.

Hunter leaned closer to Mariko, so that his helmet touched hers. He spoke quietly, knowing that the vibrations would carry the sound into her helmet. "It's not your fault, lady. You did everything you could to save the kid."

There was no answer, though he could hear Mariko's soft breathing through the helmet.

"Mariko? C'mon, lady, talk to me! Listen, the kid did his best, and it just wasn't good enough. If he'd listened to you, obeyed you like he was supposed to, maybe he'd be alive right now. But it wasn't your fault. Hell, you barely got out of it alive yourself!"

He waited in silence for an answer, then slowly straightened, moving his helmet away from hers. Over the suit radio, he heard the Colonel conclude the eulogy, and then the honor guard fired their laser rifles in a twenty-one gun salute, as the empty coffin was released from its magnetic clamps and slowly drifted away from the *Tiger's Claw*.

Bloody depressing, all of this, Hunter thought, clicking his suit into "walk cycle" to follow everyone back to the airlock. The radio channel was silent, the only sound he heard was the faint clanking of his suit's magnetic boots switching on and off, clamping the deck and releasing as he walked. In the airlock, he waited with the others for the system to cycle, then quickly stripped out of the vac suit and back into his uniform.

As he fastened his boots, he saw Mariko leaving the suit room, her face as calm and serene as the aftermath of an ice storm, no sign of tears on her elegant oriental features.

"Mariko!" Hunter yanked his other boot on and ran to catch up with her. "Hey, Mariko!"

She continued walking down the corridor, not looking at him. "Please, Ian. I wish to be alone now."

"Come on, Mariko, talk to me!"

She faced him, speaking fiercely. "You want to talk about it? Fine. We'll talk about it. Youngblood is dead. He refused my order to withdraw. Why? Because he had no faith in me as his wingleader. That's why this is my fault, because he didn't believe in me enough to obey my orders."

Hunter stared at her. "Mariko, that's not true! I hate to speak badly about someone who's dead, but that kid was an idiot! He would've been cat food sooner or later, whoever his wingleader was! Look, compare him to Jazz Colson. When I ordered him to, Jazz turned around and headed back to the *Claw*, even though he didn't want to miss out on the fight!

Jazz is going to do all right for himself, I'm not worried about him. But Youngblood, there was no way he was going to make it out there. Not a chance."

"Perhaps you could have said something about this before the boy was killed, Ian!" Angrily, Mariko wiped the tears from her eyes, glaring at him. "It is a little late to tell me this now that he's dead!"

Hunter suddenly realized that they were standing in a corridor outside the airlock and yelling at each other, with most of the other pilots of the fighter squadron for an audience. He lowered his voice. "Come on, Mariko, don't take it so hard. I'm going to keep telling you that it's not your fault until you believe it. Listen, that Colson kid is playing music over on the *Austin* tonight. We'll catch a shuttle to the ship, have a few brews, talk about it. How 'bout it, lady?"

Mariko shook her head, tears still falling from her eyes.

Jeannette Devereaux, another of the other *Claw* pilots, put her arm around Mariko's shoulders. "Mariko, I'll walk with you to the Barracks, all right?" she said in her lovely French accent. "You'll feel better tomorrow, *cheri,* I know you will."

Jeannette is sure earning her callsign "Angel" today, Hunter thought, watching them walk away. *Those two are like sisters. Maybe that's better for Mariko, to talk it out with Angel.*

Knight, Maniac, and Bossman were watching him from across the corridor. Todd "Maniac" Marshall, the youngest of the *Claw* pilots, grinned at Hunter. "Let me tell you, Hunter, you're pushing your luck, trying to make time with a lady who just had her wingman blown away," Maniac said.

"Go to hell, Todd," Hunter snarled, turning away.

"Come on, Ian, let's get out of here," Bossman said, giving Maniac a sharp look. "You want to get a beer? Are you on the duty roster again today?"

"No, I'm not," Hunter said. "Sure, let's go get a beer."

"Here you go, Hunter," Shotglass said, sliding the mug of beer down the counter to him.

"Thanks." Hunter started toward the table where Bossman and Knight were seated, then stopped in mid-stride, hearing the crackle of the ship's intercom system.

"The following pilots are to report to the flight deck immediately . . . Major Chen, Captain Khumalo, Lieutenant Marshall, Captain Devereaux, Captain St. John, Lieutenant Montclair. . . ."

Hunter slid the mug back across to Shotglass. "Ah, bloody hell. Keep it cold for me, Sam," he said, then ran after the other two pilots toward the flight deck.

"So much for gettin' the afternoon off, mates," Hunter grumbled as they hurried down the corridors to the Deck.

"Anybody know what's up?" Joe Khumalo asked, slightly out of breath.

"A strike force from the *Austin* went after those ships yesterday, the ones that Spirit and Youngblood encountered. They took them out, so there shouldn't be anything else in the area," Kien Chen said as they paused at the equipment rack to change into flight suits. He tossed Hunter's helmet to him; Hunter caught it with one hand. "Everyone was flying more patrols today, in case there were more Kilrathi fighters out there that were stranded when their Fralthis were toasted. But Tactical says that they think we took care of them all, there wasn't anything out there except debris from those two cruisers."

"So why are we doing this?" Hunter muttered, strapping on his helmet and running with the other two pilots through the hatch and onto the flight deck.

The flight deck was a beehive of activity, with more technicians than Hunter had ever seen at one time, readying all of the available fighters.

Colonel Halcyon was on the Deck near the entrance, with half a dozen pilots gathered around him. "Good, that's everyone for this launch," the Colonel said as Hunter, Bossman, and Knight joined the assembled pilots. "Listen closely, because we don't have much time. We've received a transmission from a Kilrathi Fralthi cruiser, the *Ras Nik'hra*, whose captain is apparently part of a rebellion on one of the Kilrathi worlds . . . he wants to meet with the Confederation officials to discuss an alliance of some kind. We don't have his exact position, only his in-system jump point. Tactical has calculated out his possible course . . . your ships are programmed with flight plans for interception. Whoever sights the Fralthi is to report in immediately.

"The biggest problem is that Tactical believes they've detected jump traces of other Kilrathi ships entering this system," the Colonel continued, as Hunter stared at him with mingled shock and disbelief. "If the Kilrathi realize that this captain is allying himself with the Confederation, they'll try to destroy his ship before we can help him."

"What if it is a trap, *mon Colonel*?" Angel asked seriously.

"Use your best judgment," the Colonel replied. "Don't risk yourselves. But if you can bring the *Ras Nik'hra* back intact, do it. We've never had a chance to capture a Fralthi before . . . it's very valuable to Confed High Command.

"We have several troopships of Confed Marines in the system, part of the Honor Guard for the Diplomatic Corps. We're also sending them out, in case we need a boarding party to capture the ship. Do not, I repeat, do not try to land on the *Ras Nik'hra*. That's the Marines' job, not yours."

I sure don't envy those Marine blokes, Hunter thought. *It's bad enough trying to shoot those cat ships down, but* boarding *one?*

"Everyone will fly solo patrols so we can cover the Fralthi's entire projected flight path. If you complete your patrol without encountering the Fralthi, return to the *Claw* for new orders. Good luck, everyone," the Colonel concluded. "Dismissed."

Hunter jogged toward his Rapier fighter, and saw a blond-haired face emerge from inside the cockpit. The kid . . . *what was his name? Jimmy?* . . . swung down lightly from the cockpit, and saluted Hunter. "You're ready to launch, sir," the kid said.

"Thanks, Jim," Hunter said, and climbed up the ladder into the cockpit.

"Maybe I'll see you out there, sir," the kid said.

"What?" Hunter looked down at him in surprise.

Jimmy grinned proudly. "I'm a specialist in Kilrathi engineering systems as well as our own fighters, sir. I studied on Fralthi debris back at HQ.

They're sending me with the Marines, in case we have to fly that Kilrathi ship ourselves."

"Well, take care of yourself, kid," Hunter said gruffly. "Be real careful if you go on that ship, okay? God knows what they'll have in there. Booby traps, probably."

"I will, sir!" Jimmy saluted him again, and Hunter picked up his clipboard, racing through the pre-flight checks. "Ready when you are," he said into his headset.

"You're cleared for launch, Hunter," Mississippi Steve drawled. "Good luck findin' that ship."

"I'll do m'best," Hunter replied, thumbing up the fighter's engines to taxi into launch position.

"Pilot Officer, report our current position," Kirha said, glancing up from his station.

"We are still on a direct course toward the inhabited Firekka planet," the Pilot Officer said tersely. "I am still not detecting any Terran presence . . . of course, without forward patrols, they could be waiting just outside our sensor range. I recommend that we launch fighters immediately for a long-range patrol before venturing closer to the planet, sir."

Kirha glanced at the *Thrak'hra* lord, who was pacing the Bridge. Lord Ralgha stopped at the Pilot Officer's console, looking over the Pilot Officer's shoulder at the computer displays. "Continue present course," Lord Ralgha said. "And we will not launch fighters, not yet."

My lord is nervous, Kirha thought, incredulously. *I've never seen him like this before. Even when we fought the humans in the Vega Sector, and I was certain that we were going to die, I never saw him pace like this before. Can the rest of the crew see this as well?*

"But, sir, without advance fighter patrols we're blind!" the Pilot Officer protested.

He's right, Kirha thought. *I hope that my lord knows what he's doing.* Something flickered on Kirha's computer console, and he punched up a quick diagnostic check to confirm the readout. "Lord Ralgha! I'm detecting old jump traces in our vicinity. Computer confirms them as the jump-system emissions of a Gettysburg class ship and another ship, the readings are difficult to distinguish."

Lord Ralgha strode to Kirha's station, looking down at the console. "Those are the jump traces of a Terran carrier," he said. "Do you see that pattern there, Kirha? That is created by the multiple jump engines of a carrier." The *Khantahr* deftly ran through a series of checks . . . *he knows every system on this ship,* Kirha thought, a little enviously. *That is why he is the finest captain in our fleet. Our best captain, and my liege lord. And a rebel, a traitor. If he is the best, and he chooses to hunt this path, how can I not follow?*

"There, do you see?" Lord Ralgha pointed at a numeric chart, an analysis of the faint jump engines' emissions. "A clear corollation . . . the *TCS Tiger's Claw* jumped into this system."

There was a sudden silence on the Bridge. One of the younger officers, crouched over his computer console, shuddered convulsively.

The Pilot Officer was frozen with shock, as were several others. His tail twitched once. "*The* Tiger's Claw!" the Pilot Officer said explosively. "Sir, we must launch fighters at once!"

"These traces are at least several weeks old," the lord said thoughtfully. "In all likelihood, the Terrans are no longer in this system. We will not launch fighters."

"But, sir!"

The lord turned sharply, his claws extended. His eyes glittered dangerously. "Do you question my orders, Pilot Officer?"

"Of course not, sir," the Pilot Officer said, his eyes wide with fright. "I would never question your orders." The officer slid from his chair to the floor, prostrating his belly before his commanding officer.

"Oh, get up," Lord Ralgha said in an annoyed voice. "All of you," he continued, eyeing the rest of the Bridge crew, "resume your duties." He glanced at Kirha. "Kirha, you will walk with me now. We have other tasks to attend."

Kirha keyed the computer to report any other detection of Terran jump traces, and then hurried to the lift after his liege lord.

Lord Ralgha spoke quietly as they descended into the depths of the *Ras Nik'hra*. "We cannot risk the crew firing upon the Terrans when they arrive to rendezvous with us. We will be undefended, and a single fired shot could easily result in the Terrans destroying this ship. We must avoid that at all costs."

"What will you do, my lord?" Kirha asked.

Lord Ralgha bared his teeth. "I have thought much upon this, cubling. The easiest solution, of course, would be to kill the crew. But that weighs heavily upon me . . . they have been loyal, honorable warriors in my service, and for me to kill them like animals, without the chance to die in combat . . . no, they do not deserve such a dishonorable death." He paused at the hatchway to his cabin, and keyed open the lock with his claws.

Inside the cabin, the lord removed two small laserpistols and two handheld communication units from a cabinet, handing one of each to Kirha and placing the others in his hauberk. "I have already changed the keycodes to the weapons armory, so that you and I will be the only ones aboard the ship with weapons. That should place the odds somewhat more in our favor. Kirha, your task will be to secure the Bridge. That is the only station aboard the ship that we cannot remove all the personnel from, not without endangering the entire ship. You must succeed at this. Our lives, and my honor, depend upon this."

"I will not fail you, my lord," Kirha said, his tail stiffening and twitching with nerves.

Lord Ralgha gave him a gentle shove in the direction of the lifts. "Go now. I will join you on the Bridge later."

He bowed, then started back toward the Bridge. A moment later, he heard his lord's voice broadcasted throughout the ship, echoing in the corridors: "This is Lord Ralgha nar Hhallas. All crew except the Bridge officers, report to the primary Launch Bay immediately."

Kirha felt the familiar trembling in his belly as the lift ascended toward the Bridge, and clenched the pistol more tightly. The *Khantahr*'s message repeated, and yet a third time.

What is this that I do now? he asked himself silently. *I follow my lord into treason against the Emperor, to go against all that I have believed in, for all of my life?*

I had dreams, as a little cub on Hhallas. That someday I

*would do a true heroic act, I would prove myself to all of
Kilrah, and that my lord Ralgha would reward me for it.
That he might even grant me the right to begin my own
hrai and start a clan of my own. But those were only
foolish dreams of youth, dreams of impossible glory.*

*And now what will happen to Lord Ralgha and I? We
will be traitors, outcasts from all we have known. There is
no future and no glory in it.*

*My lord Ralgha is a Thrak'hra, a noble of the empire.
Surely he knows more than I, he has greater plans for our
future. I must trust in him, for that is the only small shred of
honor left to me.*

Finally the lift doors opened and he stepped out
onto the Bridge.

The few of the officers were gathered in small
groups, talking among themselves as the lord's
message was broadcast a fourth time throughout
the ship. The Pilot Officer saw Kirha first. "Ah, the
lord's little cub is back on the Bridge," Drakj, the
Pilot, said sardonically. "So tell me, Kirha, is our
lord insane? If the Terrans find us now, we are
defenseless! What is he planning?"

"You'll learn that soon enough," Kirha said,
bringing up the pistol. "Step away from your station, Drakj'khai . . . all of you, stand away from your
stations. I do not want to kill any of you."

"What treason is this?" the Pilot Officer
demanded to know.

"No treason," Kirha said, trying to keep the pistol
from shaking in his grip. "I am my lord's sworn
officer, and am following his orders."

"And what orders are those?" the Navigation
Officer asked.

Kirha, keeping the pistol steady upon the cluster

of officers, moved to his own station and glanced down at the computer console. He lifted the comm unit to his mouth, keying it on. "My lord, the Bridge is secured, and I have detected a Terran troopship approaching. Shall I signal them?"

"Tell them that they can dock at the aft airlock," the lord's voice said over the comm.

Kirha keyed open the comm channel and spoke into it in Terran. "Terran ship, this is Kirha *hrai* Ralgha of the *Ras Nik'hra,* speaking with the voice of our *Khantahr,* Lord Ralgha *nar* Hhallas. Approach our aft airlock for docking."

The Bridge officers were staring at him in shock. The Pilot Officer was the first to react. "Treason!" he shouted, and lunged toward Kirha, claws extended.

Kirha fired a moment before the Pilot Officer's body slammed into him, and lost his grip on the pistol a moment later. The air reeked of burnt fur and flesh as he grappled with Drakj for the pistol, lying on the floor only barely beyond his grasp. Drakj's claws raked bloody furrows across Kirha's face, but still he held onto Drakj with a death-grip. With a burst of strength, Drakj hurled Kirha away from him, and Kirha's head slammed back against a console painfully. The room spun violently around him as he tried to get up, and fell back with a moan of pain. *Forgive me, my lord Ralgha,* he thought dizzily, *I did not mean to fail you . . .*

Through a haze of pain, Kirha saw the Pilot Officer, the long burn visible down his side, searing through the leather of his hauberk and his flesh, reach for the communications console. The other Bridge officers seemed frozen with shock, staring at

Kirha as Drakj punched up the controls of the comm console. "All Imperial ships, this is the *Ras Nik'hra!* Our captain has betrayed us to our enemies. Aid us now, or our ship will fall into the hands of the humans . . ." Drakj's words faded away as the Bridge blurred, dissolving into darkness . . .

Ralgha's airsuit boots clanked loudly against the metal of Launch Bay deck as he walked out before the gathered ranks of warriors. He stood for a moment, surveying the ranks of his troops assembled before him.

He saw the surprise, the shock, on the closest of his oathsworn soldiers' faces . . . *no doubt they wonder why I am wearing a spacewalking suit, complete with a sealed helmet, aboard the ship,* he thought. *This is not the usual captain's garb. Well, they will find out soon enough.* He hefted the weight of the small device in his hand, then spoke. "Soldiers of the Empire, you are sworn to me as my vassal warriors in the Emperor's service. To follow me into battle, to obey me as though I speak with the voice of the Emperor. And now I speak to you as your liege lord, to tell you that the Empire of Kilrah is corrupt and dying. How many of you have lost members of your *hrai* in this war, and for what? We have gained nothing in all these years of fighting, not territory or glory, and there is no end to this useless battle in sight.

"After I realized this truth, I joined forces with the rebel lords of Ghorah Khar in their attempts to overthrow the Emperor. To aid in this cause, I have sworn to the rebel lords that I will deliver the *Ras Nik'hra* to the Terrans."

He saw the ripple of shock move through them,

then; the looks of horror and disbelief, the narrowed eyes of the crew in the first row, their claws extending and retracting. One very young *Kilra'hra* crewman in the front rank looked as though he might faint. No Kilrathi captain had ever surrendered his ship, not in the history of their race. It was inconceivable to them . . . *and to me,* Ralgha thought. *Who would ever have dreamed that I would stand here now, trapped like a prey-animal in this conflict of Honor and duty?* As ever, the thought glimmered away, sliding like a mental prey-fish into the depths of his mind.

"All of you have served me loyally, so now I will give you a chance to live," he continued. "If you will swear to surrender to the humans, then I will grant you your lives. By Imperial law, I hold your lives in my grasp . . . you are my vassals, my sworn warriors.

"But if you do not swear to surrender to the humans . . ." He raised the small device high enough so that all could see it. " . . . then I have no other choice but to trigger this device, which will vent this Launch Bay into open space. This is your choice . . . swear to obey me now, *Kilra'hra,* or breathe vacuum."

His soldiers stood motionless with shock, except for one standing in the front rank whose tail twitched nervously.

Ralgha unclipped the comm unit from his belt and spoke into it. "Kirha! Your status?"

Kirha's voice replied through the comm. "My lord, the Bridge is secured, and I have detected a Terran troopship approaching. Shall I signal them?"

"Tell them that they can dock at the aft airlock,"

Ralgha said. He replaced the comm on his belt, and glanced at the assembled throng before him. "So, *Kilra'hra,* what do you choose? To honor your sworn oaths to me, or to die a useless death?"

He heard it then, the low murmuring that had begun during his short conversation with Kirha. A single word, whispered over and over again, now growing louder. "Treason . . . treason. . . ."

"This is treason to the Emperor!" one officer shouted from the front rank, torn between rage and disbelief. "Treason!"

Ralgha overrode his shouting. "You are sworn to *me,* Engineering Officer! Disobey me, and you are forsworn, an oathbreaker, and deserve a coward's death!"

His answer was a sea of snarling, frightened faces.

"Kill him!"

"Treachery!"

With a roar, the ranks of *Kilra'hra* surged forward. Ralgha punched the button of the airlock venting device . . . *Fools! They do not think I will kill them to save my honor?* . . . and braced himself for the explosive decompression that would follow a moment later.

With an ominous creaking noise, the fifty-foot double door of the Launch Bay began to open, then stopped. A thin whistle of escaping air could be heard over the roar of the riot on the deck, but it was not the explosive decompression that Ralgha had been told to expect. He had one brief moment to blink in surprise, and then the mob was upon him, teeth and claws reaching for him.

Accursed lowborn engineers, Ralgha thought, irritated, as he kicked the first *Kilra'hra* out of his way and ran for the exit hatchway. *What if we had needed this system as it was originally intended, for a fire in the Launch Bays? Useless, completely useless.* Another *Kilra'hra* grabbed his arm, and Ralgha backhanded him across the face, pulling free as yet another *Kilra'hra* tackled him from behind, bringing him down to his knees, tearing off his helmet in the process. *That* one received a boot in the face, falling back as Ralgha crawled toward the hatchway. *If that engineer is not dead after this ridiculous incident, I will kill him myself! Incompetency . . . nothing is more infuriating than incompetency . . .*

Ralgha shoved three of his former officers away from him, clawing for the control mechanism of the sealed hatchway as most of the remnants of his suit was torn away. The hatchway opened suddenly, spilling him and several *Kilra'hra* out into the corridor. More of his troops piled through the opening as he gained his feet and began to run toward the aft airlock.

He yanked the comm unit from his belt, shouting into it. "Kirha!" He glanced back at the *Kilra'hra* behind him, just as the first of them leaped at him. Ralgha's face slammed painfully into the deck, and blood from a cut on his forehead blinded him, filming everything in a haze of red. He kicked out wildly, trying to break free. He felt his claws rending *Kilra'hra* flesh, but could not see his opponents, or how to escape. Someone pinned his arms; he wrenched one arm free, and saw the wild-eyed face of one of his gunnery officers, not a handspan from his eyes. He kicked again, and somehow rolled free, falling over the Gunnery Officer and onto the deck. Ralgha scrambled to his feet and ran. The aft airlock was within sight now, an open hatchway at the end of the corridor.

The entire ship vibrated suddenly, echoing with the clanging noise of another ship docking against the *Ras Nik'hra*. Ralgha slid to a stop inside the airlock, trying to remember the sequence for opening the outside door. He heard human voices then, on the other side, and the sound of someone pounding on the metal skin of his ship.

He had punched in half the entry sequence when a pair of claws ripped down his back, setting his body on fire. He whirled and kicked the officer back into the arms of the others running toward him. He managed to punch in one more digit of the sequence before they brought him down like a prey animal, clawing and biting at him as he still fought to reach the airlock controls.

He tried to break free without success, held down by the weight of the bodies piled on him. Ralgha brought his fist down hard on one *Kilra'hra*'s skull, feeling the small bones breaking in his fist, and realized then that he was still clenching the comm unit. "Kirha!" he shouted into it, hoping that it hadn't been broken in the melee. "Kirha, open the airlock! OPEN THE AIRLOCK!"

Lord Ralgha. Lord Ralgha is calling, and I must obey . . . Kirha opened his eyes painfully, hearing his lord calling his name again. *Why am I on the floor of the Bridge?* He blinked and tried to sit up; an awful pain ripped through his head, followed by a wave of dizziness. He heard the *Thrak'hra* lord's voice again, and saw the comm unit lying on the floor. "Kirha!"

He sounds very strange, Kirha thought. *Is something*

wrong? "Open the airlock!" Lord Ralgha's voice continued. *"Open the airlock!"*

Kirha heard Drakj's voice, too, from somewhere above him. "Affirmative, Fralthi *Kraj'nishk*, that is our position. We need immediate assistance . . . there is rioting in the ship, and a human troopship is at the aft airlock, trying to board us."

The human troopship at the aft airlock . . .

Everything came back to Kirha in a rush . . . his lord's vow to deliver the ship to the humans, Kirha's orders to secure the Bridge, and his failure to do so. He levered himself up on one elbow, wincing at the pain in his head, then launched himself at Drakj, claws extended.

Drakj turned, his eyes wide with surprise, as Kirha sank his teeth into his enemy's throat. Drakj's scream of pain was very loud in Kirha's ears, but he held on desperately, clawing at his enemy's throat and tasting Drakj's blood in his mouth. Then, his teeth still clenched tightly, he shoved himself away from his enemy.

Kirha fell against a Bridge console, and spat out the mouthful of fur and flesh. Drakj staggered back, blood pouring from his slashed throat, then fell to the deck, the life gone from his eyes.

Kirha stood unsteadily, glaring at the other Bridge officers. One of them glanced at the laser-pistol, abandoned on the floor. "Touch it, and I will kill you," Kirha rasped, blood trickling from his mouth. The Navigations Officer knelt and presented his throat, a gesture of submission. Kirha ignored him and half-fell against the console that held internal systems controls, searching for the aft airlock control. All the systems glowed affirmative at him, a ship was securely attached to the coupling system, all he needed to do was open the exterior door.

He triggered the outside door to cycle open, overriding the system to keep the interior door open as well. Then he slid down to the floor, unable to stand any longer. He crawled the short distance to the laserpistol, retrieving it from the floor.

The small weight of the pistol felt reassuring in his grasp. "Now we wait for Lord Ralgha," he said, gesturing with the pistol at the other officers.

What an undignified way to die, Ralgha thought, struggling to claw his way free of the pile of *Kilra'hra* on top of him. He felt himself weakening from loss of blood, the pain of too many wounds slowing him even further. *I always dreamed of dying in honorable combat. Not like a hunted animal, not like this.*

Another sound penetrated through the shrieks of the mob, the sound of metal sliding on metal. A moment later, Ralgha realized what it was, as the airlock door opened behind him. He fell through the half-open door, into the airlock of the humans' ship, now filled with humans. He recognized the insignia on their woven fabric clothing as Confederation Marines, just as one of them placed the barrel of an assault gun against his face.

"Move, you dead," the human said in Kilrathi, speaking with an awful accent. "You what, tell now me?"

"Lord Ralgha *nar* Hhallas," he said. It hurt to speak, especially with the human's weapon pressed against his cheek. He could feel the blood on his face, oozing from many small claw cuts. "I bid you welcome with all honor," he added a moment later. He twisted to look through the airlock door, where his troops had stopped momentarily, staring at the sight of an armed human squadron with all their weapons aimed at the Kilrathi.

"Move and you're dead!" a small human with short golden head-fur, standing at the front of the human squadron, said in much more understandable Kilrathi. A *Kilra'hra* on the side of the airlock snarled and leaped at the small human, who whirled and fired without hesitation. The *Kilra'hra* fell dead at her feet, a smoking burn through his chest.

"All of you, paws against the walls," the small human continued. "Do it or you'll . . . or you will die in dishonor, shot like a prey animal!" The human bared its teeth in a smile. "You *macho* cat guys would really hate that, wouldn't you?"

What is this human word, macho? Ralgha wondered briefly, watching his crew to see what they would do.

None of the Kilrathi moved to obey the human.

When the first Kilra'hra *moves, all of them will attack. The humans will kill them all. I cannot allow that . . . they are my warriors, loyal to me through many battles . . . I owe them more than that.*

"You cannot win this battle, *Kilra'hra*," Ralgha said slowly. "You are unarmed, against an enemy with energy weapons. I do not wish to see all of you die for so meaningless a cause. Surrender now, and I swear on my honor as your Captain that I will see that you are treated honorably by the humans."

One of the *Kilra'hra* painfully rose to his feet, the Gunnery Officer who still had tufts of Ralgha's fur caught in his claws. He bowed once to the Captain, then turned to face the wall. Another followed his example, and a third. One by one, all of the *Kilra'hra* placed themselves against the walls, except for one young officer who was obviously too injured to stand, and the smoldering corpse on the deck.

The small gold-furred human knelt next to Ralgha. "Are you Ralgha? I'm Major Kristi Marks, Fourth Division, Confederation Marines."

"I am Lord Ralgha *nar* Hhallas, and I bid you welcome in all honor, H'hristi Mar'hkss," Ralgha said painfully. "I am *Khantahr* of this ship, the commanding officer."

"We're going to secure your ship for you, *Khantahr.* Are there any friendlies out there? Troops that are on our side?"

Ralgha nodded. "Kirha, on the Bridge. No others."

"Thank you, sir." The human spoke tersely in Terran to the others, then turned back to Ralgha. "Our medical officer will be here shortly. You look like you need immediate medical attention. We'll take you to the Sickbay aboard our ship."

"Lord Ralgha?" Kirha's voice, thin and strained, spoke through the airlock intercom. "Lord Ralgha, you must come to the Bridge at once! There is an Imperial Fralthi cruiser approaching our position . . . they are ordering us to surrender or they will destroy the ship!"

• CHAPTER FIVE

"It's a long, long way to Tipperary, it's a long way to go!"

Can't remember the next verse to that ... Lord, but I hate solo patrols, Hunter thought, unstrapping himself so he could prop his feet up on the port viewscreen. *Nothing to do but fly around hoping something will happen, and wondering if you'll be able to handle it by yourself, if something does happen!*

He leaned over to check that the Autopilot was continuing to follow the correct course, then flicked the vidscreen controls to go to multi-channel, broadcasting and receiving from all the pilots. "Hey, anybody seein' anything out there, mates?"

"Keep the channels clear, Hunter," the Colonel's voice said sternly, his image flickering on the vidscreen.

"Okay, okay," Hunter grumbled, wishing yet again that they'd let him smoke cigars when he was on patrol. Too much of a fire risk, sure, but after two hours of this, he was dying for a smoke....

"All pilots, listen closely!" the Colonel's voice crackled. "The *TCS Holmen,* one of our Marine troopships, has just reported in. They've found the *Ras Nik'hra,* and several squadrons of Marines have boarded and are taking command of the ship. And they're reporting another Fralthi is in the area, on an interception course with the ship. All pilots are to divert and assist the *Ras Nik'hra!* The coordinates are . . ."

Hunter sat up immediately, both feet hitting the floor of the fighter with a *thunk,* resetting his Auto-Nav computer as the Colonel recited the sequence of numbers. "I'm only a few minutes away from that position, *Tiger's Claw!*" he reported, strapping himself back into his chair and tightening the straps for good measure. He brought the fighter up to full speed, banking in the direction of the Fralthis.

"Affirmative, Hunter," the Colonel replied. "Bossman and Spirit are also enroute. Good luck."

"Thanks, Colonel." Hunter checked his radar . . . nothing in sight yet. He fired a test burst from his guns, resetting them from neutron guns to laser cannons so he'd have the best long-distance weapon readied, then reached over to switch to Mariko's vid channel.

"How're you doing, sweetheart?" he asked.

"We could use some help, Hunter!" she said. "The Fralthi is heavily armed."

"Hey, I'm on my way, I'll save the day! Don't you get the feeling that we've done this before?" he asked with a grin. "If I show up to rescue you many more times, people are going to start talking about us, you know!"

She smiled, and a moment later Hunter saw the battle in his forward viewscreen, two huge Fralthi firing broadsides at each other, Spirit and Hunter's tiny fighters darting between them.

"They're launching fighters!" Bossman said tersely. "One Jalthi heavy fighter heading toward us. Spirit, form on my wing! We'll take him."

"I'm with you, Major," Hunter said, switching to full guns. "I'll be on your wing in another few seconds. Watch those forward guns, those Jalthi have plenty of firepower."

Spirit spoke quietly. "Major, if we can get some dumb-fire missiles into that launch bay, they won't be able to get any more fighters off the deck."

"Affirmative on that, Spirit," Bossman said. "Be careful, Lieutenant, they'll start tracking guns on you the minute you do that . . . I want you to 'burner past this Jalthi, both of you. I'll do a hard turn and take him. You have to stop them from launching any more fighters!"

"We're on it, Bossman," Hunter said. "Spirit, I'll play decoy, you take out the launch bay!"

"Affirmative!"

The Jalthi fighter, bristling with six forward guns, banked toward them as Hunter slid into the formation next to Bossman and Spirit's fighters. Bossman's voice was tense. "Ready to break . . . NOW!"

Hunter punched in the afterburners, relaxing as acceleration slammed him back into his seat, dodging beneath the Jalthi just as it opened fire. Spirit was already ahead of him, accelerating toward the launch bay. The open space around them suddenly blossomed with heavy weapons fire as the Fralthi's guns began tracking them.

"Evasive, Spirit!" Hunter shouted. Her fighter twisted and turned sharply, still continuing toward her target. Hunter followed closely, sending bursts of cannon fire toward the Fralthi's gun turrets. The missiles arced out from Spirit's fighter and into the Fralthi's landing bay, just as a turret scored a direct hit on her right wing. She tilted away from the ship, spinning uncontrollably.

"Hunter, I'm hit in the main gyros . . . can't stabilize. . . ."

"Lady, get that *Ras Nik'hra* ship between you and this Fralthi and punch out!"

Another burst of fire from a turret caught her fighter, tearing away one of the wings. Hunter yanked on the controls and brought his fighter around, blasting the enemy turret into incandescent debris. "Come on, you bastards, shoot at me, not her!" he shouted into his comlink. An alien voice answered him, a cat face shrieking Kilrathi over the vid.

He glanced back to see Spirit recover control of her fighter, heading straight for the *Ras Nik'hra*. A moment later, Hunter realized that he was now the only target for the Fralthi, as dozens of explosions filled the space around him. He punched the 'burners a split-second later, getting out of range of the turrets.

Oh man, I feel like a bunny at a hawk convention!

"Bossman, where are you?" he called, hoping he didn't sound as frantic as he felt.

"Heading back to your position," the Major replied. "That guy took a little longer than I expected."

"Okay, draw their turret fire!" he said. "I'm going in after that hulk."

"You got it, Hunter!" the other pilot replied.

Hunter hit the afterburners for a quick fly-by, feeling the fighter shake and rattle with the proximity of the Fralthi's guns. Suddenly the fighter bounced hard to the right, and he had to fight to keep it under control and avoid spinning out. *Brushed the shields! Damn, but that thing is armed for bear! I could spend all day pounding on those shields and never get through . . .*

He accelerated beyond the cruiser and brought the fighter around again for another attack run, this time aiming at the rear of the huge ship. He could see the main thruster engine of the ship, glowing bright in the center of the five other engine nacelles. Hunter paused briefly to switch to Image-Recognition missiles, and eased back on the throttle, slowing down to only a hundred KPS. All he needed was one lucky shot. . . .

He approached slowly, feeling a trickle of sweat start down the side of his face as the Fralthi's guns swiveled to track him. *That's right, boys, I'm a sitting duck, come and get me.* . . . The targeting computer wailed shrilly as the I-R missile locked onto the Fralthi's main engine. He slammed his thumb down to launch the missile, then immediately switched to dumb-fire missiles, continuing to accelerate directly at the main engine nacelle. At the last moment he fired both dumb-fire missiles into the nacelle, banking hard to the right. Another of the engine nacelles loomed directly before him, and he twisted the ship away, diving beneath it and into open space.

Hunter looked back to see the main engine nacelle peeling away from the rest of the ship. He had a split second of horrified realization . . . *My God, I'm too close to the ship!* . . . before the Fralthi exploded into brilliant light and debris. The blast wave caught him up and hurled him forward, tumbling end over end helplessly. The Rapier's stabilizers kicked back in a few seconds later, and the fighter hung motionless in space, large pieces of debris drifting past him. Hunter just sat there for a long moment, trying to catch his breath. Then he brought the fighter around to see what was left.

Of the Imperial Fralthi, the only part of the ship that was still intact was the forward oval that he knew contained the ship's Bridge. *I hope those blokes died fast,* he thought soberly, looking at the remains of the ship. Beyond the dead Fralthi, the *Ras Nik'hra* sailed regally onward, continuing in the direction of the *Tiger's Claw.*

"Hunter, you all right?" Bossman called on the vid monitor.

"Yeah, sure." He wiped the sweat from his forehead. "Kien, where's Mariko?"

"I saw her heading toward the *Ras Nik'hra*'s landing bay."

"All right. I want to land and make sure that she's all right," he said, moving slowly toward the huge ship.

"Affirmative, Hunter, I'll stay out here as escort," Bossman said, his image fizzling out.

The ship grew larger and larger in front of him, a behemoth that dwarfed his fighter and was nearly the size of the *Austin.* He eased up on the controls as he approached the open gap of the landing bay. *"Ras Nik'hra,* do you read?" he said on the open channels. "This is Captain St. John, requesting landing permission."

A blonde woman's face appeared on the vid screen. "Captain St. John, this is Major Marks," she said. "You are cleared to land." Her image disappeared a moment later.

"Thanks," Hunter muttered under his breath. "How 'bout giving me a road map of this bloody ship?" He maneuvered for the final approach, feeling another trickle of sweat starting on his brow. *It's just like landing on any other carrier,* he told himself. *Except that it's a Kilrathi ship, I've never seen the layout of their landing bay, I don't know how much space I have to brake, or anything else about it. But other than that, it's just like landing on any other carrier. Just keep thinking that, mate!*

He brought his speed all the way down to near zero, edging into the deck at the slowest possible speed. The bay was strange, painted in odd oranges and reds, with a high curving ceiling covered with pipes and conduits. He cleared the entrance and immediately touched down, feeling the slight difference in gravity as he parked the fighter. Mariko's fighter, with the long burn mark along one side, was parked fifty feet away. Hunter killed the main engines, and checked the atmospheric readout on his cockpit panel. *Still vacuum out there, those clever cats haven't figured out how to do our magnetic shields yet,* he thought. He checked to make sure that his flight suit was still fully pressurized, then popped the cockpit.

Hunter climbed down, glancing around. The deck was deserted. He walked quickly toward the airlock, pausing for a moment to look appreciatively at the row of Dralthi fighters parked along one wall. *Those good old flying pancakes,* he thought, smiling as he studied the unusual saucer-shaped body of the Kilrathi fighters. *I've never seen one from this close before. I wonder what it'd be like to fly one of those babies?*

He continued into the airlock. Hunter stared at the complex control panel, with all of its markings in the vertical line-syllables of the Kilrathi alphabet. "Press the button marked with the two long lines and the two dotted lines," a human voice said into his helmet radio. Hunter did so, and the outer door of the airlock slid shut. A few seconds later, as the air pressure equalized, the inner airlock door opened silently.

Two Marines saluted stiffly, standing at attention. A short blonde woman with a Major's decorations on her fatigues, and two tall Kilrathi stood next to them. Hunter stepped back in spite of himself at the sight of the Kilrathi, wearing heavy leather hauberks, their ears pierced with multiple gold rings. Mariko, her hair tousled from her helmet, stood off to one side. There was a large bruise on her cheek, but otherwise she looked to be fine.

"You're okay, Spirit?" he asked, walking up to her.

"It is nothing, Ian," she said, touching her cheek self-consciously.

"Glad to hear it," he said, and kissed her exuberantly. Mariko, startled, blushed bright pink.

The taller of the two Kilrathi said something in their own growly language. The other Kilrathi bowed to Hunter and spoke in awkward, heavily-accented English. "I beg your pardon with all honor, noble sir, but my lord would know why you touch faces with the other warrior."

"Because I'll take any excuse to kiss this lady!" Hunter grinned.

"Ah, gentlemen," the Major said, clearing her throat. "We have other matters to discuss. I'm

Major Marks, currently in charge of this operation. Lord Ralgha, this is Captain Ian St. John, also known as Hunter. Hunter, this is Lord Ralgha *nar* Hhallas, Khantahr of the *Ras Nik'hra*. He wanted to meet you."

The smaller Kilrathi bowed to Hunter again. "My lord Ralgha bids you welcome in all honor, Captain Ian St. John, also known as Hunter," the feline alien said. Hunter watched the cat struggle with the human language, and realized with a start that this was a very young Kilrathi, compared to the grizzled Captain with his mane of white fur. "My lord Ralgha wishes to confirm that you were the human pilot who destroyed the Fralthi *Kraj'nishk* in valiant battle."

"Uh, yeah, mate," Hunter said, glancing at the Major, who nodded at him to continue. "That was me, I toasted it."

The younger Kilrathi spoke in his own language with the lord, then spoke again to Hunter. "Noble sir, my lord wishes to personally surrender his ship, the *Ras Nik'hra*, to you. He owes you a debt of honor, which he cannot repay. But as a small token, he wishes to give you his loyal retainer, who will serve you as his liege-lord . . . and . . ." The young Kilrathi's tail twitched suddenly. He turned back to Ralgha, speaking frantically in his own language. Even though Hunter couldn't understand a word of Kilrathi, he recognized desperation when he saw it. Lord Ralgha said something short and terse in Kilrathi. The younger Kilrathi swallowed visibly, then knelt before Hunter, raising his chin high. The two Kilrathi stared at Hunter, obviously expecting him to do something. *But what?*

"You're supposed to accept his oath of fealty, Captain," the Major said in the awkward silence.

"I'm supposed to do *what*?" Hunter said.

"We'll deal with it later, for now just say that you'll accept him as your sworn warrior." She added in an undertone, "We don't need a diplomatic incident right now, Captain. Say you'll accept him!"

"Uh, sure." Hunter said. "That is, yes. I accept you as my sworn warrior." He stared at the young Kilrathi prostrating himself at his feet, and asked, "What's your name, anyhow?"

"Kirha, my lord Captain Ian St. John, also known as Hunter," the Kilrathi replied.

"Kirha, right. Uh . . . stand up, Kirha. Tell your lord that I said thanks for the gift."

"But Captain Ian St. John, also known as Hunter . . . *you* are my lord now!"

"Why don't we continue this on the Bridge of the *Ras Nik'hra*?" the Major said. Hunter glanced at her, and saw that she was stifling a grin. Mariko, too, looked like she was enjoying all of this too much.

"What did I do to deserve this?" Hunter muttered under his breath, walking with the Major, Mariko, and the Kilrathi Captain in the direction of the Bridge, as Kirha followed respectfully behind him.

Kirha waited, in a kind of exhausted trance, for the human Hunter to do something. Anything! Either accept Kirha's oath, or tear out Kirha's throat with his claws —

Well, maybe not that. But shoot him, or something. What, didn't much matter anymore. Kirha was too tired, too bewildered by the sudden change in loyalties, and too confused to care. Just so something happened, something that did not require *him* to make a decision.

Finally, Ralgha, with Kirha translating, coached the human through the words and actions of formal oath-swearing when they reached the bridge. Hunter completed the ceremony and told him to seat himself out of the way, and Kirha permitted himself to collapse into a shock-chair on the bridge. He watched apathetically as Lord Ralgha directed the humans in the navigation and control of the ship, translating when he was called upon to do so. No longer a Kilrathi ship . . . strange. It ought to look different somehow; it ought to have turned unrecognizable and alien. Yet nothing had changed, except the figures at the consoles. Too thin, too hairless, no tails at all.

It occurred to him, in a dim sort of fashion, that he was probably in shock. Too many changes, too quickly. The Kilrathi did not care much for change; yet Kirha's life had been one long string of changes, with only his oath and his loyalties to Ralgha as a constant. Now, even that was . . . changed. . . .

At some point in the haze, they must have reached the humans' command-ship, for more of the creatures came pouring aboard, and some of them approached him. They were armed, bearing both hand weapons and things that were as long as their arms, and from their postures, they were very wary of him. They stared down at him as he continued to sit; he stared up at them, wondering what they wanted. Finally, one of them said, in badly pronounced and nearly unintelligible Kilrathi, "You, come. For questions."

Now what was that supposed to mean? Were they planning to interrogate him? Why?

He spotted the human Hunter across the room, and called out to him. Hunter looked up, startled, as the humans surrounding Kirha jumped back a pace. Hunter left the human he was speaking to and hurried across the bridge. Kirha reflected that he moved well, for a human. He would have been more graceful with a tail, however. Kirha remained sitting, since that was what Hunter had told him to do.

"What is it?" he asked. "What's the matter?"

Kirha spoke slowly and carefully, so that there would be no misunderstandings.

"These — fellow-beings of yours — seem to wish me to come with them for interrogation," he said, with as much dignity as his weariness would allow. "Is there need for this? I possess no secrets; I am permitted no secrets. I am sworn to you, is this not sufficient?"

Hunter's face-skin twisted and wrinkled, and he rubbed the side of his head. "Furball, I can't explain this properly, but just go with them. Answer their questions. It'll be easier that way."

"But my loyalty — " Kirha protested. "You have my oath!"

"I'm not questioning that, but my — uh — clan-siblings don't understand the way the oath works yet. We'll both need to explain it to them. They — uh — we don't know a lot about your customs."

"Then tell them," Kirha said, logically.

The skin of Hunter's face wrinkled still more. "Just do it, all right? They have to talk with you themselves."

Kirha flattened his ears, and got slowly to his feet, making no secret of his reluctance. The humans backed up another pace or two as he straightened to his full height, the stiffness of their posture showing their nervousness, their face-skins perfectly smooth.

One last time, he turned toward Hunter, but the human only motioned for him to go on. He flattened his ears with unhappiness, and obeyed.

First, they doctored him, which was welcome; his wounds were not as extensive as Lord Ralgha's, but they pained him. He had assumed drugs; he had feared torture. The humans administered neither, although they were as thorough as any expert Kilrathi interrogator. He assumed, when they questioned him for a long time about religion and clan-customs, that they had instruments trained on him and were establishing a base-line for truth. It was a reasonable thing to expect; even prey-species knew that physiological changes accompanied untruths.

Finally, he told them his assumption, in the vague hope that it would make them come to the point.

There were three humans doing the questioning, besides the six guarding him; they sat behind a table or console whose face he could not see. One of them laughed, that peculiar barking sound the humans used to express pleasure; the face-skin of the other two assumed various degrees of wrinkling. He understood just enough of the human tongue to make out what the first one said.

"I told you we wouldn't fool this cat for long," he said. "He's the equivalent of an ensign at the least, and fools don't last long in their Fleet."

He turned to Kirha, and continued in Kilrathi

that was almost acceptable. "Save us both a lot of time, if you would, warrior Kirha. Recite a tale that would be told to a cub, so that we can get a base-line, then we'll just ask you a few questions and you can go to your new quarters."

His new prison, he suspected. Nevertheless, he told them one of his favorite stories from childhood, the tale of "How Clan Ishta Got Its Stripes."

Oddly enough, telling the familiar story, even to these hairless ones, relaxed him. So when the first human said, "Our thanks, warrior, that was excellent, and fine tale-telling as well," he was able to respond with a gracious nod and wait for the real questions to begin with something like calm.

They soon found out for themselves that he had no military secrets of any kind — or at least, nothing that could not be discovered from the ship itself. As he had told Hunter, junior officers were permitted to know nothing more than they absolutely needed for their functions. And they found that his loyalty was now bound completely to Hunter.

They had a great deal of difficulty understanding that, and questioned him over and over, using different ways of asking the same thing, as if to trap him. Or — just perhaps — they were making sure that there was no loophole in the language that would permit his loyalty to slip. That was annoying, but to be expected. Even the interrogators of the Kilrathi sought such linguistic traps when they questioned warriors about their loyalty to their officers and Emperor.

Finally they must have decided that his oath was unbreakable, and told him that he would be taken to "somewhere safe."

Safe for whom? he wondered, but told them tiredly that he could do nothing without his liege lord's permission. He had thought they understood this by now, but evidently they did not. He had to repeat it to them several times, in the tones one reserved for cubs, that he could do *nothing* without Hunter's permission.

Finally the first one made a sound of surprise, as if he suddenly understood something.

"I've got it — " he said to the other two in the human tongue. "Look, he's not being stubborn, this is the part of the honor-code that protects him from being abused or exploited, and protects him from being used against his lord. You see what I mean?"

The second shook his head from side to side, but the third bobbed his head up and down. "This way we can't order him to do anything against his lord without Hunter knowing about it. He won't act, even if the act seems harmless, because he can't know for certain that it is harmless."

"Exactly," said the first. "And we also can't poison him or lock him away without Hunter knowing about it. Or at least, if we killed him or locked him away, his lord would presumably notice the fact that he didn't come looking for orders after a while."

The second one made one of those skin-wrinkling expressions, and growled, "All right then, get that (unknown) (unknown) rocket-jockey in here so he can give the (unknown) cat his (unknown) orders!"

Kirha presumed that the words he did not know were expletives, and filed the sounds away for later.

There was some talk on the ship's intercom, and the second one took over from the first, growling into the microphone, "I don't care if he's (unknown) the Admiral! Get him *down* here before I have him court-martialed!"

Presently, Hunter appeared, flushed and out-of-breath. He ignored the three interrogators, except for a sketchy salute. They seemed contented to be ignored, something that would not have been tolerated among Kirha's people.

"Now what's the matter?" Hunter asked unhappily, his face-skin very wrinkled indeed. "Do you have any idea what you dragged me away from? I had the most incredible — " he shook his head. "Never mind. What do you want? You're making me crazy, I hope you realize that."

Kirha ignored the last sentence as irrelevant. Hunter was already crazy; all humans were, it was a given. One did not have to be sane to be intelligent, or a worthy opponent. In fact, it often helped a warrior to be a little crazy. "You must tell me what you want me to do now, my lord," he said earnestly. "I have followed your orders, and now you must give me new ones."

"It has to be me?" Hunter replied, sounding as weary as Kirha felt. "Why can't you just do what — "

"Yes, my lord," Kirha told him firmly. "You must tell me personally exactly what you wish me to do."

Hunter made a strange, strangled sound.

"Do it, St. John," the first man said. "And make sure you cover everything he needs to do. Specifically and explicitly. Right down to when and what he can eat. And eliminate. And anything else he might need to do."

Kirha let his fur fluff a little with relief. Here, at least, was one human who understood.

Hunter sat down. Kirha raised his ears to show

his attentiveness. "All right, Kirha," Hunter said, heaving out his breath. "Let's take this from the top. First, go with these people to the place where Ralgha is. Eat what they give you, *if* it's acceptable and *if* you're hungry, and if it isn't acceptable, then tell them what you want. Sleep when you're tired. After a few days, someone will come to take you to Confed High Command. . . ."

Ralgha hoped that Kirha would be all right. Was the youngster flexible enough to accept the addition to his loyalties? His first loyalty would always be to Ralgha of course; until Ralgha took back that oath, the boy would be his before he was Hunter's. But this seemed the best and surest way to keep Kirha safe. Provided it didn't tip him over the edge with too much change, too much stress, too soon.

At least these humans had enough honor to respect a surrender and a safe-conduct. That was encouraging and promising as well. They had not subjected him to any indignities; he could probably assume they would not subject Kirha to any either.

In fact, thus far they had given him more courtesy than his own people had; they had tended to his injuries, taken him to a quite comfortable room, with chairs actually adapted for the use of beings with tails, and had left him with water and a promise of drink and food later. He could use both; the strain was beginning to tell on him.

Rest would be even more welcome, but for all three, he would have to wait until these humans had satisfied themselves concerning him.

He had several moments to reflect — but he was too tired to think, much. The rush of fighting-hormones that had borne him up was spent, and now he felt every year of his age, every cut and bruise, every now-broken and once-broken bone, every old scar that pulled fur and skin a little too tight.

He longed, suddenly, for home; for the rolling hills covered with grass, for the bitter scent of *merrgha* leaves and the munching of the herd-beasts. For the simple life of a Herdmaster, with no concerns of Empire, only the prosperity of his family.

But before he could mire himself in regrets, the door slid open, and two humans stepped through it, followed by two armed guards. By Kilrathi standards, the uniforms the humans wore were pathetically plain, but there were enough of the paltry things that passed for decorations of honor on these two to denote some importance among the humans of this ship.

Ralgha was somewhat surprised when they both addressed him in his own language, until he saw the tiny translator-units attached to their belts. Expensive technology, that — which denoted both their importance and his.

"This is Captain Thorn, kalrahr of the *Tiger's Claw*, Lord Ralgha," said the younger of the two. "I am Colonel Halcyon, leader of the squadron you surrendered to."

Ralgha nodded, but did not rise. These humans were important, but did not outrank him. Besides, he didn't want to make them nervous, and rising to his full height might do just that. He was tall, even for a Kilrathi, and still in his warrior-prime. But it was good to see the kalrahr of the squadron here; it indicated that the humans took honor seriously. This Colonel Halcyon, like a good liege-lord, was taking responsibility for what his oath-bound warriors did.

The two humans did not seem perturbed, but took seats opposite Ralgha. The guards moved to stand silently beside the entrance. "I'm here to assure you that we take your safe-conduct seriously, sir," Colonel Halcyon said. "I stand personal surety for it, in fact. Your young liegeman will be joining you when we are finished speaking, and you may verify that we have caused him no harm for yourself."

Ralgha blinked gravely, but with a sense of satisfaction. It was good; these humans *did* understand honor and decency, then.

"But we all know that you must have come to us, bringing your ship, with your own agenda," Captain Thorn said. The man had a deep, tight voice; Ralgha could hear it even through the flat tones of the translator. "Let us be honest with each other, Lord Ralgha. This is the first time that any of your people has exchanged anything with ours — except an exchange of fire. There must be something that you want from us."

This was a little more abrupt than Ralgha preferred, but such directness was not altogether unexpected. He tilted his head to one side.

"I do want something from you, human," he replied. "I want something from your alliance; something only you can give."

Carefully, slowly, with Halcyon and Thorn asking equally careful questions, he explained the situation on Ghorah Khar; the Emperor, seemingly so power-drunk that he no longer worried about the welfare of his people, and the advisors who continued to urge war upon him, when war gained them nothing, not even the good-will of the war-god. How, after all, could Sivar approve of a war that held no true victories? How could the god approve of a war in which, increasingly, the highest number of deaths were among the women and children — and in accident, not in combat. Such deaths meant nothing to Sivar — and they impoverished the Kilrathi, destroyed the hope held in the blood of the young.

Then, only when he was certain that the humans understood as much as they could, did he speak of the rebels — and made certain that they knew that there were no few of the priestesses of Sivar among them. He had to digress long enough to make them aware of the important positions the all-but-invisible females held among his people — that just because the humans never saw them, they were by no means powerless and unimportant. In fact, the day-to-day administration of government and estate-management could never succeed without them. And *they* were prominent in the rebel cause, with ample opportunity for concealing insurrection.

Finally, he flexed his shoulders and took a sip of water, then said, simply, "We have done all we can. We need help." There he stopped, every carefully-crafted word spent. He had said what he came to say. Now, it remained for the humans to make their move.

He was not expecting an immediate offer of aid, so he was not disappointed when Halcyon and Thorn exchanged looks that he could not read, and Thorn made a coughing sound.

"You have to understand that we cannot speak

for Confederation High Command," Thorn said, so slowly that Ralgha suspected he was choosing each word with the greatest of care. "We can give recommendations, we can give you support — but we do not make the decisions that will affect the entire Confederation."

"No more than would the Emperor accept such a promise if I had made it," Ralgha agreed. "We are all subject to the decisions of those who outrank us. But you *can* speed my cause, if you choose. You can even force the issue, I suspect. More than that, I would be willing to wager that your word will carry far more weight with your superiors than you will admit."

He wished he could read their faces, their body-language; he could read herd-beasts more easily than these humans.

Finally, Thorn hid his mouth behind his hand for a moment, and coughed again. "You could be correct," he said, "Although I would not care to test that." Halcyon nodded, and Thorn continued. "We will do what we can."

"Meanwhile, we must assure ourselves of you," Halcyon said. "We will send you to Confederation High Command to plead your case in person on the next available ship. And in the meantime, the Captain and I would appreciate it if you would permit us to perform a chemical interrogation on you. You understand, you can object to this if you wish, but in that case it will be that much longer before you can come before High Command."

"Of course," he replied blandly, thinking how clever they were. They would not force drugs upon him, yet if he would not agree, they would — must!

— suspect him of being a Kilrathi agent.

"I hope that your healers and interrogators are sufficiently familiar with Kilrathi metabolism to keep me from damage," he continued, keeping his voice perfectly calm. "I see no reason to refuse such an — invitation — so long as you are sure of that. I would like to be away from this system as soon as may be, at any rate. It is likely to become most uncomfortable here before long."

There was no mistaking the look of startlement on both their faces; in every species Ralgha had ever encountered, widened eyes and rapid blinking meant surprise.

"Ah — why do you say that?" Halcyon asked. Carefully.

Could they *not* know?

Perhaps not. Perhaps they were not aware of how important religion was to his people. Perhaps they had intercepted communications about the coming ceremony, but had no idea what it *meant*.

Perhaps he had better enlighten them.

"We are about to celebrate the most important religious ceremony of the year," he told them. "This is the *Sivar-Eshrad* ceremony. Every Kilrathi warship that can be released from duty will be coming here, intending to fight. And I must tell you, they will fight with a ferocity such as you have not seen before."

He closed his eyes for a moment, as the silence lengthened, until all he heard was the sigh of the ventilators.

"The site of the Holy Dedication must be taken by warfare," he continued, after much thought. "Conflict itself hallows the site; the more conflict, the holier the site, and the more pleasing in the eyes of Sivar. The results of such conflict are the appropriate sacrifices and servants for the ceremony — the sacrifices being those of the enemy killed in the fighting. Every warrior in our Empire hopes he may bring many sacrifices to Sivar's honor, and so every warrior that can will be here."

Ralgha opened his eyes, and noted that the humans had turned several shades paler. He assumed this meant that they were more than alarmed, they were horrified. And well they might be. There was an armada on the way, full of warriors keying themselves up to a berserker frenzy.

No matter what they had faced before this, it would be nothing compared to the fighting they would see now.

"I am not certain how to respond," Thorn said at last. "Thank you for the warning."

The humans exchanged more unreadable glances, then Thorn rose. "I must contact Confederation High Command," he said. "I trust you'll excuse me."

With that he left, without waiting for a response. Not that Ralgha blamed him. This had apparently come as something of a shock, and not a pleasant one.

"What of yourself, Lord Ralgha?" Halcyon asked. "Were you intending to participate in this massacre?"

Ralgha's ears curled back. "Since the death of my *hrai,* I do not care about the gods."

"Hmm." Halcyon was silent for a long moment. "I suppose that leaves it to me to escort you for questioning," Halcyon said at last. Ralgha simply rose, signifying agreement by the simple act. Halcyon rose immediately, and the guards that had been waiting silently beside the door, like so many immobile statues, suddenly came to life.

Halcyon gestured smoothly, and as the door slid open, Ralgha preceded him through it.

They walked together through the corridors of the ship, as Ralgha reflected that there were few differences between a base-ship of any species, so long as they were bipedal. His crew could probably walk in here — and if everything was labeled — have it cruising anywhere in the galaxy within a day. Three days, and they could probably fight with it.

Perhaps it was that he was so tired; perhaps that he was lost in thought. Perhaps that, now that his task was fundamentally over, he had relaxed his guard. For whatever reason, he was unprepared for violence.

Yet violence came to him.

One moment, he walked beside Halcyon, hoping that when he reached the human healers, they would see a little more to his wounds as well as drugging him. One of their kind had done his best to patch up the wounds the Kilrathi had sustained in the takeover of their own ship, but Ralgha's injuries still pained him. That was all that he was thinking of, the moment he walked into the corridor.

The next moment, he was on the deck, knocked there by Halcyon, and heat scorching past his ears told him that someone had just tried to kill him.

In the next breath, the human guards had leapt upon the man, who shouted and waved his gun wildly as he went down beneath them.

Ralgha climbed slowly to his feet, and watched

dispassionately as the human guards put restraints upon their fellow. From some of the glances thrown his way, he guessed that no few of them wished that the restraints were going on someone else — and that if the crazed human had succeeded in killing him, they would have been much happier.

Expected. But it made him feel even lonelier.

Meanwhile, Halcyon was attempting to apologize for the crewman's attack, speaking so quickly that the translator stuttered and squawked attempting to keep up with him.

"He just lost his family to the bas — to the attack on Goddard Colony," he concluded. "He hasn't been the same — "

Ralgha waved the rest of the explanation wearily away. "And I lost my entire clan to an evacuation ahead of an attack by your people," he replied, wishing at that moment that this was all over. There had just been too much death on both sides, it made no sense to reckon up who owed blood-guilt to whom. "I understand, and this in no way invalidates your safe-conduct or my surrender. At least he was more competent than the last Kilrathi who attempted my life."

And as Halcyon stared at him, mouth falling open just a little in what was probably surprise, he continued down the corridor towards the place where the healers were. The interrogation chemicals would without a doubt include some euphorics and painkillers.

Right now, he would welcome both.

● CHAPTER SIX

He was flying a Rapier fighter . . . no, it was a Kilrathi ship, very alien, with a curved cockpit roof and that weird alien writing everywhere. He scanned the controls, trying to figure out how to fly the strange craft, but nothing made much sense. And something was wrong, the alien fighter was moving strangely, rocking from side to side.

No, someone was shaking him . . .

"Go away," Hunter mumbled, his face buried in his pillow.

"Come on, Hunter, get a move on! The briefing's in ten minutes!" Hunter opened his eyes slowly, to see Joe Khumalo looking down at him with a sardonic look in his dark eyes.

"Go away, Knight. I flew a patrol at Oh-Four-hundred hours," Hunter said. "That can't even have been two hours ago! Give me a break, I can't be up for patrol."

Joe pulled his blanket off, leaving him shivering in the blast from the ventilators. "You're on the roster, Hunter. Hell, we all are. As of last night, everyone's flying patrols on a four hours on, four hours off schedule. Colonel's orders."

Hunter crawled out of his bunk, found one last clean flight suit hanging in his locker, and dressed quickly. *No time to shower, or even shave. . . .*

Joe brought over two cups of coffee from the

wardroom next door to the Barracks while Hunter was dressing, and Hunter gratefully accepted one. "Thanks, mate," he said, grimacing at the bitterness of the coffee. *This is why this guy's callsign fits him,* Hunter thought, *Because he acts like a knight and a gentleman, even in the face of a surly Aussie who hasn't had enough sleep!*

"I'll meet you at the briefing room," Knight said, starting for the door.

"I'll be there in a few," Hunter said, finishing the coffee. It didn't quite clear the fuzziness out of his brain, but was a good start. Enough so he could at least start thinking about what Joe had said.

In the week since they'd brought the renegade captain's Fralthi into a parked position next to the *Claw,* the enemy presence in the Firekka System had increased by a factor of ten. Hunter was beginning to wonder if the Kilrathi ships that were arriving in force were *all* because of the escaped Fralthi. He could understand them sending a couple ships after the *Ras Nik'hra,* to try and destroy it before the humans could take it out of the system, but the number of ships they'd been encountering ...

He was keeping a running tally of the ships they'd sighted, and a personal tally of the ships they'd destroyed, and their own losses. So far the *Tiger's Claw* and *Austin* pilots had done exceptionally well, no casualties and only a few ships damaged beyond repair, mostly because the cats didn't seem to expect any enemy presence this far out in this system. But that was bound to change eventually. Sooner or later, the Kilrathi ships were going to start comparing notes. Sooner or later, *someone* was going to send a message back to their equivalent of High Command.

And sooner or later, the Confed pilots were going to start making mistakes. Especially if he and the other pilots were flying so many patrols that they were too exhausted to think straight.

It had to break, eventually. Either the reinforcements would arrive, or they'd be recalled from this system. Hunter didn't want to think about that, knowing what was likely to happen to the Firekkans if their only defenders left.

Those bird-folks don't have any planetary defenses, any space-based defenses or interception fleet . . . they'd be sitting ducks. . . .

I hope the reinforcements get here soon, he thought grimly. *We can't leave the Firekkans to face the cats alone, but we can't hold this system by ourselves for much longer, either. We're going to start running out of missiles very soon, and fighter replacement parts, not to mention what's going to happen once the Kilrathi really start fighting back and we begin losing pilots.*

He didn't want to think about that. *But it's only a matter of time, if we continue to be so badly outnumbered. How many Kilrathi ships have we run into in the last week?*

He consulted his mental tally. Another Fralthi cruiser. Two Dorkir. A Snakier carrier. Several corvettes. And lots of enemy fighters.

And the tally was still rising . . .

It's not a strike fleet, it's a bloody invasion force! Those damned cats!

Well, time to do my part to get rid of them. He pulled on his boots, and started for the Briefing Room.

As usual, he was late. The Colonel was already at

the podium, detailing the assignments. This time, though, the Colonel didn't pause in his litany of assignments and patrol routes to chastize Hunter as he always did. He'd lost count of the number of times he'd heard the Colonel's sardonic "So glad you decided to join us, Captain St. John" comments.

He slid into an empty seat next to Knight, listening as the Colonel assigned the patrols.

"Gamma Wing is Angel and Bossman, they'll patrol the jump point area. Delta Wing is Spirit and Iceman, flying the wide patrol beyond the jump points. Epsilon Wing is Hunter and Knight, you'll stay close to the *Claw* in the usual defensive patrol. With an unknown number of enemy ships in this area, we can't risk any Kilrathi fighters getting close to the carrier."

"Babysitting duty again," Hunter whispered to Knight.

"Remember, you'll be back on duty again in four hour shifts," the Colonel continued. "Get as much sleep as you can between flights. Dismissed." The assembled pilots rose to their feet as the Colonel left the podium, starting for the flight deck.

"I think we got the defensive patrol because of you," Joe said as they walked to the flight deck, too tired to sprint the way they had a few short weeks ago.

Hunter gave him a puzzled look. "Because of me? Why's that?"

"Have you looked at yourself in the mirror yet?" Joe asked, a little grimly.

He didn't want to think about how he looked. Really, it was no worse than anyone else. "I'll be fine with another cup of coffee," Hunter muttered.

The flight deck was already busy; two Hornet fighters took off, one after the other, as Hunter mustered up a tired trot to his fighter. A tech was under the Rapier, invisible except for a pair of booted legs sticking out from beneath the wing. "Good morning, Jimmy," Hunter called, forcing himself to sound cheerful.

The face that emerged from under the ship was definitely not Jimmy's, or male. She was a pixie-faced young woman with short red hair and smudges of grease on her face. "Jimmy's not here, sir."

"And who might you be?" *One hell of a cute lady, that's who,* Hunter thought, hiding his delighted smile. He was never too tired for an attractive lady, after all.

"I'm Janet McCullough, a new technician on the *Austin,* sir. But, please, call me 'Sparks.' Everyone does." She was so cheerful she sparkled; a much-needed dose of good humor among all the exhaustion. "Jimmy's been working on the *Ras Nik'hra* for a few days. They're supposed to take the Fralthi to Confed High Command tomorrow, and they needed Jimmy to doublecheck some of the ship systems."

Hunter didn't mind dallying, a little — this was information the rest of the crew would be interested to hear. "So they're finally taking that tugboat back to Sol Station?"

She nodded. "That's what I've heard, sir."

But that left some "loose ends" unaccounted for. Some very hairy loose ends, one of which seemed determined to attach himself to Hunter. "What about the Kilrathi that we took off the ship?"

Her eyes narrowed in thought. "Most of them have already been taken out-system. I think the only ones that are left on the *Claw* are the two cooperative guys. They're still here, but under guard, of course."

"Right." *The grizzled old Captain and the young Kilrathi. What was his name? Kirha, that's right. The one that was given to me as a gift. Some gift. Now I know how the old Rajahs felt when they got those white elephants. 'Course, this time the elephant knew what was going to happen to him.* Hunter repressed a grin, remembering the shocked look on the young Kilrathi's face. *Well, he's not my problem anymore. Taking care of all of his friends out there who're trying to invade this system, that's my problem now.*

"How soon will this old bird be ready to fly?" he asked the technician, who had disappeared under the wing again.

"Just . . . another few minutes . . . sir!" came her voice from underneath. "I need to tighten . . . the fuel intake to this engine . . ."

"Take your time, sweetheart," Hunter said, leaning against the side of the fighter. After all, the longer she took, the shorter the amount of time he'd have to spend strapped in. *Could be the Colonel didn't reckon on how much down-time these Rapiers need.* "Say, you wouldn't happen to like listening to live jazz music, would you?"

Her voice came out from under the fighter with a kind of muffled quality to it. "I've heard Lieutenant Colson play several times, if that's what you're asking, sir. He's quite good."

A most excellent opening. And Hunter was going to take full advantage of it. "Yes, he is. Well, I was wondering. . . ."

"Hunter! What's taking so long? I'm waiting to launch!" Joe Khumalo's voice boomed out over the flight deck PA. Everyone on the Deck stopped working and looked up. A moment later, Khumalo's voice continued, "Oh, this is set to the loudspeaker frequency? Sorry about that, let me switch it to . . ."

"Your ship's ready for launch, sir," Sparks said, scrambling to her feet and saluting him smartly. She was flushed, and Hunter thought that her color was due as much to embarrassment as to exertion.

Well, there went his chances, right down the old tube.

"Thanks, Sparks," Hunter said, and sighed. "Great timing, Joe," he muttered, climbing up into the cockpit.

Five minutes later, he was floating free in space, gently working the controls to bring his fighter up on Knight's wing. The *Tiger's Claw* floated beside them, huge and imposing against the starfield and the silhouetted planet of Firekka. Just beyond the *Tiger's Claw* was the *Ras Nik'hra*, the captured Fralthi.

"What was taking so long on the Deck?" Knight asked, his voice a little tinny over the comlink.

"You're a married man, Joe," Hunter said, wondering if he could somehow track the girl down again, and then wondering if he'd have any time to spare for her even if he did. "You wouldn't understand. So, what's our patrol coordinates?"

Knight kept his curiosity — if he had any — to himself. "Five thousand klicks out, a diamond configuration. It shouldn't take us more than an hour."

"Good," Hunter said, yawning. "Then I'm going

to set my Nav computer and put this on Autopilot. Wake me up if anything interesting happens, okay?"

Joe sounded aghast. "Hunter!"

Couldn't the guy tell a joke when he heard one? "All right, mate, just kidding." *Did he really think I'd even consider flaking out like that?* "Setting first Nav coordinate, AutoNav on your mark?"

Knight was right back to business. "Affirmative. Two . . . one . . . mark!"

The two fighters banked simultaneously, cruising in the direction of Nav 1.

An hour later, Hunter was more bored than he'd ever been in his life. Aside from a few minutes of conversation and bad dirty jokes with the Deck Officer of the TCS *Austin,* as their patrol path brought them within sight of the smaller Gettysburg-class ship, the patrol was totally uneventful. *Totally boring,* Hunter thought. *I probably* could *have taken a nap.*

As if Knight had heard the thought, he came on-line with a crackle of static. "You need to be more serious about your job, Hunter," Joe said, as they dropped out of AutoNav, within sight of the *Tiger's Claw.* "Life isn't all jokes and beer, you know."

Be gentle on him; he's probably hoping for a promotion. "It's been that way for me so far, mate," Hunter grinned, as if he took Joe's reproachful attitude as yet another joke, then switching his vidscreen to the *Tiger's Claw* channel. "*Tiger's Claw,* we are requesting permission to land."

"Affirmative, you are clear to land," the Deck Officer reported a moment later.

"After you, Joe," Hunter said. He sat back and

watched as Knight's fighter turned smoothly into the final approach, gliding down into the Deck.

"Hunter, you are cleared to land," the Deck Officer repeated a moment later, obviously expecting Hunter to follow Knight down onto the Deck.

Little did they know . . ."Negative on that, *Tiger's Claw*, your signal is breaking up. Communications malfunction, I can't quite hear you. What were those new orders?"

"Hunter, bring that fighter down *right now!*" The Deck Officer sounded suspicious. Well, he should be. Especially if he knew Hunter by reputation.

He tried to keep a straight face, knowing that the Deck Officer could see *him* very well, even if a supposed malfunction made it impossible for him to hear the D.O. "Affirmative, *Tiger's Claw*, now proceeding with new orders." He brought the throttle up and tilted the fighter on a new course, a direct route to the floating *Ras Nik'hra*.

It's even bigger than I remember, he thought, maneuvering for final approach on the odd circular-shaped landing bay. He brought his speed all the way down, but miscalculated on his angle of approach, and bounced once off the deck as he brought the fighter to a complete stop within the Fralthi's bay.

The vidscreen still had the D.O. squawking angry orders at him as Hunter climbed out of the fighter, looking around the deck. He recognized a thin space-suited figure standing on the wing of a Dralthi fighter, looking down at an open panel. He switched on his suit's radio. "Hey, Jimmy!"

The young technician looked up, and saw Hunter. "Hunter?"

Hunter walked up to the Dralthi. "Just wanted to see how things were going for you. And get a last look at this Fralthi before they take it away. Say, that's one of the new Dralthis, isn't it?"

Jimmy nodded, the helmet of his suit bobbing slightly. "Yes, it's what we're calling a Dralthi Mark Two. It has a new weapons system, better armor, and a few other improvements." His voice brightened as he began describing the differences; Jimmy was a techno-junkie, for certain, and like all techies, he loved talking about gadgets and widgetry. "It's a lot better than the first model of Dralthi, not quite so likely to have that power overload problem the first time the shields get pounded a little too hard. That's why the older version of these fighters was so easy to kill, three or four direct hits would overload the shield generator."

"That's good to know," Hunter observed, looking at the parked fighter. *Good to know, hell. It might save our lives. Why doesn't anyone ever see that the pilots get info like this?* "I wonder how well these old girls fly?"

"I've sat in the cockpit, but haven't turned on the engines," Jimmy said. "The visibility isn't so great, and the controls are a little weird, but I think it'd fly pretty well. The wing stabilizers are kinda neat, they're—"

"Good," Hunter interrupted, climbing up onto the wing next to Jimmy. "How do you get into the cockpit?"

"Actually, you climb in from below," Jimmy said, frowning slightly. "The top of the cockpit doesn't pop off the way ours do, in fact it doesn't seem to have an ejection system, either. That'd be awful, to be trapped in a dying fighter with no way to get out."

"I guess the cats don't care much about that," Hunter said, jumping down from the wing and looking underneath the belly of the ship. "Well, Jimmy, I think I'm just going to have to take this Dralthi for a test drive. Better stand clear."

Even through the helmet faceplate, Hunter could see Jimmy's eyes widen. "But, sir — " he protested.

Hunter ignored him, popped the bottom hatch and crawled up into the fighter. *This is a peculiar way to do things,* he thought, climbing up into the cockpit and sliding over into the pilot's chair. He latched the hatch, listening as it automatically sealed to become airtight. His spacesuit readings said that the cockpit was slowly pressurizing with breathable air. *Good.* He wriggled in the seat, trying to make it feel more comfortable. The seat was made of plant fibers woven into a chair, with a large empty spot at the back of the chair . . . *probably for the cat's tail,* he decided. It was too large for him, but he strapped himself in anyhow. As his suit readouts switched to green, indicating that the cockpit was fully pressurized with breathable air, he popped open the faceplate of his helmet. The suit had twenty minutes of breathable air on the emergency tank, but there was no reason to use it now.

"Hunter, are you authorized for this?" Jimmy's voice said anxiously through the speakers in Hunter's helmet.

"Not a problem, mate!" Hunter replied, looking in perplexity at the control panel. All of the controls were labelled in the odd vertical letters of the Kilrathi language, which Hunter had never learned how to read. *But that looks like a joystick, and that looks like an air pressure gauge, I don't know what that is but I'm sure I won't need it, and that looks like an engine power gauge . . . I wonder what that switch is, next to it?*

He pressed it, and the fighter vibrated suddenly as the engines rumbled to life. "Clear!" Hunter shouted, a little too late.

"Don't worry, Hunter, I'm standing in the airlock where it's *safe*," Jimmy replied, his voice more than a little strained. Poor kid was probably wondering how he was going to explain this to his superior officers.

"You don't have any faith in me, mate?" Hunter grinned, and pulled up on the joystick slightly. The Dralthi fighter lifted a few meters off the deck. Hunter eased it forward, aiming for the circular exit of the bay. *I wonder what that switch does?* he thought, looking at a toggle that was halfway down the console. He depressed it, and the engines suddenly roared into full power. Hunter's eyes widened as the Dralthi shot from the landing bay like a bullet from a gun. He brought the speed down a moment later, and drifted in space in his alien fighter. He slowly turned the Dralthi so he could look back at the *Ras Nik'hra*, floating majestically against the starfield.

So, where to now? he asked himself. He picked a direction away from the Fralthi, and brought the speed up to a reasonable clip. The Dralthi's controls were very fine, the ship handled beautifully, if a little delicately, and it was definitely as much fun to fly as any of the Confederation fighters. Maybe even a little more fun, since it had better wing stabilizers.

Maybe that's why they built it in this "flying pancake" style,
he thought, *to spread out the stabilizers over a larger
area, make it easier to stabilize at high speed. Lousy shields
and armor on these babies, though . . . how many of these
have I toasted so far? At least five or six. That defect that
Jimmy was talking about, that's probably why they've been
so easy to kill.*

He tried the different control switches on the
front console, curious as to what they controlled.
One switch plunged the ship into total darkness,
which gave him a few panicked moments as he
fumbled to switch the lights back on. As he pushed
another button, the video monitor clicked on.
Complete with a helmeted Kilrathi face, cat whiskers and all, on the screen.

"Krajksh nai variksh h'hassrai?" the Kilrathi voice
said. Hunter instantly looked around for a Transmit button, wanting to say something long and
descriptive in English to the alien pilot, then
stopped himself, realizing just what the appearance
of the cat on a vid-screen meant. And it wasn't good.

Ah hell. *How did a cat patrol get within transmission
range of the* Tiger's Claw *and the* Austin? *They must've
slipped past our patrols somehow. That Kilrathi can't be too
far away, his vid signal is very clear.*

*Damn, damn, damn! There's no time to figure out how
to make this thing transmit on the Terran Confederation
frequencies, so I can't warn the carrier!*

Hunter looked around for the vid pickup, then
reached up for the small camera. He yanked hard,
pulling free a handful of tangled wires. *Now at least
they can't tell that there's a human in this Dralthi, at least
not until they're close enough to see the whites of my eyes.*

I have to track this patrol down ASAP!

How the hell do I get myself into these things?

He scanned the controls of the Dralthi, trying to figure out how to enable the long-distance sensors. Momentarily, he thought about just turning around and heading back to the *Claw* at top speed, then abandoned the idea. For one, there probably wasn't enough time, and for another . . .

Here he was in an enemy ship, the perfect disguise. There was no way for the enemy patrol to know that he was flying one of their ships. Maybe the situation wasn't so bad after all!

I just can't resist an opportunity like this, he thought with a grin at his own foolishness. *Who could?*

Ten minutes later, after finally figuring out how to enable the long-range sensor array, he tracked down and visually sighted the Kilrathi patrol. It was a wing of Gratha fighters in a tight V formation.

And just in time, he thought, maneuvering into a high-six position behind the enemy squadron. *We're not even five minutes away from the* Austin! *What's going on there, why didn't any of their patrols spot these blokes?*

The five Gratha suddenly accelerated, banking down in tight formation toward the waiting cruiser.

Oh, hell! They're startin' their missile run! Hunter brought his Dralthi fighter up to full speed, sliding into position behind the Kilrathi fighters. As he angled for a good firing solution, he saw a single Rapier fighter launched from the *Austin,* too late to stop the attack run.

Hunter steered the Dralthi with one hand, desperately searching for missile controls on the cockpit panel with his other hand. *I know there's a missile switch here somewhere, I know it, where in the hell is it?*

There!

He enabled the missiles and fired a split-second later, yanking the stick to veer away at the last moment as the lead Gratha was engulfed in a fireball, taking two of the closest Gratha with it. The other two Gratha banked away to avoid the explosion, aborting their missile run.

Hunter whooped and brought the Dralthi down on top of one of the Gratha, a perfect firing solution. He clicked down on the gun controls, and —

— and nothing happened.

"Jesus!" He dived away as the second Gratha came at him head-on, all guns blazing. *Ah hell! Ah bloody hell! Why didn't the guns fire? There must be a safety switch somewhere, I have to find it or I'm dead!* He shoved the stick hard to the left, twisting into a tight roll as he tried to find the gun controls. The Gratha followed as closely as it could with its wide turn radius, lumbering around to bring Hunter's fighter back into its targeting sights.

Come on, come on . . . hell! He pulled up sharply as the Dralthi shuddered with the close explosion of a missile. Hunter glanced back to see half of one of the Dralthi's wings peel away from the blast. He fought to keep the Dralthi under control, wrestling with the stick to prevent an unrecoverable roll. *I hate this fighter — lousy, cheap piece of junk — goddamned flying pancake — I should've stolen something decent, like one of those hot new Hhriss fighters —*

Another close hit, this time by the Gratha's multiple cannons. Several warning systems in the fighter began to wail simultaneously, and the Dralthi's shield readouts flickered once and died completely. Hunter worked the controls furiously, trying to use what was left of the Dralthi's superior speed and maneuvering to avoid another direct hit. Ahead of him, he could see the *Austin* Rapier fighting with the second Gratha. The other Gratha banked close to the huge Gettysburg-class cruiser in an attempt to escape the Rapier. A little too close, as it turned out: the Gratha exploded spectacularly against the side of the *Austin*. The Rapier turned tightly and 'burned directly at Hunter's Dralthi.

"Not me, mate!" Hunter yelled as the Rapier dived toward him. A moment later, the Rapier fired a missile. Hunter's eyes widened as the deadly missile accelerated right toward him.

The missile passed overhead just above his cockpit, and he glanced back in time to see it slam into the Gratha on his tail. The Gratha spun out of control and exploded.

He turned back to look at the Rapier, and realized in horror that it was still on a direct collision course with him. A split-second later, the Rapier rolled neatly, flying inverted a couple meters over Hunter's head, so close that Hunter could see the pilot's helmet with the musical notes surrounding the name JAZZ.

"Good work, Colson!" Hunter shouted, even though he knew there was no way Jazz could hear him. *Not bad for a kid,* Hunter thought with a grin, as he pulled up on the stick to bring the Dralthi up in a tight turn to avoid the looming *Austin* ahead of him.

It didn't.

"What?" Hunter shoved hard at the stick. The Dralthi didn't change course, continuing on a straight line for the *Austin*. "Goddammit, this isn't fair!" he yelled. *I'm going to make a lovely wet spot on the side of the ship, just like that Gratha . . . can't find an emergency brake on this damn ship, there's no ejection unit, nothing . . .* Desperate, he punched all com channels open.

"Mates, if you're listening on the Kilrathi channels . . . grab me with a pickup beam or I'm history!" *And if they're not listening . . .*

He unstrapped himself from the pilot's chair, and sealed his helmet's faceplate, making sure that the suit was still airtight and hadn't been holed during the dogfight. He quickly slid down to the Dralthi's exit hatch. A very long two seconds later, he had the hatch unfastened and shoved it open. All the air in the cockpit rushed out past him, blasting him through the hatch and into open space. He spun uncontrollably in his suit, still carried by his momentum directly toward the silvery hull of the *Austin*. He shut his eyes, thinking: *Oh God, this is going to hurt . . .*

Something wrenched him to a complete stop, and his face jammed against the faceplate of his helmet. He swore, feeling the blood running from where his nose had impacted the helmet, and blinked. The *Austin* was a hundred feet in front of him; as he watched, the Dralthi crashed into the side of the ship, disintegrating on impact. As for himself, he was continuing to drift along the side of the cruiser, slowly spinning as the tractor beam pulled him through space.

Thank God I don't get spacesick, he thought, closing his eyes for a moment. The sudden silence and calm quieted his rapid heartbeat, and he felt himself relaxing, breathing slower and easier.

Just drifting — this isn't too bad, just to be alone out here

— I think I owe that Austin tractor operator a drink . . . or two, or three . . .

A few seconds later, the tractor beam from the *Austin*, as gentle as a lover's touch, brought him to the immense Flight Deck entrance. The tractor beam cut off as he was only a few meters from the entrance . . . he continued to drift through the magnetic shield, which crackled momentarily around him, and into the waiting hands of the Flight Deck crew. They helped him regain his feet, and he unfastened his helmet and took it off. "Thanks, mates," he said, wiping the sweat and blood off his face.

He was suddenly aware of the crowd gathered around him, and the sound of loud cheering and clapping. A moment later the crowd parted to admit two uniformed officers. Hunter recognized Commander James Reilly, the Executive Officer of the ship, and Major Petrenkov, commander of the *Austin*'s fighter squadron. The last time Hunter had seen these two officers was when the Military Police had carried him off the ship for being drunk and disorderly in the *Austin*'s rec room.

"Captain St. John, we meet again," the Executive Officer of the *Austin* said, smiling. "You've had an exciting day, haven't you?"

They always smiled when you turned a screw-up into a victory. It was only when it stayed a screw-up that you got into trouble.

Hunter snapped off a sharp salute, then wiped more blood from his nose. "Yes, sir. It's been a very exciting day. And it's not even lunch-time yet."

"I know," the Exec said dryly.

There was a question that he had to ask, that had

been plaguing him since all of this had started. "What happened to your patrols, Commander? This ship could've been blown away and you'd never have known what hit you!"

"We're quite aware of that, Captain," the Exec said, exchanging a glance with Major Petrenkov. "But there are circumstances you're not aware of . . ."

"Hunter's right, sir," the Major said in a tight voice. "My failures nearly got everyone on this ship killed. If it wasn't for Hunter, we'd be dead now. You should accept my resignation."

"As I've already said, I won't let you resign, Nikolai. At least not until we've returned to Confed High Command," Commander Reilly said quietly.

"Then I hope you'll accept it once we're back at Sol Station, sir," the Major said bleakly.

"Clear the deck! Incoming fighter!" the loudspeakers blared. Hunter followed the rest of the crowd in a quick jog to the safety zone, away from the main deck approach. He managed to catch up to Commander Reilly near the airlock.

After all, he had a reputation for audacity. So why *not* put his two cents in with the Commander? "Commander, since it looks like you're going to be needing a new squadron commander anyhow . . . we have a few good people on the *Claw* that you should consider. Such as — "

"I've already thought about it, Captain," the Exec said. "If you'd like to talk about it in the Rec Room, I'd like to hear your suggestions."

Hunter kept his grin to himself. Once again, audacity paid off. "It'd be my pleasure, sir. As I remember, your Rec Room serves a very good Aussie beer."

The Rapier fighter glided in for a smooth landing. The pilot popped the canopy even before the fighter had completely stopped. Hunter saw Jazz Colson's grin even at this distance, as the crowd of Deck crew surrounded him, cheering wildly.

"Damn, but that boy is good," Hunter said, cheerfully acknowledging excellence, even when it wasn't his own. He wiped at the trickle of blood from his nose again. "I think he'll go far."

"I'm sure he will," the Exec said. "Well, then, let's go get that beer, shall we?"

Four hours later, after lunch with Commander Reilly and the Captain of the *Austin*, and then hoisting several beers with Jazz Colson and some of his friends, Hunter caught a lift back to the *Tiger's Claw* aboard a shuttle with several technicians.

Now I have to find Angel. This news can't wait another five minutes.

Disembarking from the shuttle, Hunter scanned the Flight Deck for Jeannette Devereaux, but didn't see her near the parked fighters. And there weren't many parked fighters, either . . . looked like everything flyable was out on a mission right now, which was unusual.

Well — unusual for Standard Operating Procedure. Not unusual considering the past few days. Funny, he wasn't tired anymore. All that adrenaline must've knocked him into his second wind.

Meanwhile, he needed to find Angel. He waved to Cafrelli, who was working on a disassembled fighter engine on the far side of the Deck, and headed for the Barracks. *Maybe she's asleep, if she just got in from the early morning patrol.*

The Barracks were completely deserted except for Maniac, who was sprawled out on his bunk, snoring. Hunter thought about whether or not he should let Marshall continue sleeping for about two seconds, then shook the boy awake.

"Wh-wha?" Maniac muttered, rubbing his eyes.

"Where's Angel, Todd?"

Maniac gave him a look that he couldn't quite interpret. "I saw her walking with the Colonel to his office," he said, yawning, but with a funny side glance at Hunter. "What happened to your nose, Hunter? No, don't bother telling me . . . just go away, I want to get some sleep."

Then the kid just rolled over, away from him. No small talk, no "where've you been — "

"All right, mate," Hunter said, pulling his hand away and walking off, mulling over what Todd had just said. Strange. Very strange. It didn't make much sense. The only reason anyone went to the Colonel's office was if they were in some kind of trouble, about to get reamed out for one offense or another. Hunter knew that well enough; he'd been in the Colonel's office often enough that he'd memorized the interior decor. But Angel wasn't like him, she was a straightforward, skilled, "by the book" kind of pilot, with a perfect record for all her years in the Navy. That's *why* he had this terrific bit of news to tell her . . .

He left the Barracks and walked down the corridors. On impulse, he headed for the Rec Room. He knew the place would be empty, since the bartender, Shotglass, didn't go on shift for another couple hours, and all you could get at this hour was the awful sugar-water drinks from the automatic dispenser. *But just on the off-chance . . . Angel actually likes that horrible soda they have there, hell if I know why.*

And his luck was up. He smiled as he walked through the door and spotted her. Angel was seated alone at one of the tables, a glass of pink soda in front of her. He slid into the seat across from her, unable to keep the grin off his face. "Lady, have I got news for you . . ." he began, and stopped.

She was crying. Not loudly, or obviously. But there were tears coursing silently down her face. He froze, his heart suddenly in his throat, and reached across to take one of her hands in his. "What's wrong, sweetheart?" he asked, as gently as he could. Whatever it was — it had to be the worst of news.

"Bossman's dead, Hunter," she said.

"Oh, damn," he breathed. "Not Kien." Kien, who was always as steady as rock, one of the best pilots in the squadron. Hunter remembered all the nights spent drinking beer in the Rec Room, the missions where they'd fought together against the cats, the times that they'd saved each others' lives. "How did it happen?" he asked.

Her voice was very quiet, thick with tears, the accent that made her sound so charming now making her sound as if she were a tragic heroine in a play. But the tragedy was real, and this wasn't theatre. "We were patrolling the jump point area, as per our orders." She sniffed, and her voice faltered. "There was no warning. Suddenly a Kilrathi strike force began appearing around us. A Fralthi cruiser, several corvettes, two Lumbari tankers. Bossman knew that the corvettes would overtake us if we ran, that there was no way to outrun them, so he . . ."

She almost broke, then, and Hunter tightened his hold on her hand. She steadied herself. "He ordered me to return to the *Claw*, and he started on an attack run on the Fralthi. He kept them busy long enough for me to get out of range; he kept transmitting as much information to me as he could, telling me the number of fighters, their exact course, how many more ships were jumping in . . . then he said, 'Angel, tell my wife I love her.' There was a burst of static on the comm, and then, nothing."

She looked up for a moment, but Hunter sensed that she didn't really see him. He wasn't sure he wanted to know what she *was* seeing. "I wanted to go back, but I knew that one of us had to survive, one of us had to warn the carrier. . . ."

"You did what you had to, sweetheart," Hunter said, knowing that wasn't enough, that it wouldn't have been enough for *him*, but knowing that he had to say it. Maybe if enough people told her that enough times, she might start to believe it.

"But he was so alone, he died alone out there, I should have been there with him." She wiped the tears from her face, but more streamed from her eyes to replace them. "It was so awful, *mon ami*, knowing that Bossman was dying and there was nothing I could do to help him. . . ." Her voice broke on a sob, and she buried her face in her free hand.

He didn't know what else to say, so he sat there, silently holding her hand, giving her something to hold onto, and wishing he could offer more comfort than that. After a few minutes, she looked up at him and tried to smile. "So, you came running in here wanting to tell me something. What was the news you were so eager to tell, Hunter? And . . . what happened to your nose?"

"Oh, it's nothing much," he said diffidently. *Maybe* — maybe this will help her, a little. Prove to her that the rest of us know she always does her top best. "Just a little promotion for you. The Captain of the *Austin* would like you to take over command of their fighter squadron."

"What?" Angel's eyes were wide, the tears still on her face, but a little more life coming into her expression. "You are joking, *non?*"

He patted her hand. "It's not confirmed yet, but the Top Hat says that he doesn't see any reason why Confed HQ wouldn't sign the papers. I was there when he called Colonel Halcyon about it. Halc says that he's sorry to see you leave, but he's glad that you're getting the promotion." *That must've been just before she came back from her patrol with the news that Bossman was dead.*

"But it should not be me!" She wiped at her eyes, the bleakness returning. "It should be someone who is better than I. Bossman should have been the one for this."

He had to say something, anything. "Angel, it hurts, knowing that he's dead, but we've got to keep going without him. They need you on the *Austin*. You've got the talent for working with people." He searched for the reasons he'd given the Commander for recommending her, and gave them to her, earnestly. "You can be a leader, which Knight can't. You can make people do things because they want to, not because they've been ordered, which Ice can't. You've got things —

qualities — that us rocket-jockeys just don't share, things that make you a leader, and us the guys in the fighters." He continued in a quieter voice. "And you care about the people around you, which matters more than anything."

"Why didn't you ask for this position yourself?" she asked, bewildered, but whether she was surprised by his vehemence or the circumstances, he couldn't tell.

He shook his head. "What, me in charge of a bunch of pilots? You've got to be crazy, sweetheart. Why, that'd be like putting Maniac in charge of a squadron! Someone would have to be a complete lunatic to do that!" He smiled gently at her. "No, you're perfect for this, and you know it."

He sat up abruptly in his chair as the loudspeaker in the Rec Room began to blare noisily: "All pilots, report to the Briefing Room immediately."

"How 'bout you, lady?" he asked.

She shook her head. *"Non,* Colonel Halcyon did not want me to fly any more missions today."

Good for the Colonel. "Will you be all right, sweetheart?"

She nodded, slowly. "I think so," she said quietly. "Thank you, Hunter. For — everything."

He stood up, and then impulsively bent to kiss her. "I'll look for you later, okay?"

I can guess why Halcyon didn't want her to fly any missions today, he thought, walking briskly toward the Briefing Room, and just as pleased that the adrenaline charge was still holding. He was going to pay for this later, but that was later, and this was now. Besides, maybe the medics could give him a shot or something to supercharge him. That ought to make up for the green goop. *Old Halc knows that if he sent Angel out right now, she might deliberately try to get herself killed. Survivor guilt, that's what the psychs call it.*

He thought back about the wingmen he'd flown with, and how he'd felt when Littlehawk had crashed on the Flight Deck after they'd both been shot up badly during a Vega mission. He'd seen the fireball as he was on final approach to the carrier, and had aborted his landing run just in time to avoid becoming part of the disaster. He couldn't remember exactly how he'd felt when he had finally landed several hours later, after they'd cleared the debris off the Flight Deck, but he remembered that he'd done nothing but drink for the next few days after that.

He grabbed a seat in the back of the room. Spirit was seated next to him; he leaned close to her and whispered, "What's going on here? I thought we were offduty after two back-to-back patrols! I was going to get some sleep!"

"You didn't hear the news?" she whispered back. From the look on her face, he didn't think it was good news.

"What news?" he asked, not wanting to know, but aware that he needed to know.

"Five carriers, three light cruisers, four tankerships, and at least eight corvettes jumped into the system in the last hour." She looked as if she hardly believed it herself. "The *Tiger's Claw* and the *Austin* are retreating out-system while we wait to hear from Confed High Command as to what we're supposed to do next."

He felt as if someone had just hit him with a bottle, and the adrenaline drained right out of him, leaving him numb with shock. "What in the hell is going on here? This is a backwater system, there isn't anything here the Kilrathi could want!"

Spirit shook her head. "No one is saying what's going on, Hunter. But the brass knows. They've been closeted with that renegade Kilrathi captain, talking about all of this."

Retreat — He'd just been thinking about that. And what it meant. "And we can't abandon the Firekkans! They're a peaceful species, they don't have a navy or any planetary or space-based defenses. They're going to be helpless against a Kilrathi invasion!"

"Shh," she whispered, as Colonel Halcyon strode up to the podium.

The Colonel looked as exhausted as any of them, or even more so. "As all of you have already heard, we lost Bossman this morning. He died heroically, giving Angel enough time to warn us that this system is being overrun by a huge number of Kilrathi ships, who are arriving here for a Kilrathi religious ceremony called the *Sivar-Eshrad*. There's no way we can fight that many ships, so we are in the middle of a strategic withdrawal, but we are *not* abandoning the Firekka System. The Firekkans are evacuating as many of their people as they can, and we'll assist that in any way possible. As soon as we have enough reinforcements, we'll start taking on these Kilrathi forces directly.

"But until then, we're going to use a different tactic. Some of you may have heard about Hunter's joyride out to the *Austin* earlier this morning . . ."

Hunter studied the ceiling intently as the other pilots turned to look at him.

" . . . because of the success of his tactics, we're

going to use the Dralthi fighters in our next missions, to confuse and evade the enemy," the Colonel said. "The technical crew aboard the *Ras Nik'hra* is readying the fighters for us now."

"Like hell!" Hunter swore, loud enough that the Colonel paused to glare at him. "I'm never getting into one of those pieces of junk ever again — sir!" he added politely.

The Colonel sighed, then continued, pretending that he had not heard Hunter's outburst. Which was just as well. It would be hard to get High Command to uphold a court-martial for insubordination on a pilot who had already flown back-to-back missions and narrowly escaped a crash to boot.

Hunter knew that; so did the Colonel. So did everyone else. "These are the wing assignments. Knight and Iceman are Alpha Wing. . . ."

• CHAPTER SEVEN

The Dralthi fighter slowed as it banked through the clouds, tilting down toward the main Firekka continent. Hunter glanced at his sensors, doublechecking that there were no Kilrathi ships in the area. He'd passed a couple Kilrathi heavy troopships on his way in, parked in orbit above, but no other ships.

They're off trying to find out where the Tiger's Claw *is,* he thought soberly. *I'll have to be damn careful on my way out of here, that I don't lead them back to the* Claw *and the* Austin.

It was still night as he brought the Dralthi in for a landing on the shuttlecraft field, with just a hint of golden light touching the edge of the horizon. A heavy wind blew across the field, making the Dralthi wobble unsteadily as he set it down. The wind was hot and dust-laden, stinging his face as he crawled out through the bottom hatch.

Several Firekkans were wheeling down to land around the Dralthi. For a moment he thought something was wrong with them, they were moving less gracefully than he'd seen them fly before. Then he realized why, as the heavy assault rifles slung over the Firekkans' chests were brought up to aim at him.

"Hey, don't shoot me, mates!" he said, raising his

hands above his head. "I'm here to see K'Kai. You know K'Kai? K'Kai?"

They glared at him suspiciously, their beady eyes blinking as they stared at him over their assault rifles.

It'd be real stupid to evade all of those Kilrathi patrols and get here just to be shot by some of K'Kai's people, wouldn't it? he thought. "Come on, mates, just let me see K'Kai, all right?"

Finally one of them nodded, and gestured with the rifle for Hunter to start walking.

Hunter stopped at the edge of the field, looking across the rope bridge at what was left of K'Kai's hometown, silhouetted in the early morning light. The tall, elegant towers that he had admired so much before were now scorched and blackened, marked by dozens of explosions. Half the towers were missing the top portion of their expanses, others had awful holes blown out of them.

The sight made his heart ache, made him yearn for a Kilrathi ship in his sights with all missiles ready to fire. The Firekkan behind him prodded him in the back with a rifle barrel, and he started across the woven bridge, which had somehow survived the attack.

The Firekkans brought him to one of the tall towers. He ducked inside the entrance, looking around.

One Firekkan lay on the floor, his torso wrapped in bloody bandages. Another Firekkan knelt over a third, applying bandages to a wing that was torn nearly in half. Hunter swallowed, looking away.

"Hun-ter?" a familiar voice said from above him.

K'Kai dropped down to the floor in front of him.

He was relieved to see that she seemed to be unharmed, except for a small bandage wrapped around her right thigh.

"Hello, K'Kai," he said.

She canted her head to look at him curiously. "Why are you here, Hun-ter? All the other Terrans have gone from Firekka."

"I borrowed one of our captured Dralthis and flew through the Kilrathi fleet," he said. At her alarmed look, he added, "Don't worry, they're used to me doing that kind of thing by now. It was a long flight here from where the *Tiger's Claw* is hidden, but the Dralthi's little nuclear powerplant held up just fine." He shifted awkwardly. "I just . . . I had to see you again, K'Kai. We're evacuating from this system. The brass knows why the cats are trying to capture your planet now, it has something to do with a weird religious ceremony of the Kilrathi. There's nothing we can do, and the Confed won't send in any reinforcements. Oh, they've got some crazy plan of sending down some Marines to crash the Kilrathi party, disrupting the religious ceremony. But they won't give us enough troops to defend your planet."

"I know, Hun-ter," she said quietly. "Your dip-lo-mats, they told us this before they left Firekka. The Kilrathi have already landed here," she continued. "Two days ago, here and on the northern continent. We fought them off, using the weapons given to us by your people, but they will be back. Eventually they will win . . . my people are good fighters, but not against the technology of the Kilrathi."

"Come with me, K'Kai," Hunter urged. "I'll take

you off-planet, get you out of this mess. You know what the Kilrathi are going to do to your planet and your people, once they start landing here in force."

"And that is why I must stay," she said firmly, raising her head on her long neck. "I am coordinating the evacuation, sending as many of our people to safety as we can. Many of the flock leaders are dead. My people are often confused, frightened. This is my home, Hun-ter . . . I cannot leave here, not now. Not when they need me."

"I understand," he said, slowly, knowing she was right — and was showing a lot more responsibility than he would have. "But I wish you'd reconsider. You know that there's only one way this fight can end."

"I know." K'Kai bobbed her head, opening her beak in a silent Firekkan laugh. "But we will make it as costly for the Kilrathi as we can." She glanced through the open door at the brightening golden light. "You had better go, Hun-ter. The Kilrathi attack us at dawn, always. We will go to shelter soon."

He clasped her clawed hand. "Take care of yourself, K'Kai."

"Farewell, Hun-ter," she said. She walked with him out of the tower, standing at the tower entrance as he trudged toward the parked Dralthi.

She was still standing on the barren rock when he lifted, the Dralthi wobbling in the heavy winds. He held the fighter in an unsteady hover for a long moment, looking down at her, the solemn profile of the alien woman, standing tall and proud, then kicked in the Dralthi's engines. The Dralthi leaped upward, gaining acceleration as it arced up through the atmosphere.

He saw the wing of sixteen Jalthi approaching, the Kilrathi fighters' wings weighted down with their bomb-loads. They passed by him at top speed, banking down for their attack run on the planet below. For one quixotic moment, he thought about turning on them, but knew that he'd never manage to kill them all or even survive the attempt. K'Kai's duty was with her people; his was on the *Claw,* and to live to defend it. Hunter held the Dralthi on course, heading back into open space toward the distant *Tiger's Claw.* He glanced back at the planet of Firekka and rubbed at his eyes.

They were still stinging, and a moment later, they were running.

It was the dust that was making his eyes tear, he decided. Nothing more.

He wasn't crying.

He couldn't be crying.

The rest of the flight back to the *Tiger's Claw* was uneventful. Hunter didn't sight any other Kilrathi ships, which was fortunate . . . he didn't think he'd be able to keep himself from opening fire on them, if there was even half a chance he could do it and survive.

The time stretched out endlessly as the Dralthi fighter soared through open space. *I'm going to catch hell for this when I get back on the ship,* he thought. *They're probably wondering what happened to me, why a two-hour patrol has taken me twenty hours. I'll have to do some fast talking when I get back.*

But that shouldn't be too much of a problem. The Colonel was used to it by now.

He nodded, imagining the exact words the

Colonel would use. It would probably be a rather choice speech. The Colonel had an excellent command of the English language, and knew exactly when to use it. And somehow Hunter seemed to bring out the — best? — of it.

He was going to deserve a dressing-down, even he had to admit it. But hell, the Colonel seemed to secretly enjoy it all, though Hunter was sure he'd never say that. Colonel Halcyon would probably be bored to tears if he didn't have Hunter around to keep things interesting on the *Claw!*

After hours of navigating across the system and past enemy patrols, he began his final approach to the *Claw's* hidden position in the asteroids.

Except that the carrier wasn't there.

Surprise.

The punch-line from a comedian's joke sprang into his head. *I was born in Chicago. My folks moved to New York right after I was born, and it took me months to track them down.*

Don't panic, he told himself, looking around wildly at the drifting asteroids. *Check the Nav charts, maybe I made a mistake. I could've miscalculated my course, the ship is probably close, somewhere nearby in these rocks. Just don't panic. . . .*

He ran a quick computer calculation on his course, triangulating his position.

No. He was in the right location. The *Claw* wasn't.

He fought the impulse to scream, or hyperventilate, or pound his head against the side of the cockpit. None of that would help him much in this situation. *Oh God, they've jumped out-system and left me here. I'm stranded, no way to get back to Vega in this little fighter, I can't jump and follow them out-system, I've got nowhere to go.*

His heart pounded, and suddenly he wasn't tired at all. Just in a total state of panic. That was all. *Calm down. Just stay calm, mate. Think this through, you've got to make some good decisions here. One, I can turn around and head back to Firekka. K'Kai's people can probably hide me somewhere, until . . . until . . . hell, it could be years before the Confederation comes back to Firekka! God knows how long it'll take for those fat-assed idiots at Confed High Command to decide what to do about our feathered friends.*

And in the meantime, the Kilrathi will be swarming all over that planet. Odds are that I'd get captured eventually and sent to some hellhole of a prison camp. . . .

His stomach turned over at the thought; it was always a fear that had hidden in the back of his mind, that he could be captured by the enemy. *Anything but that. I'd rather die.*

Or . . . it's several hours to the jump point out of this system. Maybe the Claw *hasn't jumped out yet. If I fly like the wind, maybe I can get there in time.*

His hands moved quickly, setting a new course for the jump point. His hands were shaking, but he ignored that, bringing the Dralthi up to full speed on a direct route to the out-system jump. He was too tense to sit back and let the fighter fly itself on AutoNav. Instead, he switched through the Confederation comm channels continuously, searching for any sign that there were other humans in the system. There was something else he'd noticed: the air gauge slowly drifting down into the red zone.

If they aren't there, I won't have enough breathable air to get back to Firekka. The fighter's nuclear engine's good for another million klicks, but I'll be out of air in a few hours.

I could turn around right now, head back to Firekka . . . no. I'll take that risk. Just don't leave me here alone, mates . . . please, don't leave me here. . . .

Two hours later, he was approaching the jump point. His stomach sank as he realized that there was no sign of the *Claw* ahead of him.

I'm dead now. I'm still living and breathing, but I'm dead. I should just take off my helmet and pop the hatch, and get it over with.

The comm screen suddenly crackled into life, a woman's face speaking sharply in English. "Kilrathi fighter, identify yourself immediately or be destroyed!"

What? Oh God — oh God! Thank you thank you thank you — "I'm Captain Ian St. John! Don't leave without me, mates!" He scanned the space around him desperately . . . there! Off to starboard, coming in from a different Nav course, was the *Claw*, shining silver and green with the carrier's bright red numbers visible on the metal deck in front of the landing bay. He'd never seen anything so beautiful in all his life.

"Land immediately, Captain, we are on final countdown for out-system jump!"

"Yes, ma'am!" Hunter brought the Dralthi up to full speed and then punched in the afterburners as well, aiming for the ship. He skimmed over the *Claw's* deck and the huge numbers, heading directly toward the landing bay like a bat out of hell. At the last instant, he slammed on the reverse-brakes.

Never tried this particular trick before. I sure hope it works!

The Dralthi screamed at the punishment as the fighter decelerated sharply in the space of a couple seconds. Hunter aimed the ship toward the open landing bay, hoping that there was no one parked in his path.

The Dralthi's top scraped against the ceiling of the Flight Deck, then bounced hard against the deck floor. Hunter fought to keep the craft from rolling, and kept full pressure on the brakes. The fighter slowed, bounced again, then settled down onto the Deck. A split second later, he felt the gut-wrenching twist of a Jump.

I cut that a little too close, I think.

He sat for a moment in the Dralthi's cockpit, feeling relief wash over him like a wave, then hurried through the procedure of shutting down the engines and a final check before popping the fighter's exit hatch.

Jimmy Cafrelli was waiting for him outside the hatch, relief and exhaustion warring on his face. "We thought you were dead, sir!"

"Not yet, Jimmy. Maybe next week." Hunter swung down through the hatch and onto the firm metal of the Flight Deck. _I'd kiss that Deck if I didn't know my mates would never let me forget it for the next ten years._

"Not a bad landing," Iceman's sardonic voice observed. Hunter turned to see the veteran pilot striding toward him. "Did you realize that you broke off the starboard cannon when you hit the ceiling, Ian?"

Hunter glanced at the wing involuntarily. It wasn't just the cannon that was broken . . . half the wing was scattered all over the Deck. "Oops," he said, and grinned, too full of relief himself to feel anything else. He patted the cold metal of the

Dralthi's hull. "Poor old girl, I put her through a lot today."

"You're on jump arrival patrol in two minutes," Iceman continued, one eyebrow raised sardonically. "With me. The Colonel seemed convinced you were going to show up. Ready for another flight?"

"I can handle it," Hunter said. Right now, he could handle anything. Nothing like thinking you were dead — then finding out that you were going to live, after all. . . ."Are the fighters ready?"

Iceman pointed across the Deck; he began to run toward the parked Rapiers, Hunter hard on his heels.

"Maniac's back on the Flight Roster," Iceman called as they ran.

"What?" Hunter asked, out of breath.

"The Colonel said that we need all hands," Iceman explained. "Even one as insane as Maniac. I wanted to warn you, Hunter. He is as crazy as ever. You could get him as wingman at any point."

"Terrific," Hunter muttered, looking at the row of Rapiers lined up for launch position on the deck. "That's all I need right now, a lunatic flying on my wing."

"At least we're back in Confederation space now, Hunter," Iceman said. "Our own home ground again."

"We were supposed to be in Confed space, back on Firekka, mate," Hunter said suddenly. "But I guess no one wants to remember that."

Now that he was no longer worried about his own survival, he had a moment to think about someone else's. "And now we've left the Firekkans there to face the Kilrathi on their own." He didn't look to see if Iceman paid any attention, or even heard him; instead he glanced back through the open landing bay, wondering if one of those million points of lights was the Firekka system, K'Kai's homeworld, hidden among the other stars. "Good luck, K'Kai," he whispered, as he climbed into the cockpit of the Rapier fighter.

"First group, move as close as you can to the landed ships while second group flies in from above . . ." K'Kai traced out a map with one curved claw on the dirt of the cave. The dust of the cave irritated her sensitive eyes, but it was something she had learned to ignore in these last days, as she had learned to live without the comforts of her home. At least her friends and family were with her, all having survived the torching of their tower homes by the alien Kilrathi. All armed with the assault rifles given to them by the humans, and bearing the marks and wounds of the long weeks of war against the Kilrathi.

Her sister Kree'Kai was a fine flock-leader, wise and a good counselor to her people. But Kree'Kai was no war-leader, and it was K'Kai, with her knowledge of space combat, who had been chosen as *Shenrikke,* to lead the flyers of Firekka against the Kilrathi invasion.

There is no one else. All the humans have gone, even Hun-ter, leaving us alone against the felines. Well, that was not strictly true. The humans had returned long enough to stage their attack against the Kilrathi religious ceremony, but then they departed, and for many days now, the Firekkans had been on their own. *Maybe they will be back, maybe not. It does not matter. We will fight on, with or without them.*

K'Kai pointed at one particular Kilrathi ship in her diagram, a large warship bristling with gun turrets. "We think this is their command center for the landing group. Focus your attack on anyone from that ship. Flock-leaders must be very careful." She gave Kree'Kai and several other flock-leaders a very sharp glance. "Because the Kilrathi have captured enough of our people that they surely know who our leaders are."

"You speak for yourself as well, K'Kai," Kree'Kai said seriously. "The Kilrathi must know that you are war-leader for all the flocks. Why else have they targeted our flock over the others in this area?"

"I will be careful, too," K'Kai agreed. "We have inflicted great casualties upon our enemies, with our inferior weapons but good tactics and knowledge of our homeworld. We cannot risk any carelessness now. Any questions?"

There was a long silence, and K'Kai spoke again, quietly. "Good. All of you, be ready to attack at sunset. Rest now, for a few minutes, then move to your positions."

She crouched, staring at the map drawn in the dirt, as the others moved away to their tasks.

"How long will you stare at the dirt, sister?" Kree'Kai said, grooming K'Kai's neck with her beak.

"There is something wrong here," K'Kai said at last. "They have brought all their landing ships here, to this valley, from all over the continent. They must know that we will attack. But there are few troops in the valley below, and only a handful of watchmen. It does not make any sense."

"K'Kai!"

The shout echoed through the cave. K'Kai spread her wings and launched herself toward the mouth of the cave, fluttering to a stop just inside the entrance. "What is it?"

"Look, in the valley!"

K'Kai's sharp eyes focused on the flames of the Kilrathi ship engines, raising clouds of dust from the valley floor. "They're leaving!"

Kilrathi footsoldiers were moving quickly onto the ships, which began to depart, one lifting every few seconds. A Kilrathi corvette glided in from the north, coming to a stop next to the largest of the ships. A moment later, Kilrathi soldiers emerged, guiding a group of Firekkans into the hold of the larger ship.

"Rikik!" Kree'Kai shrieked suddenly, pointing at the Firekkan prisoners. "They have Rikik!"

"Kree'Kai, wait!" K'Kai shouted, as her sister dived from the cliff's edge, heading straight down toward the valley. "Don't!"

Kree'Kai ignored her; ignored everything except the furred enemy — and the tiny figure among the taller prisoners. Her daughter —

She would not stop, not now.

"After her! Quickly! They know we're here now!" K'Kai called, and dozens of Firekkan warriors launched from the nearby cliffs, screaming battle cries at their enemy.

The gun turrets on the stationary Kilrathi ships swiveled, tracking the fast-moving flyers. Cannons boomed, sending energy bolts crackling into the cliff walls, rocks shattering and falling around them. K'Kai leaped from the cliff a moment before her perch disintegrated into falling rubble, and banked steeply down toward the Kilrathi squadron.

Kree'Kai was nearly in range to fire . . . K'Kai could see her aiming her assault rifle at one of the Kilrathi guards . . .

. . . another ship cannon fired, only a few meters from Kree'Kai as she swept past. For a horrible second, the Firekkan flock-leader was outlined in blue light, burning alive, and then she was gone.

K'Kai didn't stop to think, or grieve. There was no time, not if they were to rescue the captives. The small huddle of terrified Firekkans, being herded into the hold of one of the Kilrathi ships, stared up at the wing of Firekkan warriors descending down toward them. K'Kai heard her niece screaming her mother's name, as a Kilrathi guard shoved her into the airlock of the ship. The other Firekkans were forced inside as well; K'Kai recognized a dozen other flock-leaders and leader-kindred, captured from towers around the continent. *Hostages. They are taking hostages with them!*

She fired her assault rifle just as the airlock door slid shut; the energy bolt glanced uselessly off the thick metal, searing into the ground. A faint rumbling from beyond the metal skin of the ship warned her of what was about to happen.

"Back! Get back!" she screamed, flying away with all her strength and speed as the engines of the ship roared into life, blasting the area around it. She glanced back to see another Firekkan warrior who had not moved quickly enough, his wings on fire as he fell helplessly toward the ground.

A few seconds later, K'Kai landed on a high ledge, turning to look back at the valley. The last Kilrathi ships were lifting, ponderously moving upward through the sky. On other ledges, she saw Firekkans waving their rifles and shouting defiance at the departing Kilrathi ships.

Another Firekkan, his wings scorched and feathers blackened, landed awkwardly on the ledge next to her. In silence, they watched as the last Kilrathi ship disappeared into the night sky above them.

"The Kilrathi are gone, K'Kai. Is it over now?" the young fighter asked.

"No," she said slowly. "It is not over. I do not know if it will ever be over, not now. . . ."

● CHAPTER EIGHT

Ralgha watched his young liegeman pace, noting that Kirha's movements had become as predictable and repetitive as those of any caged beast. Thirteen steps to the wall, a reflexive twitch of his tail the moment before he turned, a lift of his chin as he turned. Then thirteen steps to the door, pulling up a little short, a pause to stare at the portal in case it opened (it never did), then an abrupt turn that left scratches on the floor from his claws, to pace back to the wall again. It was as well that this place had no fiber mats upon the floor, for the little cub would have torn that particular spot to shreds by now.

Ralgha had learned in his earlier captivity that such mind-numbing occupations did nothing to make the time seem any shorter. Instead of useless pacing, he varied his waking hours, doing nothing at the same time from day to day, not even eating. There were the exercises he had learned to keep a body in shape using a limited space — very useful on shipboard, when a captain could not take the time to go to an exercise room. Ralgha usually persuaded the younger male to share those exercises with him, for even Kirha could see their value. They kept his body supple, if not his mind.

There were other things to occupy Ralgha's attention. The chiefest was the computer terminal with limited access, so thoughtfully provided by their captors, through which he improved his command of the hairless ones' language and learned the ways in which they thought by reading their literature, philosophy and holy texts. The humans were fascinating; controlled more by their biology than they would admit, and yet less controlled than the Kilrathi, in many ways. And so many religions . . . many contradicting each other. Completely fascinating. It was as if the humans were, themselves, composed of many species.

Or as if, as one of their figures of literature had said, they could believe in several impossible things before breakfast.

He had other things from his own culture to occupy him, and make the place seem less alien. There were the meditations, for instance — things some of the priestesses had taught him, meant to focus thought and self-discipline as well as to relax.

He even learned a number of the humans' games and played them against the computer.

And if their games were any indication of their abilities as strategists, there was no wonder that they had fought his people to a deadlock. They were excellent strategists. He had always maintained that, but it was pleasant to have his opinion so confirmed.

Their little room held nothing else of interest; two bunks, three chairs, the desk, a closet for cleansing and elimination, evidently designed for multi-species use and elementary, but adequate. The walls were gray and could not be marked, the floor bare metal. The air carried no scent but that of the humans, and even that was faint. Someone must have deduced that too strong a human-scent would make both of the Kilrathi edgy and nervous.

He had expected to be sent to High Command as soon as Kirha joined him, but shortly after the youngster was escorted through the door, Captain Thorn sent a messenger with a kind of apology. It would not be possible to send the Kilrathi out of the Firekkan system at this time. He was sorry that he could not deliver the message in person, but Ralgha was a ship commander, and he must know that the ship and crew came before other considerations. It was phrased more diplomatically than that, of course, but that was the gist of the message.

Reading between the lines, and knowing what he did, Ralgha had no difficulty in interpreting the ambiguous message. The Kilrathi had arrived in force, and sooner than Ralgha had expected. The Prince must have decided to act quickly once word of Ralgha's defection reached him. It would be impossible to say without information he would *certainly* not get whether the problem was that no pilot could be spared to shuttle the two Kilrathi out, or whether the Kilrathi fleet had so invaded that system that no ship could escape them. And in any case, it hardly mattered. He and Ralgha were now bound to the *Tiger's Claw* and would share the fate of its human cargo.

He could guess some things; alarms that meant Kilrathi fighters had penetrated near enough to threaten the *Claw* itself, the dimming or flickering of lights that showed enormous power-drains on the ship's systems. Shudderings as the *Claw* maneuvered — or perhaps took a hit?

But mostly he and Kirha were left alone, to their

own devices, with their meal arriving once a day, promptly, an hour after waking. As he himself had specified. The Kilrathi still followed their carnivorous instincts; eating only once a day, but gorging, then lying torpid for an hour or so. Kirha usually ate when he did, out of deference for his lord, and Ralgha varied the time to give the cub's day that little change that kept him from becoming mad with boredom.

Ralgha had been playing one of the games, something called *Go*, when the game itself suddenly froze on the screen, one piece holding in transition. Before Ralgha had a chance to react, the screen blanked, showing only the blinking cursor in the upper corner.

Then, before he could snarl in frustration and beat the terminal in the side, the cursor began to move, and a message appeared in its wake.

Commander Thorn would like to speak with you. Write "/send" and your reply.

It was not in the characters of written Kilrathi, but rather, scribed in the humans' written words. So, they had figured out that he could read their texts, hmm? He had assumed they were monitoring what this terminal was accessing, limited as the range was. Somewhere, some bored technician had noticed he had been calling up human texts.

And had made the appropriate deduction.

The abrupt character of the message was certainly typical of a bored tech of whatever species. Sometimes Ralgha thought that computer technicians were a species apart from all others, that it mattered not at all what their exterior shape was, for their minds were all alike. Precise, quick to recognize patterns, but with no interest for anything beyond their arcane little universe of numbers and electrons.

I shall speak to him, Ralgha typed, prefacing the message with the "/send" as instructed.

"Settle down, young one," he advised Kirha. "One of the humans is coming to call upon us, and if you are standing or pacing, you may make him nervous."

Kirha had barely settled into a chair when the door slid open, admitting Captain Thorn and the ubiquitous set of guards. They made the tiny room seem very crowded.

"We've got a situation," the human said without preamble, "and I was hoping you would explain it."

"Would?" Ralgha asked dryly, noting with no surprise that the Captain was not wearing his translator — and *was* speaking in his own language, rather than in Kilrathi. So the tech must have reported Ralgha's growing command of the human tongue to his superiors. "Would?" he repeated, in slow, deliberate human speech, "Or *could?*"

Thorn started to grimace, and stopped himself, which gave the odd effect of looking as if his entire face spasmed. "Perhaps a little of both," he admitted.

He did not sit down. Ralgha did not rise. Kirha had come to stand behind him, in the position normally taken by a personal guard.

Ralgha watched the Captain a moment longer, establishing the dynamic between them — the Captain, as the petitioner, himself as the courted. "I will try," he said, then. "What is this 'situation' of yours?"

There was a softening of the Captain's posture that made Ralgha think he had relaxed. "We sent Marines down to Firekka to try and disrupt the *Sivar-Eshrad*," he said shortly. "It seemed like a logical move, since your people place such store by the ceremony. We succeeded in that plan — and now —"

"Now the leader — who is probably the so-ambitious young Prince Thrakhath — is withdrawing his troops," Ralgha interrupted, and suppressed a purr of amusement at the widening of the human's eyes.

"How did you know that?" Thorn demanded, startled.

"There is no other choice for him. He must," Ralgha replied. He looked up at his young liegeman. "Tell the human, Kirha, why the Prince must withdraw, since the ceremony has been corrupted."

Kirha's forehead wrinkled, as he tried to find the human words to express Kilrathi concepts. "If the ceremony is corrupted, it is because Sivar is displeased and has rejected the ceremony and those who sponsored the ceremony," he said, haltingly. "The warriors that perished in the battle to take Firekka are no longer Sivar's favored servants; they are simply his fighters, standing between the Light of Sivar and the Great Dark which ever threatens the Light and seeks to devour souls. Because the ceremony was corrupted, those that survived cannot dedicate themselves to Sivar for the coming year, and they fear their souls will be lost in the Great Dark if they perish in combat."

"Does this mean that — that they're retreating because they think that Sivar has forsaken them?" the human asked, haltingly.

Ralgha nodded agreement, as the human shook his head; not in negation, Ralgha thought, but in unbelief.

In a way, Ralgha was torn. He was angry that the ceremony had been disrupted, and burned for those who had been so betrayed — yet this would not have happened if the Prince and the Emperor were not already corrupt. The humans were not the cause, only the means.

He must keep telling himself that. Sivar had simply used them to express his displeasure.

"So, fearing that their souls will be lost, there is no inducement Thrakhath can offer to make them fight," Ralgha continued. "If he attempts to force them, they will revolt. They are now as fearful as cublings in the moon-dark, and every ill that befalls them will be attributed to the loss of Sivar's favor. They are as eager now to escape with a whole skin as they once were to die."

He allowed the tips of his canines to show, for this part of the situation pleased him very much indeed. "This will not look well for the Prince, for he chose the site and he led the expedition. Sivar's displeasure falls the hardest upon him. The priestesses will be encouraging unhappiness with him."

The priestesses would not forget that the Prince ordered some of their number taken for questioning. No. That might have been the biggest mistake of the Prince's life. While no Kilrathi could be happy with this situation, the priestesses of Sivar must be purring with a certain bitter satisfaction at this turn of events. Surely they had been whispering warnings that any who interferred with Sivar's chosen would suffer Sivar's displeasure.

Now what had been whispered could be shouted.

"They will be retreating as quickly as the war-ships can carry them," Kirha said at last, after a long silence in which the hiss of the ventilator was the only sound. "They will be turning back towards conquered space, where there are temples wherein they might try to make their amends to the god. Until they can be purified, they will go to the Great Dark, if they die." His neck-ruff stood on end, for *that* prospect was not one any Kilrathi would face happily.

"Were I the commanding officer of this vessel," Ralgha said, "I would do the same as they; retreat-ing, regrouping and bringing in reinforcements. I would not pursue them, for they are desperate, and only a fool presses on the desperate. Remember that even a herd-beast will fight when cornered. Remember that the desperate are eager only to escape and will pay any price to do so. Only when I had a substantial strength would I return. Then I would consolidate the victory."

He yawned a little, then, and his eyes narrowed in satisfaction as Thorn slowly nodded.

"Thank you," the Captain said, in Kilrathi. "Thank you, Lord Ralgha. I think it is possible that your meeting with High Command can take place soon."

And with that, he was gone. The door slid shut behind his guards.

Ralgha's polite cough at Kirha's astonished expression covered his very real satisfaction. He had preserved the lives of warriors who had done *him* no harm, and might be induced to swear fealty at some point to him. He had saved the humans more casualties — which they would sustain, if they pressed their advantage. It was a better outcome than he could have reasonably expected.

But best of all, the Prince would doubtless survive, and would have a great deal to account for to the Emperor. The Emperor's displeasure was going to fall heavily on him — and on any who were his favorites. The repercussions of this disaster would echo down along the chain of command, affecting anyone who was partisan to the Prince's cause. They all, from the Prince downward, might well find themselves piloting fighters on the frontlines.

The ancient texts said, "Revenge is best when cultured, gathered at the proper time, and lingered over."

He would linger over this scrap of vengeance for a very long time. Perhaps it would wash away the bitterness of knowledge.

The sure and certain knowledge of his own hand in this disaster for his people.

Nothing had been heard from K'Kai since the Confederation forces had to abandon the planet. In the few moments that Hunter had free to think about something other than the next thirty seconds, he'd worried about her. The Kilrathi were unlikely to look kindly on a Firekkan space-ship captain; they did not permit their subject races to have command of much in the way of technology, as it made them easier to keep under their thumb. K'Kai and Larrhi represented the "aberrant" traits that the Kilrathi wanted removed from their subject races — Larrhi was out of their reach, but if K'Kai didn't have the sense to hide what she was, Hunter wouldn't give her any odds at all for surviving.

He only hoped K'Kai had the sense to hide her ship, scatter her crew, and pretend to be whatever the Firekkan equivalent of a dirt farmer was.

After a while, he no longer had time to hope anything, other than to hope that he would survive the next engagement himself.

The moment he had lost flight controls of that Dralthi and ditched her, he had been absolutely positive that he wouldn't even do that. And the same when he thought he'd lost the *Claw*. Those experiences had shaken him in ways he still was coming to terms with. He'd never had to confront his own mortality quite so closely before. In better times, he'd have had a chance to retreat to sickbay and shake for a few days — but he couldn't be spared, and he was no sooner back on the *Claw* then someone was throwing him into a fighter again, and sending him out.

He could have broken, as Maniac was threatening to do at any moment, as dozens of others had. Somehow, he didn't. He still didn't know why.

Suddenly, it was over, and the *Claw* was in retreat — but oddly enough, not because they had lost, but because they had won. The Kilrathi were retreating in disorder, but the Confederation was not pursuing. Halcyon explained it to them, but frankly, Hunter was too tired and too overloaded to understand even a tenth of it. It was enough that the fighting was over for now, and that they had won. *He* wasn't so gung-ho that he wanted to chase after the cats. Let them run. Hunter went to his bunk, fell asleep, and slept dreamlessly for three days straight. He was not the only fighter pilot to do so.

In the days and weeks that followed, he had far more leisure to think about K'Kai and her crew than he would have liked. He kept thinking about that final farewell — and hoping she had survived.

A leave down on good old Earth would do very little to make him forget, when all was said and done. It would be a relief when the orders came, sending the *Claw* and her crews back to Firekka. At least he would know, one way or another, what had happened to her.

"Read 'em and weep, guys," Blair said, spreading out his cards. Two kings, three queens; Hunter whistled softly in admiration. Amazing; Blair had been enjoying an incredible run of luck lately — well, in cards, anyway. His lovelife was pretty barren, or so Hunter had heard. Not that his had been much better, but Hunter wasn't going to complain. He was afraid he'd used up most of his lifetime quota of luck just surviving that Dralthi ejection. He hadn't played many card games or chased any lovely ladies since; he hadn't wanted to use up any luck he'd had left. Flying with Maniac as occasional wingman was taking up more than enough of that remaining luck.

For the first time in his life, *he* was superstitious. Maybe it would wear off, in time. The psychs said it would. "Just let things ride," they told him.

Blair sat back in his chair, grinning, as the rest of the poker players threw down their cards with varying degrees of chagrin and disgust. No one had anything like that hand. Blair raked in his winnings, his grin broadening, and invited the other players to try their luck again.

Jazz grimaced, and bowed out. Blair lifted an eyebrow in Hunter's direction, a clear invitation to take the chair Jazz was vacating. But before Hunter had to make any kind of disclaimer, one of the fighter-pilots newly assigned to the *Claw* stuck his head into the room and spotted him.

"St. John, Halcyon wants you on Flight Deck A-5, ASAP." He vanished before Hunter could ask why, or what the Colonel wanted. He looked at Blair, shrugged wordlessly, and followed in the messenger's wake.

The Flight Deck in question was empty, the squadron housed there currently out on patrol, looking for Kilrathi stragglers.

Empty? No — not quite. Off on the side, out of the way of the fighters that would be returning shortly, was a battered, tired-looking freighter, a small one, but still Jump-capable. The model was an old one — outmoded, but somehow familiar.

Familiar, then all at once, he *knew*. Knew it before he glimpsed plumes, beaks, or Firekkan writing, half-erased, on the freighter's nose.

"*K'Kai!*" he shouted, breaking into a run. A dozen beaked heads swiveled in his direction; a chorus of excited squawks arose as the Firekkan crew spotted him. They began running, wings half-spread, converging on him.

In moments, he was surrounded by excited Firekkans, most of them showing signs of distress as well as excitement, and all of them the worse for wear. Most were missing feathers; many had injuries both old and new. He was half afraid of what he would find when he finally reached K'Kai herself.

But as he managed to work his way through the

agitated flock, he caught a glimpse of her in excited conversation with Colonel Halcyon. The Colonel didn't seem to be catching more than one word in four, she was speaking so quickly, and he greeted Hunter's appearance with the pleasure of a drowning man on seeing a life-preserver.

"St. John, get over here!" the Colonel shouted over the din, then reached out and grabbed Hunter by the uniform sleeve and dragged him through the mob of Firekkans. "Here, K'Kai, tell Hunter what you want — "

And with that set of instructions, the Colonel beat a hasty retreat.

"But — " Hunter said desperately after the Colonel's retreating back. "But I — "

Too late.

K'Kai and her entire crew surrounded him, gabbling at the tops of their lungs, until he finally lost patience with them all.

"*Shut UP!*" he roared. A blessed silence descended, as the Firekkans rolled wide, startled eyes at him. He turned to K'Kai. "Right. What happened? What's wrong?"

K'Kai shook her feathers, and stared at him out of wide, half-stunned eyes. A couple of the others made little meeping noises, but he ignored them. Finally she clacked her beak a couple of times, and began speaking. Slower, this time.

Even so, it took Hunter several tries and a lot of cross-questioning to get the whole story out of her. When he did, he didn't blame her or her flock for being upset.

The Kilrathi had taken hostages — not something they did, normally, but evidently the ambitious Prince Thrakhath had thought it would be advantageous to his plans to have hostages . . . or perhaps they were only prized slaves. In view of the disastrous Sivar Eshrad ceremony, the total subjugation of Firekka had been the Prince's only remaining means of saving face.

One of those nests was K'Kai's family, and one of the hostages her young niece Rikik. Rikik's mother had been killed during the battle to rescue the hostages, and that had made Rikik, young as she was, the titular head of the flock. Her very youth made her a good hostage; she was so frightened and vulnerable that no adult Firekkan would resist the Kilrathi Prince's orders, knowing that she would suffer if they rebelled.

One of the first orders had been to pinion every adult so that they could not fly. K'Kai had the bright notion to make the Kilrathi think that removing only the first two secondaries on each wing would make Firekkans ground-bound — and once she sped the idea through the nests, the rest went along with the ruse. They planted the misinformation in their own records, and feigned their loss of flight when the feathers were removed, taking to the air only within the nest, or where they were certain no Kilrathi could observe them.

The Kilrathi Prince neither knew nor cared that pinioning every adult would cripple them, make it impossible for them to reach feeding-platforms and sleep-perches within the nest. His orders grew progressively crueler, but with their leaders in Kilrathi hands, there was nothing the avians could do but obey, and fight a covert battle to retake their world, letting the Kilrathi think that the fighters were from outside the city, as Hunter had seen for himself.

"And they departed from Firekka," K'Kai concluded. She shook her head. "But the first ship off-world took with it not only the Prince, but his hostages. They took our flock leaders with them! They said that if Firekka could not be theirs to conquer, then they would see to it that it would not ally with you! That was what I came here to tell you — those leaders who are left will cancel the treaty! They will not risk the lives of our flock leaders!"

With each sentence, she grew shriller and shriller, until at last she was shrieking again. As Hunter tried to calm her down, his mind was really on her alarming news.

The Confederation needed Firekka. Not for any strategic reason . . . the planet was too isolated from the rest of Terran space to make any real difference in the war . . . but for political reasons. The Confed had sworn to protect Firekka against the Kilrathi, and hadn't. If the Firekkans broke the treaty, how many other Confed planets would follow?

"Come on, K'Kai," he said. "You and me have a sudden date with Captain Thorn."

He bullied and wheedled his way to the Captain, but once there, Thorn made it clear that this was not a matter for a lowly pilot, flock-friend or not. So he had to leave K'Kai there, without knowing what Thorn would do for her.

But he had confidence in the Captain, and as much in K'Kai. She was in good hands. Thorn would get her to Confed High Command, and see that she spoke to the right people.

Something would be done.

Something would be done!

• CHAPTER NINE

"Meal time, kitty," the human voice said, shoving a bowl and a mug through the slot in his cell door.

The human's words and a terrible smell awakened Kirha from a sound sleep on the floor. The smell was coming from the mug, which smelled of rotting plants of some kind. He moved closer to the door and stared at the contents of the mug, a foul bubbling yellow liquid, then at the bowl. It was filled with a strange mixture of plants and roots, not real food. He could see some meat mixed in with it, but the meat was brown and looked terrible, nothing that he could eat.

What had happened to those humans from the ship, the ones who had known what a Kilrathi warrior needed? From decent food and decent quarters, he had come to this — burned trash and treatment he would not have given to a slave.

He heard the footsteps walking away, and held back his rage. A warrior of Kilrah did not lose his dignity by shrieking at empty walls. Kirha sat back on his haunches, steadfastly ignoring the hunger gnawing at his innards, and waited.

It had been like this since the Kilrathi retreat, and their arrival at Sol, when they had separated him from Ralgha. He had not seen Ralgha, nor his lord the human called Hunter, since.

Where is my liege lord? he wondered. *How can he leave me here in this awful place?*

Has he completely forgotten me?

He leaped to his feet and stalked the length of his cell, pacing angrily. The cell was tiny, and empty but for a white plastic source of water in the corner, another odd plastic fixture attached to the wall, and a strange elevated pile of compressed fabric in the corner, which he assumed was the necessary, since nothing else in the cell even vaguely looked usable for that purpose. The place he and Ralgha had shared had a necessary, one recognizable as such. This cell had nothing of the sort. The end result was a foul odor that Kirha could do nothing about, but which only added to the humiliation of his incarceration.

Lord Ralgha would have been kinder to let me die, he thought sadly, curling up on the floor for another nap.

Another sound awakened him, and he blinked at the bright light streaming in from the hallway. Someone was standing in the open cell doorway, a tall human. This human had longer head-fur than most of the humans, a tawny gold fur that was nearly the same color as the fur of Major H'hristy Mar'kss, but he also had fur on his face. His chin was bare, but there was a small line of golden fur beneath his nose that extended down the sides of his mouth. That mouth was frowning now, as he stepped into the cell.

"I'faith, it reeks like the devil in here!" the human said, his words oddly accented and more difficult for Kirha to understand. "Dinna someone ever come in to clean this place, laddie?"

Was this another interrogation? He thought they had ended with that, since no one had come to take him to the interrogation room for several eights of hours. He hated it every time they came to take him away. The drugs they gave him made him dizzy and sick, and they always asked the same questions, over and over again. Kirha knew none of the answers to them. Fleet movements, battle plans, any of it.

This human, though, seemed different. Instead of the pair of human guards that always tied his arms behind him before taking him to the inter-rogation room, this human only closed the cell door, then turned to stare at Kirha.

"So why aren't ye eating any food, laddie?" the human male asked. "The brig guards tell me that ye haven't eaten anything in two days now."

Kirha was uncertain whether he should answer the human. After all, this was one of the enemy . . . or was he? Captain Ian St. John, also known as Hunter, was human, and Kirha would have gladly answered any of his questions without hesitation. Perhaps he ought to honor the human's request for an answer, if only not to risk bringing shame or disgrace upon his liege lord.

"They have not given me anything to eat!" Kirha said, trying to keep the anger out of his voice. "I would like to eat, but they do not give me any food!"

The human sat down on the bunk across from him. "Well, that's not what they're sayin'. Duke said that they gave you some beef stew yesterday, and again this morning, and you haven't touched it. See, there it is, sittin' on the floor. They even gave you a beer, I see, in the hopes that it'd help your appetite."

It seemed the stranger was at least asking questions. "I do not know what this 'beef stew' is, but what they gave me was *harakh*, not food for a warrior! Am I a prey-species, to be fed roots and berries?"

"Ah, I see," the human said, baring his teeth in a smile. "That was an easy mistake for the guards to make. You're the first Kilrathi prisoner we've had on Sol Station. Usually captured Kilrathi are held on the fleet ships and then transported directly to a prisoner camp, not here to Sol Station. You're a unique case, lad . . . and your Captain wasn't here long enough to eat a meal before they took him down planet-side. So, Kilrathi warrior, what would you rather eat?"

Oh, this was better. Like the humans upon the ship, the *Claw of the Tiger.* Humans who would listen to him, not order him about. Humans like the one called Hunter. "Meat. Fresh meat, not burned in a fire. And no plants or roots mixed it with it. And I would like some *arakh* leaves," he added hopefully.

"*Arakh* leaves? I remember hearing about those, it's like catnip for you Kilrathi. All right, I'll see what I can arrange." The human walked to the platform against the wall, and his nose wrinkled. "Lord!" He glanced at Kirha. "You're not sleeping in this, are you?"

Kirha straightened in quiet dignity. "Of course not. I sleep on the floor, as no one has provided me with sleeping furs."

The human had an odd expression on his face. "Why don't you use the john, boyo?"

John? He searched through his memories of human vocabulary, but that word was not familiar to him, except in that it was one of his liege lord's honorifics. "I do not understand," Kirha said.

The human crossed over to the white plastic pool of water, pressing the switch that Kirha had discovered would replenish the water supply. "Use this, laddie."

Kirha's lip curled in disgust. "I would not foul my drinking water, human! Do you think I am completely uncivilized?"

The human's mouth twitched. "I see where the problem is now. They must've given you visiting alien VIP quarters on the *Claw;* you've been stuck in a human brig, here. This," he said, pointing at the odd fixture on the wall, "Is the water supply. You press these knobs here, and that'll provide hot and cold running water. You use this," he continued, pointing at the other fixture, "For yer, er, biological needs. Ah — elimination. And that," he pointed at the pile of compressed fabric which Kirha had clawed apart, "Is what you sleep on. Understood?"

The human glanced at a small mechanical device strapped to his wrist. "I have to be at a meeting shortly, or we could continue this fascinatin' discussion of human versus Kilrathi household technology. I'll send someone to bring ye a new mattress, and make sure that they start feeding ye something you can eat." He walked to the door and pressed his palm to the lock. Nothing happened. He pressed his palm to it again, then hit it once with his closed fist. "Let me out, boys, I have to meet with Commodore Steward in five minutes."

"Of course, Major Taggart," a human voice said from the other side, and the cell door slid open a moment later.

The strange gold-furred human paused in the doorway, looking back at Kirha. "Don't I even get a thank-you from you, laddie? For keeping you from starving yourself to death?"

Kirha spoke stiffly. "I would rather be dead, but my former liege-lord refused my request. That is why I am a prisoner here now."

The human raised one bit of eye-fur, while the other remained as it was. It gave his face a most peculiar look. "Hmmm. Well, if ye need anything, boyo, call for me. My name is James Taggart, but everyone calls me Paladin."

Some small courtesy is required now, Kirha thought, *even though I do not wish to extend any honors to these humans.* "Thank you, James Taggart, whom everyone calls Paladin," he said gravely.

The human's mouth quirked into what Kirha now knew was a small smile, then the door closed behind him and Kirha was alone again in his cell.

This human was honorable, however. As he had said, edible food began arriving on a regular schedule. Some time later, two of the guards entered the cell to remove the fouled fabric and replace it with another. Kirha could not bring himself to sleep on the odd platform, but he did follow the human's instructions for his personal hygiene. The air in the cell stayed fresh, the fresh meat tasted good, and Kirha's spirits rose for the first time since the surrender of the *Ras Nik'hra.*

The only factor that still depressed him was that there was *still* no sign of his liege lord. *But at least I will be strong and fit when he requires my services again,* Kirha thought, consoling himself. He had been keeping up the exercises that Ralgha had taught him. *To fail one's lord out of physical weakness would be the greatest shame of all.*

The golden-furred human came back several eights of hours later, in the company of another human, one with a long mane of reddish head-fur. This human was younger, and dressed differently, in a garment that hung loosely around his legs. With a start, Kirha realized that it was female. Discerning between human males and human females was still difficult for him. He and Lord Ralgha had not known that the Major aboard the *Ras Nik'hra* was female until someone had corrected his speech for him.

"This is our boy, Kirha," the man said. "He's all yours, Gwen. His English is excellent, so ye won't hae to worry about speaking in that throat-hurtin' Kilrathi language."

"Thanks, boss," she said, studying Kirha intently. Kirha stared back at her, equally curious.

"Are you being treated well?" she asked. "Is there anything we can do for you?"

He hesitated before asking. It was a show of weakness, to request something from his enemies rather than demand it, as he had before. But who was his enemy now? The distinction had blurred in his mind past all recognition.

And besides, his liege-lord had given him orders to ask for what he needed.

"I would like to see my liege-lord," Kirha said, hoping the desperation was not showing in his voice.

"Lord Ralgha?" Paladin asked. "I thought I told ye, lad. He's not here, lad, he's down on Earth."

"Not Lord Ralgha," Kirha said. "Captain Ian St. John, also known as Hunter, is my liege-lord now. Lord Ralgha is only my overlord."

"What?" The human laughed out loud. "Hunter? Ye must be joking!"

"I am very serious, James Taggart, whom everyone calls Paladin," Kirha said stiffly. "Captain Ian St. John, also known as Hunter, is my liege-lord now."

"How did you end up swearing loyalty to a human?" the female asked curiously. "This wasn't in any of the reports . . ."

"Lord Ralgha *nar* Hhallas was my sworn liege-lord, and I served him aboard the *Ras Nik'hra*," Kirha explained. "When my Lord Ralgha surrendered the ship to Captain Ian St. John, also known as Hunter, he gave my fealty as an honor-gift as well. So Captain Ian St. John, also known as Hunter, became my liege-lord. Lord Ralgha is still my overlord, but he cannot command me to disobey Captain Ian St. John, also known as Hunter."

"Unbelievable," Paladin said, shaking his head.

"Stranger things have been known to happen, Paladin," the woman murmured.

"I know. Well, laddie, this makes matters even more interesting. By the way, when you're talking about 'Captain Ian St. John, also known as Hunter,' you can just call him 'Hunter.' "

"It would not be disrespectful toward my liege lord?" Kirha asked, concerned.

"Not at all. In fact, I'm sure that Hunter would prefer it. Captain Ian St. John, also known as Hunter, is a bit of a mouthful. And since I've never formally introduced myself . . . I'm Major James

Taggart, formerly of the Confederation Navy. But as I said before, you can call me Paladin."

"I'm Gwen," the female said. "My full name is Gweneviere Larson, but no one ever calls me that."

"I am Kirha *hrai* Ralgha *nar* Hhallas," Kirha said, then hesitated. "No, my name is now Kirha *hrai* Hunter . . . what is my lord Hunter's home planet?"

"He's an Aussie," Paladin said.

"Then my name is now Kirha *hrai* Hunter *nar* Aussie," Kirha said with some satisfaction. At last, an identity! It made him feel — a little more secure.

"Is it all right if we just call ye Kirha?" Paladin asked. His face appeared very strange, as if he was struggling not to laugh. "Kirha *hrai* Hunter *nar* Aussie is just as bad as Captain Ian St. John, also known as Hunter."

"If it would not dishonor my lord Hunter," Kirha said seriously.

"I don't think it would; we humans tend to use the short versions of our names, 'cept on formal occasions. In fact," Paladin said, exchanging a glance with Gwen, "I'm friends with your lord Hunter, and I know that he would be very pleased that you're bein' friendly with us, talking to us now."

"I am glad to act in a way that honors my lord Hunter," Kirha said. "But how can I know that this is what he wishes me to do, if he is not here to order me himself?"

"Excuse us for a minute here, laddie," Paladin said, and he and the female moved away from Kirha, closer to the closed cell door.

"What do ye think, lass?" Kirha heard Paladin whisper to the female, so quietly that Kirha, listening closely, could barely hear his words.

"We know that the Kilrathi take their honor very seriously," she said. "This could be for real, the first time that a Kilrathi is totally loyal to a human. It's a marvelous opportunity for Intelligence."

"Do you think he'd willingly help us?" the male said. Kirha controlled his indignation. How could they doubt his loyalty?

"It's worth a try," the female whispered back. "Certainly the interrogators haven't managed to get any good information out of him."

Paladin turned back to Kirha, speaking louder. "Tell me more about this oath of fealty to, ah, your lord Hunter. What does this mean, exactly?"

Kirha could not keep a look of surprise off his face. Everyone knew what an oath of fealty meant, even the littlest cub in a *hrai*! He thought about it for a minute before speaking.

Then again — these two were not Kilrathi. They were not taught of honor and fealty from cubhood. What they were taught, he did not know — but if he were fortunate, they might know something *like* it.

Perhaps, if he explained himself, they would find Hunter and bring him here. "It means that I am sworn to him and his *hrai* for all of my life, and all my descendants' lives. That I am his to command, and will defend his honor and life with my own, and obey any order without question."

"So . . . Ralgha . . . was your earlier lord? And when he told you to surrender to the humans, you did?" Paladin seemed — more curious than anything else.

"Of course," Kirha said, surprised at the question.

"And this didn't bother you?" he persisted. "Does

it bother you now, to be talkin' with two humans?"

Kirha bared his teeth. "I would rather rip out your throat than talk to you, human, but that would probably not please my lord Hunter."

"I hope the tapes are catching all of this," Gwen murmured, so quietly that Kirha could barely hear her. "This boy may not be of much use militarily, but we've never captured anyone who would talk about their social system before."

"Maybe you're right. But, then again . . . what do you know of Ghorah Khar, lad?" Paladin asked louder, his eyes suddenly intent.

"It is a beautiful planet, one of the loveliest that the Empire has colonized," Kirha said, remembering.

"What do you know of the rebellion on Ghorah Khar?" This from the female. Understandably; the priestesses were at the heart of the rebellion. She would want to know what other females were engaged in.

"Only what Lord Ralgha *nar* Hhallas told me," Kirha said, hunching his shoulders. "Which is very little."

"But you know Ghorah Khar?" Paladin persisted. "The layout of the towns, the location of the starport, all of that?"

"Of course," Kirha said, beginning to be annoyed with all of these inane questions. "The *Ras Nik'hra* landed there many times."

"So we can cross-correlate Ralgha's information with his," Gwen murmured quietly.

"That we can, lass. That we can." The human male's eyes glinted. "We're going to have some questions for you, Kirha lad. Answer them and your lord Hunter will be very happy with you."

His human lord . . . the change in loyalties was
dizzying to Kirha. It had been so much easier
before, when he was sworn to Lord Ralgha, and
loyal to the Emperor. Now all he knew was that
there was a single center to his universe . . . and that
center was somewhere else, doubtless far away
from him. Even Lord Ralgha, whose orders he was
permitted to follow, providing they did not con-
tradict Hunter's, was far from him. He had never
felt quite so alone. "I want — I want to see my liege
lord," Kirha said, stubbornly. "I want to hear from
my lord Hunter that I am to help you with this."

Paladin nodded. "I can arrange that for ye.
Hunter's down on Earth, on leave and visiting his
family in Sydney. I saw him a week ago when he
stopped on the Station before heading downside, but
he'll be back up in Sol Station shortly, before catching
a lift back to wherever it is that the *Tiger's Claw* is currently stationed. I'll tell him to drop by and see you."

Kirha resisted the impulse to prostrate himself
before the human, he was that overwhelmed with
relief and gratitude. "Thank you, James Taggart.
Thank you."

"Don't thank me, laddie," the human male said,
then showed his teeth in a human grin. "Or if you
want to thank me, we could get a head start on
these questions . . ."

"I will answer your questions when you bring my
liege lord to me, and he gives me permission to do
so," Kirha replied, stubbornly. "That is my right
and my duty."

"Deal," the human said, and extended his
smooth-skinned hand to Kirha, who looked at it,

not understanding. "Humans shake hands when they've sworn on oath," Paladin explained.

Uncertainly, Kirha shook the other's hand, keeping his claws sheathed so as not to draw blood from the human's fragile skin. "Upon my honor, I swear it," he said.

"Good," Paladin said. "Verra good. Now, maybe while we're waiting for your lord Hunter, maybe you can start thinking of everything you know about that spaceport on Ghorah Khar. . . ."

K'Kai stalked through the strange metal corridors of the Sol-Central space station without trying to hide her agitation. Humans and nonhumans alike cleared out of her way. Just as well; she was ready to moult, she was so frustrated.

At Hunter's advice, she had taken her case before Confederation High Command, demanding that they do something to free the hostages the Kilrathi had taken. Threatening them with the cancellation of the treaty. Warning them that even if the treaty was not canceled, they could never be sure of what her people might or might not do if their flock-leaders were threatened.

The humans of High Command had made soothing noises; she refused to be soothed. They had made vague promises; with stubborn insistance, she had forced them to turn those vague promises into ones with a little more detail.

But now — now it didn't look as if they had any intention of following through on those promises. Day followed day, with no indication that a rescue attempt was even in the planning stages. With each day that passed, she grew more and more upset, thinking of little Rikik in the claws of those meat-eaters. Today's meeting had been the same as all the others — she had been told that with all the Kilrathi encroachments into the human-controlled areas of Enigma Sector, there just weren't any troops to spare for a rescue attempt. If nothing happened soon, she would have to consider making her own — probably doomed — attempt. Right now — now, she could only prowl the corridors, working out her frustrations, walking until she was exhausted and could finally sleep.

Only to dream of poor little Rikik . . .

An odd noise in the corridor ahead of her caught her attention; the sounds of claws amid the boots. Claws?

Curious, she lengthened her stride, and found herself following a very odd gathering; human guards escorting what could only be a young Kilrathi!

She stopped dead in her tracks, frozen in place with astonishment, and the party vanished around a turn ahead of her. She continued to stand there, ignoring the stares of those who had to push by her, trying to think what such a thing could mean.

Hadn't Hunter said something about Kilrathi prisoners?

No, not prisoners; defectors. One of them had somehow gotten himself attached to Hunter, who had found the experience something less than amusing.

She clacked her beak a little, thinking of Hunter's face and how he had looked when he had described that unwelcome responsibility. He had not been happy about his role as Kilrathi-lord.

Well, that was too bad for him. But she wondered

if she could do something with this young Kilrathi.
Perhaps he could help her, or maybe he could tell
her something that would either force the Confederation to act, or make her own rescue attempt a
little less suicidal.

There was only one way to find out; arrange an
interview with this Kilrathi, if she could.

She turned abruptly, frightening a human clerk
who had not expected her to move so quickly. He
made an odd yipping noise and jumped backwards.
She ignored him, heading straight back to her
quarters and the computer console there.

Now to see if all that observation of humans had
paid off; her sister always claimed she could
manipulate her way into or out of any situation, so
maybe it was time to see if her persuasiveness could
work on humans. . . .

And if it worked on Kilrathi too.

K'Kai took her place cautiously across the table
from Kirha, the youngest of the two Kilrathi defectors, and Hunter's little problem. He seemed
uneasy; the more so since there were no guards at
this meeting. The Kilrathi had given his sworn oath
that he would not harm K'Kai, and it seemed that
the humans trusted him to keep that word.

Interesting. Perhaps he even feared her, what she
might do to him. Certainly, she thought cynically,
the humans guarding him would not move in to
stop her with any degree of haste.

The Kilrathi's ears were flattened, and his whiskers twitching. That might be the sign of nerves —
or it might be the sign that he was holding himself
back from making a meal out of K'Kai. Either

possibility was likely. K'Kai clicked her tongue a little with impatience.

"I am not going to stab you with my beak, you know," she said abruptly in the humans' language.

The feline's ears flattened a little more, then raised slowly. "What, you would try to fight me?" he said contemptuously in accented Terran. "I think not. You are a prey-species, and inherently inferior to the Kilrathi."

"Well, that must be why your people on Firekka were so confident that they ordered all of my people to be made flightless," K'Kai retorted. "Or was it just that they were so lazy they didn't want dinner to be able to fly out of reach?"

The Kilrathi stared at her for a moment, clearly nonplussed, then began to make a kind of gurgling sound she deduced was laughter. "You have a sharp wit, feathered one," he said. "You must take care that it does not cut you."

"Ah, but those of us with claws and beaks, and teeth worth talking about, are better prepared for sharpness in anything, are we not?" K'Kai said archly. "Not like these pathetic humans. Their weapons and their wit have to be manufactured."

The gurgling increased, and the feline's ears rose and unfolded. "Too true," he said. "My clan-lord finds their games and storytelling amusing, but I find them dull creatures."

K'Kai made the appropriate responses of commiseration, and then added, "Part of the problem may be that they are not creatures of a flock or pack. They do not understand the balances that must be worked out among one's kin. They cannot understand how these balances both keep the pack alive against outsiders, and keep the pack from destroying itself from within."

"Too true." The Kilrathi hung his head, and stared at the table-top. "I try to understand these creatures, and understanding eludes me. I have more in common with you, feathered one, than with them."

"Really?" K'Kai replied ingenuously. *Even if I am a prey-species, Kilrathi?* She took a quick inventory. "Hmm. You could be right. We both have claws. Beak — well, you have fangs, and this *is* a weapon if I choose to use it. Body-coverings, unlike the furless and unfeathered humans. A similar social structure. Perhaps you are speaking more truly than you know, Kilrathi . . ."

"Cease the mindless chatter, Firekkan," the feline growled — and yet, there was no anger or malice in his voice. "You wished to see me. Surely it was for some purpose other than curiosity."

K'Kai thought he looked as if he was thinking; wondering if he should say something further, or wait until she revealed herself. Her purpose at the moment was to keep him curious. When she didn't answer, he leaned back in his seat, tail swishing on the floor behind him.

"You are not like the craven humans who keep me penned here," he said at last. "And you are not as I thought your people would be. I am not certain what to make of you — what category you fall into. And I find myself wondering if you understand what these humans cannot."

"What is that?" she asked, accepting the challenge. "Wait, shall I guess? You want me to say or do things that will tell me whether or not I understand honor in the purest sense."

She puffed up her chest-feathers, glad now that she had taken the extra training from the Confed language tapes allowed her to speak with authority outside the nests.

"Do I understand honor?" she asked, as his eyes grew wider and wider. "Is that what you wanted to ask me? I cannot blame you; the humans have a very different sense of honor from you and I. They frequently make promises they hope they will not have to keep, they use language that will not bind them to anything if they can help it. They have a class of folk who do nothing but find ways to exploit or be rid of those promises. Whereas among both our peoples, a promise is binding, for all time." Then she cackled. "And so *we* have a class of peoples who devote themselves to keep us out of any such entangling promises! I would probably find the same class among the Kilrathi, eh?"

The gurgle became a full-voiced howl of amusement. "You are the most entertaining creature to cross this threshold in many long days. I believe I like you. What do you call yourself?"

"K'Kai," she replied carefully. "And you?"

"Kirha," the Kilrathi replied. "I make you free of my name."

That last had a sound of formula about it, and she replied the same way. "I make you free of mine." Then, slyly, "And of something else as well."

She had checked with the medics on this one; they had been interrogating Kirha often enough to know what would and would not affect him — and what he might enjoy. Firekka's Finest was under the heading of "things he might enjoy." The alcohol content was something Kilrathi metabolized easily enough, and they liked their food raw, but spiced. So she had brought a few bottles of her favorite brew with her. Just in case.

She placed the first green glass bottle carefully on the table between them, with a Firekkan drinking-vase of iridescent blue glass and a Kilrathi cup of red-glazed porcelain, more like a deep saucer than a cup, because the felines lapped up their drinks with their tongues. He eyed the bottle with mingled interest and suspicion.

"Check the cup, or use one of your own," she suggested. "We will be sharing the bottle, in any case. We call it 'Firekka's Finest.' I checked with the medics and there is not anything in there to which you should react badly. It might even settle your stomach." When he continued to hesitate, she cocked her head sideways. "Hun-ter liked it well enough. Or is not the custom among the Kilrathi to share a drink as well as common interests?"

She opened the bottle and poured herself a drink, sticking her beak down into the long neck of the vase for a quick sip. Kirha growled and poured himself a cupful, raising it to his mouth, his eyes daring her to laugh at him as he lapped up a cautious sample.

His eyes widened, his pupils dilated. He raised his head and stared at her.

"Not to your taste?" she asked, oddly disappointed.

He coughed, and blinked. "Quite the — opposite," he replied. "I wondered why the Prince had chosen your world for the *Sivar-Eshrad. Now* I know. Once he had Firekka in his claws, he could bring in his house agents and proceed to accrue a private fortune from this — " he raised the cup a little " — and all without the Emperor ever knowing he was doing so!"

"Well, your Prince had a few surprises awaiting him," K'Kai said proudly. "Firekkans may look peaceful, but we know how to defend ourselves."

"If you can brew this, I must believe you! This is truly a drink worthy of warriors!" Kirha bent to his cup again, his tongue rapidly lapping up every drop in the basin. He came up for air, looking as if he would be very happy for another round.

Clucking happily to herself, K'Kai obliged him, pouring another for herself. As she did so, Kirha's whiskers lifted and his eyes narrowed in what she had been told was the Kilrathi expression of pleasure. "By Sivar, K'Kai, this elixir of yours *is* settling my stomach! I'd begun to think that this venture of my lord's was going to be nothing but an endless hell of interrogation and stomach-aches!"

"Do not stint yourself, there's plenty more where that bottle came from," K'Kai said helpfully. "And I can get more to you. I suspect a cup with a meal should help, after those ridiculous drugs upset you."

Kirha growled — or maybe purred. Or a combination of both. "Right now, if you do not mind a seasoning of truth, I should like very much to become intoxicated."

K'Kai cackled, startling him. "That was my idea precisely," she told him. "I am as frustrated in what I came here to do as you are — and since it is the humans who are causing that, I felt very disinclined to have my intoxication with any of *them*."

"So you chose me as a drinking partner?" Kirha

shook his head, his words just a little slurred. "I fear you are not stating even an eighth part of the truth."

He had finished his third cup by then, and K'Kai her third vase, and the bottle was half empty. She poured them both another round.

"The truth is, I thought we both had a lot more in common with each other than with the naked bipeds of Sol," she said. "We both understand honor; you are imprisoned, even though you have given your word to serve Hun-ter — I am treated like a prisoner, since I cannot leave until I get an answer from High Command and they won't *give* me an answer."

His eyes glazed a little as he tried to follow that convoluted statement. "We are two aliens in a sea of deceitful hairless apes," he agreed. "To fellowship!"

He raised his cup; she brought up her vase, and they drained the vessels. She poured again. Her ears were beginning to buzz, and she felt pleasantly relaxed and warm; like soaring effortlessly in a hot thermal.

"So what is it that you want from the apes?" he asked at last.

She narrowed her own eyes, and stared down at her vase. "When the Kilrathi Prince left my planet, he took some of my people with him as hostages," she said bitterly, and his eyes widened and ears flattened. "My niece was one of them. I want to get them back, sun scorch it! But High Command keeps saying that they cannot do anything!" She took a long pull of Finest. *"Won't,* is more like it."

"I begin to see why my lord Ralgha brought us to this pass," he said, as he followed her example. "The Prince should *not* have done that. It is dishonorable; it violates the Warrior's Code to hide behind hostages! He will cause the fury of Sivar to follow him and his blood to the eighth generation!"

"I wish the fury of Sivar would scorch the butts of the flightless mudbrains in the human High Command," K'Kai replied. She looked up at him, and noticed that there seemed to be two of him for a moment. No doubt about it, this was a particularly strong batch of the Finest. "What is the use of a treaty if it does not work both ways?"

"For a female, you speak very strongly. But it is true . . . you have been treated with less than full honor," he agreed. His words ran together a bit, with a bit of hissing on the sibilants. His eyes began to cross, and K'Kai rather thought he was as drunk as she was. Maybe more. "I have been treated with less than full honor. We should become intoxicated." He hiccuped, and his eyes crossed a little more. "Correction. We *are* intoxicated. We should continue the state."

K'Kai poured, carefully, into the cup he held out to her. "I will drink to that," she said. "Oh, I will drink to that!"

● CHAPTER TEN

Hunter walked through the corridors of Sol Station, glancing at the color-strips on the metal walls to make sure that he was still headed in the direction of the transient officers' barracks. By this time tomorrow, he'd be on his way back to the *Tiger's Claw,* just in time for the beginning of their new assignment in the Enigma Sector. One of the Tactical Officers from the *Claw,* who'd joined him for a few drinks in the San Francisco Terminal as they waited for the shuttle departure, had said something about a possible mission behind enemy lines. The Tactical Officer had been drunk enough to talk, though sober enough to realize when he'd said too much. But that tidbit of information was enough for Hunter to start making guesses. It could be an attack against Ghorah Khar or one of the other Kilrathi colonies, or maybe even the Kilrathi sector command at K'Tithrak Mang.

It's 'bout time we took the fight to the cat's doorstep! He smiled to himself. *'Cause it's a long, long way to Tipperary, but my heart's right there. . . .*

"Hunter, lad!" someone called to him, a man's voice thick with a Scottish brogue.

He recognized the voice instantly and turned. "Paladin! What are you doing here, mate? I thought they'd retired you!"

Paladin ran his hand through his silvering blond hair. "Nae, they're not gettin' rid of me just yet. I've been reassigned to Sol Station for a few months, before I head out for my new assignment."

"New assignment?" Hunter frowned. "But you're over the age limit for fighter pilots!"

"Who said I'd be a fighter pilot, lad?" Paladin grinned.

Hunter shook his head. "It's just like you to talk without sayin' anything, old man. All right, so what gives?"

"We shouldn't talk here in the hallway," the older Scotsman said. He caught Hunter's elbow, steering him down another corridor. "Besides, there's someone else ye need to talk to. So, how was your downside leave, Ian?"

Hunter shook his head. "Guess you hadn't heard, mate. I spent most of my leave in Brisbane with my family, at the memorial service for my kid brother. He was a Marine, went down with the assault on Firekka and didn't come back . . . I didn't even know that until afterwards. We weren't close, hadn't talked in years, but it was still a shock. Grandma didn't handle it too well." Hunter's mouth quirked in a wry smile. "She's an amazing lady, though, she'll get through it okay. She's getting up in years, but still rides all over the hills every day with the ranchhands. Then I stayed with Mum and Dad in Sydney. And I spent a couple days in San Francisco, visiting Bossman's wife and daughter. She moved there to be closer to her parents." He shook his head; it hadn't been an easy visit for any of them, especially after watching them lower his kid brother into the ground in Brisbane, but it had been one he'd needed to make. "She's a tough lady, she'll survive this okay. She and Angel have been corresponding these last few months. I think it's been good for both of them." He glanced around, suddenly realizing where Paladin was leading him. "Hey, James! This is the detention area. What are we doing here?"

Paladin gave him a sideways glance. "Do ye remember those Kilrathi that defected to our side, back in the Firekka system?"

"Of course." He nodded. "I met Lord Ralgha, and another cat, Kirha. What does this have to do with anything?"

Another odd look. "Do ye remember that other cat swearin' fealty to ye?"

Hunter shrugged. "He did something weird, some kind of Kilrathi ritual."

Paladin pressed his palm against the door lock. "Hunter, I want you to meet Kirha *hrai* Hunter nar Aussie."

The door slid open, and Hunter could see a broad-shouldered Kilrathi standing inside. The Kilrathi made an odd sound and immediately knelt at Hunter's feet, his whiskers nearly touching Hunter's boot. "My lord Hunter, you are here!" the cat said in heavily accented English, his tail quivering. And he sounded — pleased. No, not pleased — something more than merely "pleased."

Hunter stared down in shock at the Kilrathi kneeling in front of him, and then at Paladin, who was apparently trying hard not to laugh but failing miserably. The Scotsman's laughter rang loud and clear through the halls of the Detention area.

*   *   *

"This has to be a joke," Kirha's liege lord said, as Kirha knelt respectfully, awaiting his orders. "This *is* a joke, right, mate?"

The other human was still laughing. Kirha thought this was very poor manners, to make so much noise at such a serious moment, when a sworn warrior was reunited with his liege lord, but obviously his lord was not bothered by it, so he held his peace.

"His name is Kirha," the other human, James Taggart, whom everyone called Paladin, commented, still making outlandish noises. "Actually, his name is Kirha *hrai* Hunter nar Aussie. He's named himself after you, Hunter."

"Uh, why is he on the floor?" Kirha's liege lord asked.

"My lord, I will not rise until you have given me permission," Kirha said quietly.

"You . . . you can get up," his lord said, and Kirha rose to his feet, standing at attention, his belly trembling with excitement.

"As my lord wishes," he said, carefully enunciating the human words.

"I'm not your — dammit, James, stop laughing!" his lord said, glaring at the other human.

"As ye wish, m'lord," Paladin said in a serious tone, then dissolved into laughter again.

"Ignore that Scottish idiot," his lord instructed Kirha. "Now let's talk about this, mate. Back on that *Ras Nik'hra* ship, after the fight with the other Fralthi — I didn't know exactly what was going on with that weird Kilrathi ceremony about oaths and fealty, but I went along with it because Major Marks said I had to. So quit staring at me with those lovesick Kilrathi eyes, because I am not your lord!"

Kirha lowered his eyes respectfully as Paladin spoke. "Oh yes, ye are, Hunter," the human male said. "Kirha, tell him what ye told me about liege lords and sworn warriors, lad!"

Kirha stared down at the plain plastic of the floor, not answering.

"Kirha? Laddie, why won't ye talk to me?" Paladin persisted.

"Come on, Kirha, talk to the man!" Hunter said.

"But, my lord, you ordered me to ignore him," Kirha said, confused. He glanced up at his lord, then quickly lowered his eyes again, remembering his orders not to stare at his liege lord.

"This doesn't make any sense," Hunter began. "All right, Kirha, you can talk to anyone you want to. And stop staring at the floor!"

"As my lord wishes," Kirha said respectfully.

"I can't deal with this," Kirha's lord said wearily. "I just can't. Kirha, it's been fun meeting with you, mate, but I'm — "

"Actually, Ian, I need a favor of ye," Paladin said, rubbing one finger along the edge of the fur on his face. "I want to ask Kirha some questions about Ghorah Khar, and apparently I need your permission to do this. If ye'd be so kind . . ."

Hunter sighed. "Sure. Kirha, if James or anyone else asks you any questions, please answer them truthfully. All right?"

"Of course, my lord Hunter," Kirha replied, relieved to at last have gotten a simple order from his lord.

"Good." He blew his breath out hugely. "Kirha, it's been fun, but I have to go get drunk before I get on a ship tomorrow."

Leave? He was going to leave? "But you cannot leave without me, my lord!" Kirha protested, suddenly alarmed.

Hunter stared at him, his eyes gone round. "What?"

"You are my liege lord," Kirha explained as calmly as he could. *To be abandoned here again, a shame and a dishonor! I belong with my liege lord!* "My place is fighting by your side, defending your life and honor from your enemies."

His liege lord was fixing his gaze at Kirha, his mouth dropping open. Kirha dropped his gaze, not wanting to offend.

"Actually, Hunter won't be leavin' without ye, Kirha, at least not for another few days," Paladin said, smiling again. Kirha's lord looked at him with widened eyes. "Since I need your help with Kirha, here, I've requested that they not ship ye off for another few days, Hunter. I already set up a bunk for you on-Station."

Kirha's lord glanced from Kirha to the other human. "But you can't change my assignment, James. I'm an active duty pilot! They need me back on the *Tiger's Claw!* It would take an Admiral's orders to do that!"

Paladin patted his jacket pocket. "I have those orders right here, Ian. Signed by Commodore Steward, at my request."

Kirha's lord seemed not so much agitated as surprised. Kirha was relieved. He would have hated to kill this Paladin, who had acted honorably in all ways to Kirha — but if Paladin offended Hunter, he would have to. "What in the hell are you doing, James? What kind of assignment have they given you?"

Paladin made a clucking sound. "Ever hear of something called the Special Operations division?"

"But that's Intelligence! You're not an Intelligence agent—" His lord faltered in mid-sentence, staring at the other human. "What in the hell have you gotten yourself into, James?"

"Well, it involves a very high-tech ship disguised as a freighter that they've assigned to me, which I've named the *Bonnie Heather,* and which will be ready for our first assignment in another couple days, and my fine assistant, who'll you'll meet in the next few days, and some little political problems in the Kilrathi Empire. I can't explain too much of it, but I'll tell you what I can. Kirha, we'll be back tomorrow, Hunter and I, to talk more about all of this."

"As my lord wishes," Kirha said, bowing to his human lord.

"I need a drink," his liege said, looking down at Kirha with an indescribable expression on his face. "No, strike that. I need a couple drinks —*several* drinks—"

By the next evening, Hunter wished he'd never seen the *Ras Nik'hra,* never heard of Kirha or Lord Ralgha, and certainly wished that Paladin had retired off to Scotland instead of getting involved in . . . *whatever this is,* he thought, *that James won't tell me about. Didn't matter how many drinks I bought for the man last night, all he'd say was that Commodore Steward recruited him for Special Operations, and that he has to learn as much as possible about Kilrathi internal affairs from Kirha, and then he's going to fly that freighter of his off on some special missions. It doesn't make much sense to me. The closest anyone ever gets to seeing Kilrathi internal affairs is when we make a raid across enemy lines . . .*

. . . back to some godawful prison camp . . .

He banished that thought, that small fear that always lurked in the mind of a fighter pilot. *Anyhow, none of this is very important to the progress of the war! Now Paladin's trying to get more information about this Ghorah Khar planet. It's behind enemy lines, the Kilrathi hold it securely. So who cares?*

He leaned back against the wall, and closed his eyes wearily as Paladin continued. "How many people live near the spaceport of Ghorah Khar, Kirha?"

Kirha hunched his head down, which seemed to be the equivalent of a shrug. "Not many. I have not seen more than a few dozen in the city markets."

Hunter straightened, opening his eyes. Kirha, he wasn't surprised to note, looked as exhausted and bored as he did. *Poor little kitty, stuck in a cell and forced to answer questions for hour after hour.* "James, I think Kirha's referring to humans in the spaceport, not Kilrathi."

Kirha bowed his head. "I beg my liege lord's forgiveness. When James Taggart said 'people,' I did think that he meant humans, not Kilrathi."

"Don't get upset about it, kid. Just tell him the correct number." Hunter leaned back against the wall.

It was so strange to him. Kirha was a Kilrathi, one of the enemy, but he didn't *feel* like an enemy anymore. Maybe it was the way Kirha kept looking to him for approval, like a little kid waiting his Grandma's encouragement. Certainly Kirha *looked* like a menace, all six feet of furred muscle with lots of claws and teeth, but he didn't act like one.

Learn something new every day, Hunter thought wryly.

Paladin made a note, and continued. "Tell me about the town around the spaceport. Are there many nobles that live there?"

"Yes, James Taggart, there are several *hrai* — " Kirha paused, then shook his head. "I do not know how to translate *hrai* into your language. It is one's parents, siblings, and vassals, the focus of one's honor."

"Sounds like a clan or sept to me," Hunter commented from the side of the room. "How many people — I mean, Kilrathi — are in these *hrai*?"

Kirha seemed to think about it for a moment. "Usually, at least a hundred. But sometimes they are very small. Lord Ralgha's *hrai* is only himself and I. And I am sworn to lord Hunter; his will must always be first. This is very sad."

The cell door slid open unexpectedly. Hunter blinked at the brighter light, and the silhouetted figure standing in the doorway. The woman, a gorgeous redhead wearing a non-regulation dress that showed most of her lovely legs, walked into the cell toward Paladin. "James, the Commodore wants to ask you some more questions about Ghorah Khar. He wants to . . ." She paused, seeing Hunter there for the first time. "I'm sorry, I didn't realize there was anyone else here. I don't think we've ever met," she said, smiling at him. "I'm Lieutenant Gwen Larson, Major Taggart's assistant."

"Captain Ian St. John," he said, clambering to his feet. "A pleasure to meet you, miss." *A real pleasure. She's the loveliest lady I've seen in a long time. Maybe I should try to transfer into Paladin's Special Operations division?*

"Well, I'd better nae keep the Commodore waitin'," Paladin said, stretching for a moment. "I'll be back later, lads." The cell door closed behind him.

"How are you doing, Kirha?" Lieutenant Larson asked, looking at the Kilrathi curled up on the floor.

"I am very tired," Kirha said. "So many questions about Ghorah Khar. I do not understand why you humans are so interested in that planet, or the rebellion there."

Rebellion? Hunter managed to keep a grin off his face. *So that's what's going on here!* He took a half-smoked cigar from his pocket, lighting it before asking, "So, what's this about a rebellion?"

"The lords of Ghorah Khar are rebelling against the Empire," Kirha began, as Gwen interrupted, "It's not really any of your concern, Captain."

"Why do you say that, miss?" Hunter asked, with just a hint of challenge in his voice.

It worked. "I just — I thought a pilot like you, from one of the best fighter squadrons in the fleet, would be more interested in tactics and fleet maneuvers, not politics," she said awkwardly.

He hid a grin. "Oh, I'm full of surprises. But how did you know that I'm from the *Tiger's Claw*?"

"I have my own surprises, too," she said with a hint of a smile. "That's my job, after all."

"You're too pretty to be a spy," he said, and instantly regretted it. "I meant, you're — "

"They hired me for my brains, not my looks, Captain." She laughed. "Though sometimes the looks come in handy. Besides, I'm not a spy," she added. "I'm an officer in Special Operations — a technical specialist, actually."

He tried to regain the ground he'd lost. "So you know all about me, but I don't know anything about you. I need to do something about that lack of information about you. Maybe over a few beers on the Observation Deck?"

"This does not make any sense to me," Kirha said suddenly, from where he was curled on the floor. "You are talking but saying very little. Is there a purpose to this?"

"Oh, mate, we've been talking about quite a bit, just not about anything you'd understand." Hunter grinned, and Gwen blushed a faint pink. "So, Gwen, how 'bout it?"

She hesitated. "I have a meeting at five o'clock with the General Staff . . ."

"So, seven o'clock?"

She smiled. "Agreed. It's a weakness of mine, I can't say no to a handsome pilot."

"I'll have to remember that," he said, and grinned as her blush deepened.

"Can you please explain this to me, my lord Hunter?" Kirha asked. "Is there a reason for this kind of conversation, where you talk about very little?"

"I'd better get back to the office," Gwen said, moving to the door. "As much as I'd like to hear you explain flirting to a Kilrathi refugee, I have to get some work done today. See you at seven?"

"You bet." He watched her walk away with an admiring gaze, until the cell door closed behind her. "That's one hell of a lady," he said, sitting down on the floor across from Kirha and relighting his cigar.

"I still do not understand, my lord," Kirha said. "In fact, very little of that conversation made any sense to me."

"It's human behavior," Hunter said, trying to think of a simple way to explain it. "I think Lieutenant Larson is very attractive, and she seems to like me a little. But you can't rush into these things. You need to talk a little, say something funny, make a good first impression, and then ask for a date."

"A date?" Kirha was clearly confused. "What has a calendar to do with anything?"

"That's . . . a different meaning for the word. This kind of 'date' is when you go out together, maybe have dinner or drinks, so you can get to know each other better, decide whether you're right for each other." He never thought he'd find himself explaining semantics to an overgrown tomcat!

"Ah, now I understand. You wish her to be your . . ." Kirha paused, apparently searching for a word. "You wish to create offspring with her?"

Hunter laughed. "We humans usually take some time before making that decision, Kirha. It's not something you want to rush into, really. You want to spend a good amount of time with a lady before you start thinkin' about anything permanent. Though that Gwen, she's definitely the kind of girl you can take home to meet the family."

"It will take me eights of years to understand humans," Kirha said, his ears drooping a little. "Over the next few years, I am certain that I will always be asking you these questions. I hope my curiosity will not annoy you, my lord."

Hunter sat upright. "Wait a second, furball! You're not going to be with me for years. More like another week, maybe! Then I'll head back to the *Tiger's Claw,* and they'll probably send you to a

POW camp somewhere. You'll probably go home eventually, if we ever do a prisoner exchange."

"But you cannot let them do that! My place is with you!" Kirha protested. His tail was lashing from side to side, a sign of agitation. "You are my liege lord!"

"I'm just a human pilot, Kirha," Hunter said, shaking his head. "You don't need a liege lord, you can be your own man . . . well, Kilrathi. You don't need to follow anyone around." He sought desperately for an explanation. "Besides — I have orders of my own to follow. I have — I have liege lords myself, and they've given *me* orders. And those orders — well, they mean that you have to go into detention, and I — go to the *Claw.*"

Kirha was very agitated, his ears flat to his skull, his head hunched way down between his shoulders. "But, my lord! You cannot! If I am not with you, how can I defend your honor? If I am locked up in a camp, I cannot serve as your sworn warrior! It is the obligation of a liege lord to allow his warriors to serve him, to fight at his side, to die gloriously for his honor!"

The cat was taking his imminent departure a little too hard. *You'd think he'd be happy to be with his mates again, with other Kilrathi, instead of all of these humans. I swear I'll never understand these furballs.* "Listen, Kirha, you need to understand . . ." he began, then stopped. There was some noise in the hall, muffled by the closed door. It sounded like someone was screaming at the top of their voice, and more shouting. "Excuse me for a minute, Kirha," he said, getting to his feet and moving to the door. He palmed the lock and stepped out into the corridor.

The tall Firekkan and the human guard continued arguing loudly, the Firekkan reverting into the rasping and clicking sounds of her native language every few seconds. They both completely ignored Hunter, standing in the corridor not ten feet away from them, until Hunter shouted, loudly enough to ring the walls: "K'Kai! What in the hell are you doing here?"

The Firekkan woman turned quickly, nearly hitting the guard with one of her folded wings. "Hun-ter!" A moment later, Hunter was caught up in a feathered embrace that nearly lifted him off his feet, K'Kai's beak riffling through his hair in that "grooming and looking for lice" maneuver he remembered so well from his stay on Firekka. After a moment, K'Kai stepped back, looking at him curiously.

"Why are *you* here, Hun-ter? The *Tiger's Claw* is very far away, busy in the Enig-ma Sec-tor."

"Hey, I asked first!" He grinned. "I was on shore leave on Earth, then got corralled into some extra work here on the station. I'll be heading out in a few days. But you, you're here . . . does that mean . . . ?"

K'Kai bobbed her head. "Yes. And I came here, as you said I must, to ask for help. This . . . *kk'r'kki* . . ." she said in her own language, giving the guard a foul look. "He would not let me speak with Ma-dzor Dzames Taggart. I must speak with him, and soon."

Paladin? Why did K'Kai need to meet with someone from Special Ops? He felt a chill in the pit of his stomach. "What's going on, K'Kai?"

"You do not know, Hun-ter?" Her claws opened and closed angrily. "I come for help, but the

Confeds do nothing! We sign a treaty with them, and they do nothing!"

"What?" *What in the hell is going on here?*

"She's not authorized to be here, sir," the human guard said. "Last time she was here, she had an authorization, but this time she doesn't. I keep telling her that she has to leave immediately, but she'd heard that Major Taggart was interrogating a prisoner here, and refused to leave."

"Damn straight, she shouldn't be here, at least not standing around in the hallway," Hunter said. "In case you didn't figure it out, mate, she's a diplomat from a Confederation planet. We'll just wait for Major Taggart in Kirha's cell, out of our way." He tugged at K'Kai's arm.

"But, sir!"

Hunter palmed open the lock, escorted K'Kai through the doorway, and then shut it in the face of the guard's protests. Kirha straightened from his position on the floor at the sight of the Firekkan and Hunter, then relaxed again. "Milady K'Kai," Kirha said respectfully, his tail twitching.

"You know each other?" Hunter glanced from Kirha to K'Kai.

"I asked for permission to meet Kir-ha," K'Kai said. "I wished to speak with a Kilrathi. All other Kilrathi I have met, it has only been in battle, not conversation."

"Hmmm." He sat down on the bunk, gestured for K'Kai to sit next to him. "So, tell me what's going on with your family. All the details you didn't tell me when I took you to the Colonel."

K'Kai folded her wings tightly around her. "When the Kilrathi left my planet, they killed many of my people, and took hostages. My sister, our flock-leader, and her mate were killed, and they took my niece Rikik with them, and many others of our leaders." Her large eyes blinked rapidly. "Your Confederation people, they do not understand. They say: We cannot help you now. You must choose other leaders. But we cannot. Firekkans are not like humans, we do not choose flock-leaders. Flock-leaders are born, bred for their tasks. They have the authority, the way ... way of command. It is part of their bodies and minds. There are human words for this. . . ." K'Kai was silent for a moment, apparently trying to remember. "Charisma? No, that speaks only of personality. It is more than that ... part of their bearing, coloration, scents ..."

"Pheromones," Hunter supplied. "That must be part of it."

"Yes." K'Kai clicked her beak together sharply. "And the Confederation, they do not understand. Without our leaders, we have no future. We will do anything to get our leaders back, even submit to the Kilrathi. I have told them, but they do not listen."

"Why won't the Confed do anything? They could send a rescue mission, a strike force —"

"Oh, many excuses, Hun-ter. This week it is because there is another covert operation that is about to begin, and they do not have the personnel. That is why I wished to speak with Taggart, since he is the one who is in charge of the covert operation. The week before, there were Kilrathi fleet maneuvers near this Gho-rah Khar Station, so that they said it was too risky. Next week, they will have another good excuse, I am certain!"

"Ghorah Khar?" Hunter asked. "Ghorah Khar,

the place that's in the middle of a rebellion right now?"

"Yes. Gho-rah Khar. You are a good flock-friend, Hun-ter. Is there nothing you can do to help my people? Perhaps if you talked to this Commodore Stew-art?"

"I can try, K'Kai. Don't know if it'll do much help, though."

Kirha spoke up from where he was curled on the floor. "The taking of hostages is dishonorable, not the act of a true warrior. My people — no, Prince Thrakhath — must have done this for political reasons, for there is no honor in it."

"I wish you could tell them, Kir-ha!" K'Kai said fervently.

Kirha made that shrugging motion, but this time, helplessly. "As you know, milady K'Kai, I am little more than a hostage myself here. My lord Hunter says that I will not be freed for some time, many eights of days. Besides, I could not act without the orders of my lord Hunter, who has told me that I am to remain here until they take me to a war-captives camp."

"Whither thou goest, I shall follow." Hunter thought about it for a moment. "Kirha, what you just said . . . does that mean that you haven't even thought about making an escape?"

"I would not disobey my lord," Kirha said, looking slightly affronted at the idea.

"I think I'm starting to figure out all of the 'liege lord' business, mate. So, if I ordered you to bang your head against the wall, you'd do it without question?"

"I might question the wisdom of the order," Kirha said, showing teeth in a Kilrathi grin.

"Because if I hurt myself, then I would no longer be able to defend your honor. But if you truly wished it, I would do it."

"You would. You know, it's crazy. You're a Kilrathi, one of our enemies, but I believe you." Hunter felt a strange delight welling up in him, an anticipation. It was like standing on the edge of a mountain, the icy wind in his face, a moment before leaping off into space. "Kirha, if I ordered you to go to that Ghorah Khar space station and rescue K'Kai's people, would you do it?"

"Of course, my lord," Kirha said, a little stiffly. "I would never disobey your orders!"

"Right you are, mate." Hunter grinned. "So, there we have it. The solution to your problem, K'Kai."

"And what is that?" she asked, obviously baffled.

"You want the Confed to supply a covert op to rescue your people from the Ghorah Khar station. That kind of op would need a Kilrathi specialist, someone who could get us past the guards and defenses. And you'd need someone to fly you there, a top pilot. And you'd need a specialized covert ops ship for the mission . . ." He stood suddenly, scanning the walls of the small cell. "Just a minute while I deal with something here . . ." He moved to the side of the washbasin, then carefully pried the mirror away from the wall. As he'd suspected, behind the reflective plastic was a small vid pickup. Hunter tugged at the wires running from the vidlink, pulling them free from the device. A small red glowing light on the top of the vid pickup faded to darkness. "There," he said, satisfied. "Now we can continue this conversation in private."

Kirha was staring at him in surprise. "The humans were monitoring me?"

"Standard ops procedure for detention cells," Hunter said. He grinned. "I should know, I've been in enough of them. I always disable 'em after I've been thrown in the brig . . . I hate havin' people watching me."

K'Kai tilted her head to look at him, a puzzled tone in her voice. "So, Hun-ter, what were you saying before? Are you going to suggest to the Confederation how they should do this operation?" K'Kai asked.

"I'll do better than that, lady," he said, with a broad grin. "I'll get your people out myself. Call me crazy, but I trust Kirha, here . . . after hearing him talk for the last few days, I really do believe that he'll obey my orders, not betray us to the cats. And he's one of them, he can get us behind enemy lines. So we'll break Kirha here out of detention. That shouldn't be too hard, I'll forge some orders that we're taking him off to be interrogated. There's no way a Kilrathi could escape off-station on his own, so that shouldn't be too difficult. Then we'll go to where Paladin's ship, the *Bonnie Heather,* is docked, and we'll give her a maiden voyage like no other ship has ever had. A mission behind enemy lines to rescue the leaders of Firekka. What do you say to that, K'Kai?"

"I would say that you are one insane human, Hun-ter," the Firekkan said thoughtfully. "But as there seems to be no other way to save Rikik and the others, I think it is what we must do."

"Kirha?"

"You are my liege lord, my reason for being," the

Kilrathi said, so seriously that Hunter couldn't laugh at the absurd words. "I would follow you to death and beyond, if that were in my power."

"Let's hope it doesn't come to that. If all goes well, you'll just be following me to Ghorah Khar and back again. So, next stop, the *Bonnie Heather*. It should be abandoned, unless — well, James said that he and Gwen were getting the ship ready to depart in another few days. So they might be there, and maybe some workmen. I'd better pick up a pistol from Ordnance, just in case."

"You would not shoot Taggart, would you, Hunter?" K'Kai asked, sounding alarmed.

"Not a chance." He grinned. "But scaring the wits out of him by holding him at gunpoint will start to make up for all those times that he got me into trouble with the MPs when we were on shore leave . . . or maybe I was the one who got him into trouble . . . anyhow, doesn't matter. We've got a plan, let's get moving!"

● CHAPTER ELEVEN

"Y'know, mates, he really isn't going to like this," Hunter said, eyeing the open airlock of the *Bonnie Heather.* It was one thing to have a crazy plan, and another to actually do something about it. He was having second thoughts. The three of them huddled in a mostly vacant equipment bay, about a hundred meters from the *Heather.* Close quarters, and Hunter was afraid that in a few moments, either K'Kai's feathers or Kirha's fur was going to make him sneeze. Paladin tended to react quickly to unusual sounds, and given his new profession and probable training, Hunter wasn't too anxious to see *how* he reacted to an assumed threat. It would probably be something on the order of "shoot first, and apologize to the survivors."

"So?" K'Kai hissed back. "Whether or not he likes this is a matter of complete indifference to me, so long as we take his ship."

"Yeah, but you don't have to live with him, after. *I* will. Provided the court-martial leaves enough of me for him to take his piece out of." Hunter watched the lock with acquisitive gloom. He'd heard stories from the techs in the past few days about the *Bonnie Heather,* the stuff she supposedly carried. It was almost worth the dual risk of Paladin's wrath and a Confed court-martial to get a chance to fly her.

Almost.

"Is it time *yet?*" Kirha growled. Hunter checked his watch. There was a little something he'd learned from *his* days as a tech; how to check the power-drain an in-dock ship was placing on tech services. As long as a ship wasn't drydocked, she was plugged into the *Claw* by umbilical, giving her ship's water and power, saving the strain on her own resources. But that drain varied depending on what was being used. An empty ship, or one full of sleeping people, didn't have a quarter of the drain a ship with two techno-junkies like Paladin and Gwen awake in it had. He'd watched and waited in the tech bay until the drain from the *Heather* dropped to almost nothing, then got the other two, figuring on two hours for Paladin to settle into a really deep sleep.

It was about that, now — and his nose *really* itched. Better move out before he sneezed.

"Now remember," he cautioned them both. "We make like commandos only until we're past the lock. Then *walk normally,* don't try to sneak."

"I still don't understand why," K'Kai complained in a whisper. "If we walk normally, won't Paladin hear us?"

Kirha gave her a withering look — and Hunter realized that now he was able to read the Kilrathi's expressions! Well, that was *some* progress, anyway!

"You are dealing with a trained warrior-hunter, oh brain-wiped one!" he hissed back. "If he hears you trying to be silent, his sleeping mind will assume that you are an enemy attempting to slip past him! If he hears beings walking normally, his mind will assume they are friends and all is well."

K'Kai shook her head. "Mammals," she muttered.

Hunter ignored both of them, concentrating on reaching his next goal, the tech bay directly in front of the airlock, timing his sprint for the moment the surveillance camera was sweeping away from him. He wasn't supposed to be here. More importantly, neither were K'Kai and Kirha. He could be brought up on charges just for bringing them in here.

Especially Kirha . . .

He ran, the other two shutting up and following him like a pair of shadows, and all three reached the safe haven of the bay just as the camera began its sweep back toward them. They pressed into the back of the bay, hoping that the shadows cast by equipment were enough to conceal them. No point in having an I-R sweep in here; too much hot equipment to confuse it. Somewhere, a bored tech watched about twenty of these screens, keeping an eye peeled for movement, looking for people who didn't belong, a nicety of purpose no computer could replicate.

Of course, if luck was *really* with him, one of the other fighter pilots was having a little rendezvous in his fighter, unaware that there even *was* a camera up there with a sentient watching what it showed. That was another thing he'd learned when he was a tech, before signing up for Flight School. Although . . . probably no one else was selling tickets to the other techs anymore, not after what they'd done to Hardesty.

Sometimes Hunter wondered if Hardesty was ever going to get off that garbage scow.

He shook off the irrelevant thoughts and tensed for his last dash up to the airlock. This one was going to take careful timing, since they were within pickup range of two cameras now. He watched them, timing them —

Then he was off, dashing up the ramp, plastering himself against the side of the lock and making room for K'Kai and Kirha. Waiting for an alarm, heart pounding, adrenaline drying his mouth.

Nothing.

With a "thank you" to fickle Lady Luck, he moved into the *Heather,* gun at the ready, but making no attempt to muffle his footsteps. The ship was shadow-shrouded, all the lights dimmed down to almost nothing, with only the red and green pin-points of equipment and controls shining at full strength. Past the control room, past something that looked like a techno-fiend's dream, a little room crammed with more equipment and tools than Hunter had ever seen in his life in one place — half of which he didn't even recognize. If he remembered the layout right, the bunkrooms should be at the end of this little corridor —

Sure enough; from behind one of the two doors came the unmistakable sound of snoring. Hunter decided to take that one, and nodded to the others to take Gwen's. Paladin, if he was armed in the assumed safety of his own ship, might be less likely to take a pot-shot at a human outline.

Three things occurred to him as he prepared to kick the door open. The first, that Paladin's reflexes might be too hard-wired by now to *prevent* him from taking a shot at anything breaking down the door. The second, that it would be just like Paladin to have set up a recording of a man snoring to decoy enemies into thinking he was asleep.

And third, that the door just might be locked, and he was about to break his foot.

By then, of course, it was too late; he was committed, and his foot hit the door with a solid _thud_. It slammed open a moment later, the second door slamming open as a kind of echo, and Hunter was in the room, down on one knee, gun trained on a very sleepy and startled Paladin.

He fumbled for the light-switch beside the door and turned it on, flooding the room with light, and feeling incredibly pleased with himself. He, Hunter, had just taken old hot-shot super-spy Paladin down, all by himself!

Paladin blinked, wincing away from the light. "Bloody hell, Hunter, what d'you think you're doing?" he slurred, his voice thick with interrupted sleep. "Dammit, you just broke up the best dream I've had in weeks! I had _three_ gorgeous flight attendants in here and — "

Hunter rose slowly to his feet, and Paladin broke off as the gun in his hand finally registered.

"I'm hijacking your ship, mate," he said, cheerfully. "Surprise!"

Hunter sat on the only chair in the tiny bunkroom. Gwen sat on the floor beside the bed, her face reflecting an interesting mix of annoyance and amusement. K'Kai stood on one leg beside Hunter, in what Hunter knew was her "resting" posture, and Kirha filled the entire doorway. Neither Gwen nor Paladin were going to get out past him.

Right now, Paladin didn't act as if he wanted to. Somehow he had persuaded Hunter — mostly by sheer force of personality — to have Gwen brought in so "we can all talk about this." What there was to talk about, Hunter wasn't sure; the original plan was to tie them both up and leave them in a maintenance closet for someone to find, figuring that by then he and the others would be long gone. But Paladin was welcome to try to talk them out of this if he wanted. Let *him* come up against K'Kai's desperation and Kirha's precious honor. Hunter didn't give him the chance of a fighter against a carrier.

After a few moments of useless persuasion, Paladin seemed to come to the same conclusion. He looked from one to the other of them, and nodded just a little. "You three really *are* set on doin' this, aren't you?"

K'Kai jerked her beak up in her equivalent of a nod. Kirha set his hindclaws into the carpet. "Try and stop us," he growled. "This is a matter of Honor, hairless ape!"

Paladin sighed, and leaned back against the bulkhead. "All right then, I won't be tryin' to stop ye," he replied. "In fact, I'd like to go with ye."

"What?" Hunter's jaw dropped. "You have got to be kidding! You're out of your mind!"

"You're out of *your* mind if you think you can run the *Bonnie Heather* without either me or Gwen, boyo — but I won't ask Gwen to be in on this."

She looked up at him sardonically. "That's good, 'cause I'm not stupid, I'm not crazy, I'm not expendable, and I'm not going. Not even for you, boss."

"There's too many things in here that you don't know — ye canna tell what they do," Paladin continued. "Push the wrong button or sequence of buttons, and you could find yourself broadcastin' wide-band to the Kilrathi, telling them — "

Here he spit out a collection of snarls and hisses that had Kirha flattening his ears down to his skull, eyes narrowed and claws extended. "You leave my clan-mother out of this, you promiscuous ape!" the Kilrathi snarled. "Your father had to beg for leavings from the beast-tenders, and your birth-mother serviced sewage workers!"

Paladin chuckled, and Kirha suddenly shook his head, as if he had only that moment remembered where he was. "I — er — " Kirha spluttered, ears coming up and flushing at the tips with what Hunter thought was probably embarrassment.

"Dinna worry about it, Kirha," Paladin said good-naturedly. "I was just givin' Hunter a graphic example of what he could get into without me along."

"Very — graphic," Kirha said stiffly. "There is no worse insult than that you just spat at me."

"And keyed up as you were, sure, you reacted without thinkin', as any trained and keyed-up warrior would," Paladin replied soothingly. "Just as any fighter pilot would, if *that* came over his com unit."

Hunter, who had watched Kirha's sudden anger with a certain amount of awe, took the point. "So what if we *do* take you with us?" he asked. "What's that gain us, besides your expertise? I don't think that's much of a gain, considering that we'll have to be watching you every damn second!"

But Paladin only shook his head. "Nae, you won't. My pledge is as good as Kirha's on this, and you know it, Hunter, me boy. I've been wantin' to rattle around in that part of Kilrathi space ever since I got this crazed assignment, and this is better than waitin' for permission from High Command." He grinned crookedly. "You know what they say; it's easier to apologize than get permission."

"Besides," Hunter replied dryly, "you can always blame us for forcing you if you get into hot water over this."

Paladin's grin widened.

"Oh *hell*," Gwen said suddenly. "You might as well count me in on this too."

Hunter looked at her in surprise. So did Paladin, but she ignored him.

"I don't want to stick around and face the music if all of you go haring off on this wild adventure. Besides, I didn't have anything else planned for the next couple of weeks," she said, shrugging. "If we can still stand each other when this is over — " She winked at him, and to his amazement, she had a definitely flirtatious gleam in her eye. "Besides, this way I have three chaperones in case you get frisky."

"Me?" he said innocently. "Frisky? Why, I'm a perfect gentleman!"

"Bloody hell! In your dreams, lad," Paladin muttered, and it seemed to Hunter that he just might be a little put out that Gwen was giving Hunter the eye.

Hunter looked at his partners-in-crime. "What do you think?" he asked.

K'Kai dropped her leg down to the floor, and fluffed her feathers. "I think that two more very sneaky fighters — whose ship, after all, this is — make a good addition."

Kirha lifted his chin and his ears. "I think that Paladin's Honor is as true as that of any of my people," he replied. "Hunter, you as my liege-lord clearly admire him. I do not know this female, but she has treated me with honor, and if he and you speak for her, then that is enough. I think we should let them come with us."

Hunter grinned ruefully; he still wasn't sure it was a good idea — but he wasn't sure any of this was a good idea. And he was clearly outvoted.

"All right, Paladin," he said, holstering his hand-weapon with a sigh, "Just how do you start this bucket of bolts, anyway? Let's get this show on the road."

Five days later . . .

Gwen's hands flew over the console at her station, as Hunter watched in admiration. He wished *he* was that good; she didn't even seem to look at anything; she was just aware of it all.

"Cat patrol in sensor range," she said crisply, long before the warning beacon and while the patrol-ships were nothing more than vague blips among the asteroids. In fact, Hunter wasn't quite sure how she knew they *were* patrol-fighters, but a moment later the onboard computer system had identified and red-tagged them.

"Right," Hunter said, reaching for a sequence of keys on his console.

"I could get us past them," Kirha offered, before he actually touched anything. "Past the first squadron, at least. I was personally oathsworn to Lord Ralgha; I doubt that any of them have anything close to my rank. They will not dare nay-say me, for fear of a challenge, if I say that I am a civilian inspector, coming to make a review of — of supply records at the base. Or something religious, an acolyte of the priestesses of Sivar, to cleanse them of the taint of the failed ceremony."

For a moment longer, Paladin hesitated. Then he shook his head. "Nae," he said, keying in a sequence too fast for Hunter to follow what he'd done. "Nae, thank you, Kirha, but we canna take the chance that — that your rank would overawe them. I've got all the latest codes, and I have a computer program that will simulate a Kilrathi on the outgoin' video signal. Gettin' onto the station isn't going to be a problem."

Hunter heard what he didn't say; that even with Kirha's oaths, Paladin still wasn't going to trust Kirha entirely.

Kirha looked as if he would like to object to this, but by then the Kilrathi ship was hailing them and it was too late. Paladin hit another sequence of keys, and answered the hail.

In — so far as Hunter could tell — near-flawless Kilrathi.

He didn't understand more than one word in ten, but Kirha leaned over and translated for him, in a whisper too soft for the pickups to register. "He says that we are fighter pilots, that we captured and boarded this human ship, and we wish to bring it to the station. He is very good; what slips he makes could be counted to being a lower-class fighter from the deep country, or having been born and raised on a colony world, far from Kilrah."

There was the inevitable pause, as the fighter squadron on Gwen's screens surrounded them and their leader checked back with the station. Hunter's gut clenched in an involuntary reaction to being surrounded like that. All it would take would be one order from the station. . . .

But the deception held.

The leader came back, ears erect, eyes relaxed, and barked a short order that even Hunter understood. Paladin jerked his chin up in an affirmative, and barked back, before cutting off communication. Out of the corner of his eye, Hunter saw the fighters on Gwen's screen peel off and reform on their leader, then shoot off in the direction of the asteroid belt again.

Paladin leaned back into his chair with a grin. "Permission to dock," he said cheerfully. "Aye. Piece of cake, lads."

"Huh," Kirha replied sardonically, "Now it only remains to be seen — just what kind of 'cake' it is. The mission is not over yet, hairless one." Then he said something in Kilrathi that Hunter could not make out at all.

Paladin only shrugged. "So they say." He turned back to his console.

Hunter looked at Gwen with a lifted eyebrow. "What was that last bit?" he asked, as Kirha bent to the docking-task that Paladin had assigned him, monitoring the Kilrathi equivalent of civilian com frequencies.

"The equivalent of our saying, 'The opera isn't over until the fat lady sings,' " Gwen told him. "Just a lot grimmer. What he said was, 'The hunt is not complete until the quarry's heart has been ripped from his chest and eaten.' "

"Lordy," Hunter replied, taken a bit aback. "That's a bit extreme."

"So are they," Gwen reminded him, "So are they.

Some day, maybe we'll understand why." Then she bent to her own task, prompting Hunter to do the same.

Kirha went to the airlock when they had docked, to wave away the helpful low-class techs and maintenance crew who came to give him a hand. Hunter stood just out of sight, armed with a hand-weapon, in case Kirha couldn't handle them.

Or in case he turned his coat — but after all this, Hunter didn't think it too likely. Not Kirha, anyway. Only God himself knew what was going on in Ralgha's mind. Presumably, the higher in rank a Kilrathi got, the easier it was to find excuses to justify a little bending of the Honor. Then a little more, and maybe a chip or two in the old Honor-armor . . . certainly power was a force for corruption, and Hunter doubted that it was any different for the cats than it was for any other sentient race.

The techs were easily cowed by Kirha's growling assertion that the ship was too dangerous to come near yet, before he and his crew had disarmed all the traps the promiscuous, mating-out-of-season, tailless, hairless apes had put in place when they abandoned their ship. Kirha bounced down the interior ramp with a certain amount of jauntiness in his step, and pride in his carriage. "*Very* low-rank," he said to Hunter. "I convinced them to go away and stay away until we called, my lord. I think they were just as pleased, once I mentioned traps. The whole area will probably become mysteriously deserted as they find reasons to be elsewhere. Low-rankers like that have no sense of pride."

Hunter didn't point out that they *did* appear to

have a healthy sense of self-preservation. He was just grateful that Kirha had found a way to get rid of them without a fuss.

They had entered the control room in time for Paladin to hear most of it, and the news brought a healthy grin to Paladin's handsome face. "Good work, Kirha," he said. "You're a bright lad, an' that's sure. Let's take that advantage while we've got it. We might just get in, get the hostages, and get out before they even notice we're gone."

Gwen made a face, suggesting to Hunter that the young tech thought Paladin was overestimating his luck-quotient by far too much, but Hunter kept his mouth shut. For one thing, it had finally hit home while Kirha was talking to the maintenance cats that this was *Kilrathi* territory, a cat-station. They were in enemy hands. And if they were discovered . . .

Mingled fear and excitement dried his mouth and made his hands tremble a little, and he took a deep breath to steady himself. *Take it easy, old boy,* he told himself. *This isn't the first tight one you've ever been in, and it won't be the last.* Paladin acted as if he was on hostile stations all the time, moving cautiously out the lock, and gesturing for the rest to follow, with no sign of emotion on his face. Maybe he was. Maybe none of this bothered him in the least.

Maybe cows could cruise the asteroids.

Hunter followed Gwen out of the lock, with K'Kai and Kirha bringing up the rear. He only hoped K'Kai could keep a tight hold on *her* nerves. Her people tended to be excitable, and this was not the time for K'Kai to go berserk on him.

Paladin glanced around the docking area, looking

for something; in a moment he found it, and the rest followed him as he hurried over to it. A computer console, Hunter saw, looking over his shoulder, with a strip across the top for station bulletins to scroll constantly. Presumably it was like the ones in their own docking bays, giving access to a great deal of information about the station. Things like — the maps of the detention areas, for instance.

Kirha craned his neck to see over Paladin's shoulder, and let out a hiss of alarm.

Paladin looked up from his search, as Kirha pointed to the string of Kilrathi characters scrolling across the screen much too fast for Hunter to even make out what they were. "Those are scramble-commands for ground troops!" Kirha growled, half in anger, half in dismay. "They are being ordered to this docking bay to attack the crew of the ship here!"

"Evidently your codes weren't quite accurate, boss," Gwen said, as Paladin swore in Gaelic. "Now what? We haven't got more than a couple of minutes at most before the welcoming committee arrives."

"They have not sounded the alarms," Kirha said flatly. "This means that they must wish not to alert us. They must want us alive, to question. Before they kill us, of course."

"Of course," Hunter said weakly.

"Fighting our way past them will be difficult," the young Kilrathi continued, unperturbed. "There must be at least four squadrons on the way here."

"We'll split up," Paladin said, suddenly. "Aye, that's it. Hunter, you and Kirha make a run for the prisoners — Kirha, the computer says that they're here — "

He pointed at the console screen, and Kirha nodded. "I can find that," the young Kilrathi said confidently.

"Meanwhile, K'Kai, Gwen and I will be tryin' to divert 'em. We'll meet back here."

"Oh thanks, boss," Gwen replied under her breath. Hunter didn't think Paladin heard.

"All right, let's move!" Paladin said, turning to run toward the entrance to the docking bay. Before Hunter could say anything, Kirha had grabbed him by the arm.

"Quickly, in here!" Kirha pulled Hunter back into a shadowy alcove of the docking bay, as the heavy footfalls of a Kilrathi squadron ran past, not fifteen feet away. Kirha started up the odd tilted plastic pole next to them, glancing down a moment later. "You do not wish to follow me, my lord? But this is the best way to the prisoner area!"

"It's not that," Hunter said, swallowing nervously as he looked up at the pole, which followed the curving ceiling a hundred feet overhead. *You'd have to be a monkey to climb that and not fall . . . or a cat. . . .* "Never mind, I can do it," he said firmly. *Just keep repeating that to yourself, Hunter, and maybe you'll make it. There's no going back now, anyhow.* He grabbed the pole, trying not to show his surprise at the feel of the warm, rough plastic against his bare hands, then began to climb.

It was slow going, especially when he was hanging upside-down in the shadows of the ceiling, looking down at the Kilrathi troops who were now thoroughly searching the *Bonnie Heather* for any other intruders, but hadn't figured out that all they had to do was look up at the ceiling to spot two of them. *And ten seconds after that it'll be "Ready, Aim, and Fire . . ."* Hunter banished the thought, concentrating on holding onto the pole and shimmying forward, a few inches at a time. Kirha, clinging to the pole a few feet ahead of him, seemed baffled by his liege lord's inability to scramble effortlessly up the pole. *It's called evolutionary differences, kitty, having fingers instead of claws,* Hunter thought as he struggled upward.

An endless amount of time later, he was still wrapped around the pole, watching Kirha pry open an access hatch and pull himself through. "Hey, Kirha," Hunter whispered, barely loud enough to be heard, "You mind helping your liege lord through this?" There was no way Hunter could let go of the pole long enough to scramble through the hatch. Kirha reached back through, easily pulling Hunter from the pole and through the hatch. *He's stronger than he looks,* Hunter thought, startled. "Thanks, mate," he murmured, closing the hatch behind him. "Now, which way from here?"

"Most of these stations have the detention areas on the fourth level," Kirha whispered back. "Some of them have it on the sixth level, though. We should check the fourth level first, which is directly above us."

"Sounds good," Hunter whispered back. He followed Kirha down the corridor, then up a twisting hall that led up to the fourth level. There was a closed hatchway at the end of a corridor; Kirha and Hunter moved quickly toward it, then Kirha paused, very close to an odd-looking plastic plate on the closed hatch. "There is a code sequence for this, but I cannot remember what it is."

"K'rakh drish'kai rai h'ra!" a loud Kilrathi voice said, and Hunter whirled.

"Oh, hell," he said, looking down a Kilrathi assault rifle barrel. There were five of them, all aimed at him. The Kilrathi behind the guns were staring at him, and at Kirha. "Uh, Kirha," he said, nudging his comrade, who was staring back at the Kilrathi soldiers. "Can you say something to them?"

"Ja'lra rash'nakh h'rai?" one of the Kilrathi said angrily, stepping forward and glaring at Kirha.

That bloke must be the leader. Lord, he's nearly seven feet tall and almost as wide! "What was he saying, mate?" Hunter whispered to Kirha.

"He is asking why I am consorting with a human, my lord," Kirha whispered back. He spoke louder in Kilrathi, a speech that went on and on as Hunter glanced nervously at the Kilrathi, who were intently listening to what Kirha had to say.

"What did you say to him?" Hunter asked, as Kirha concluded his rather long speech.

"I told him that you are my liege lord, that you are the finest, most honorable, most noble lord I have ever known, that even though you are human, your word is as the Kilrathi Emperor's to me, and that I and my descendants will be loyal to you for all eternity."

Hunter saw the way the Kilrathi's claws were extending and retracting as Kirha finished his explanation. "Uh, Kirha, you don't need to lay it on quite *that* thick, mate . . ."

The huge Kilrathi snarled something in his own language, and Kirha nodded, replying in the same unintelligible words. They spoke for another few seconds. Then the big Kilrathi handed his rifle to one of the others, and began stripping off his weapons belt, laying it and his belt knife to the ground.

"This is good," Kirha said, nodding. "Very good."

"What's so good about it, Kirha?" Hunter asked, totally baffled.

"He doesn't believe that a human can be an honorable liege lord to a Kilrathi," Kirha explained. "To prove this, he has offered to fight you to the death in single combat. He commands the others, and says that they will not harm us if you fight him."

"I'm supposed to fight *him*?" Hunter said, his voice squeaking a little on the last word, as he stared at the huge Kilrathi, now stripped down to his hauberk, who was grinning toothily at him. "Are you nuts, mate?"

"You must fight him, my lord," Kirha said earnestly. "This is now a duel of honor. You must prove that you are worthy to be a liege lord."

"What if I don't fight?"

"Then you are only an inferior member of a prey-species, and I am a traitor, and they will kill us both right now. You, for being human, and me, for betraying the honor of the Kilrathi Empire," Kirha said, glancing at the surrounding Kilrathi warriors. "You had probably better fight him, my lord Hunter."

"You and I are going to have a long talk about this 'liege lord' business, Kirha," Hunter said. "If I survive this," he added. The tall Kilrathi moved to stand in front of him, smiling to show his many pointed, white teeth and flexing his broad muscles, visible even beneath his thick coat of fur.

"Yes, my lord," Kirha said obediently.

"We can't hold them off!" Gwen said desperately, firing her pistol back down through the hatchway. The Kilrathi squadron ducked back around the corner, and Gwen punched the airlock controls to shut the hatch, then smashed the control panel with the butt of her pistol, sealing the door shut from the inside.

"Keep running!" Paladin said urgently. He glanced back, to see K'Kai struggling to keep up with them. Running was not a usual activity for a Firekkan, but there was not enough room in these narrow halls for her to spread her wings and fly.

"In here!" Paladin shoved open another hatchway, and brought up his pistol to fire with deadly accuracy through the doorway at the Kilrathi seated in the room. The air crackled with the snap of the energy weapon. Startled, the Kilrathi did not have time to return fire . . . one slumped over a computer panel, then the other fell to the deck. "Quickly!" Paladin shouted. K'Kai and Gwen dived through after him, and Paladin slammed the lock shut.

"I've studied captured diagrams of these stations," Paladin said, looking around the small room. "This is a control room, maybe an Environmental Station. If we can figure out what works here, maybe we can turn these odds in our favor."

Why are you bothering to be optimistic about this, James? he asked himself. *This mission is insane, suicide, and you know it. We'll die here, this won't help anyone. . . .*

I have to keep going, until it's obvious that we're going to be captured. His hand brushed against the holstered pistol on his belt. *Then I'll have to make sure that the cats don't capture me alive. I know too much about our Intelligence operations.*

I shouldna let Hunter do this, I could've triggered the alarms on the Heather and stopped it all before it began. But I wanted so much to get a glimpse of Ghorah Khar, to see whether or not the real mission can succeed later.

Now we're all going to pay for my stupidity.

"K'Kai, cover the door. Check those guards, Gwen," Paladin instructed the woman, who complied. "I'll try to figure out how to work these controls . . ."

"James, look out!"

Paladin heard Gwen's warning a half-second before a blue energy bolt seared into the console next to him. He leaped toward the Kilrathi who was struggling on the floor with Gwen. The Kilrathi, bleeding badly from a burn across his chest, held a pistol in his hand. Paladin reached them just as the Kilrathi shoved Gwen away from him and fired the gun directly at her, a blinding burst of blue fire. A moment later, James was fighting to wrest the gun from the Kilrathi.

A heavy backhand from the Kilrathi caught him across the face, and he stumbled backwards into a computer console. The Kilrathi raised his gun to fire . . .

Point-blank range, he can't miss — there's nowhere to go, nothing to hide behind —

K'Kai leaped into the air, spreading her wings to dive down onto the Kilrathi. Both landed hard on the deck, the Kilrathi's head slamming onto the edge of a console as he fell. Paladin could hear the *crunch* across the room. K'Kai rose to her feet a moment later, but the Kilrathi lay motionless on the deck, his neck twisted at an unnatural angle.

"Thanks, K'Kai," he breathed, and moved quickly to where Gwen was lying on the floor, not moving. "Gwen, lass?" He knelt by her, turning her over gently. His breath caught.

Gwen's face and chest were horribly burned, blackened down to the bone in several places. Her eyes were untouched and open, blankly staring.

Paladin spoke very softly, checking her unburnt wrist for a pulse. "Come on, lass, don't do this to me. Gwen, look at me, look at me. Please, Gwen . . ."

"She is dead, Taggart," K'Kai said above him. He glanced up to look at her inscrutable alien face, blurred through the tears in his eyes. "You cannot help her now."

"She can't be dead. This wasn't supposed to happen, it should have been me . . . she's so young, only a child . . . Gwen, lass, you canna die on me, girl!" Paladin's arms tightened around her, burying his face against her scorched red hair. He felt numb, frozen, unable to think. *This shouldn't hae happened, not to Gwen. A young lass, with everything in the world to live for. It should have been me, a useless old man, not her . . . not her . . .*

"Taggart, there are other lives at stake here," K'Kai began.

"Shut up!" Paladin snarled at her, holding Gwen's body against him, tears brimming over his eyes, his stomach clenched with grief.

The Firekkan leaned in close and bit his ear.

Paladin yelped and swung his fist at her, but she ducked back out of range. He felt the blood trickling hotly down his face, the pain drying his tears and breaking him out of his grief, throwing him instead into anger. *Hell, that bitch!*

"Gwen is dead, but we are still alive, and we have work to do!" K'Kai said angrily. "Get back on your feet and help me find my people, or I will do more than bite you!"

Her cold, reasoned words shocked him back into thinking again. *She's right. Gwen's dead, but we can't give up yet.*

"You're — you're right," Paladin said slowly, looking down at the woman in his arms. He set Gwen's body on the deck, gently closing her open, staring eyes. Then he straightened, crossing to one of the computer consoles. "We — we need something that'll slow down those Kilrathi troops, give us a chance to get the hostages and get back off the station. Do any of these controls make sense to you, K'Kai?"

"No, Dzames."

He stared at them, talking as much to himself as to her. "I recognize these symbols. That's the temperature controls. We could raise or lower the temperature, but that wouldn't really help us ... wait! Over there, those switches. They look like they're emergency seal controls in case of an environmental accident." His eyes raced over the keys as he spoke, pointing out what he was talking about to K'Kai. "We can seal off this section of the station, prevent the Kilrathi from bringing more troops into this area. The only risk is that we'd cut off Hunter and Kirha as well." He studied the controls, desperately trying to remember the layout of the station that he had studied for endless hours. "No, if we hit them here, and here, Hunter will still be able to get through to the detention areas."

"A good plan," K'Kai agreed, and together they set the controls for the worst possible environmental accident that could occur on a station, multiple breaches of the station's hull.

"And that gauge over there. I bet that's the artificial gravity controls."

"It could be," K'Kai said, studying the console.

"Your people are flyers. They'd be able to move pretty damn fast in zero gravity, better than the Kilrathi."

"That is true," K'Kai agreed, her eyes brightening. "Indeed we move well on my freighter."

"I'm sure they'll have backup systems, but a few minutes of zero-gee might allow Hunter and Kirha a better chance of getting the hostages out, not to mention giving us a better chance to fight our way back onto the ship." He paused a moment, trying to think of any holes in the hastily-made plan. There were probably dozens, but at this point it hardly mattered. "It's worth a try, and I can't see anything else here that'll help. We can shut down the gravity and use that surprise to get out of here. Grab onto something, I'm going to switch the gravity off . . . now!"

He held onto the edge of the console as he pulled the switch, and a split-second later felt the familiar stomach-twisting weightlessness of zero gravity. Gwen's body gently floated up from the floor, the Kilrathi corpses drifting through the air beyond her.

"We must hurry, Major," K'Kai said from the hatchway.

"I know," he replied, pulling himself across the console toward the floating body. "Goodbye, Gwen," he said, holding her unburnt hand in his for a long moment, and pressing it to his lips. He turned and pushed off in the direction of the hatchway. "On three, K'Kai," he said, grabbing onto the edge of the hatch. "One, two . . . three!" He punched the control to unlock the hatch and kicked it open. The three Kilrathi floating helplessly in the corridor tried to bring up their assault rifles, but too late . . . a few seconds later, Paladin and K'Kai were moving past the lifeless bodies, heading back toward the *Bonnie Heather.*

● CHAPTER TWELVE

"Can't we talk about this some more?" Hunter asked, staring at the huge Kilrathi warrior.

Kirha obligingly translated for him, and the big Kilrathi replied in the same language. "He says the time for talk is past, now you must prove yourself worthy to be a liege lord of Kilrah."

"Oh, hell," Hunter said with a sigh, looking up at his opponent. "Somehow I was hoping that he'd settle for a friendly game of cards instead." Hunter glanced at Kirha, then suddenly snap-kicked the huge Kilrathi between the legs without warning. The Kilrathi stood there for a moment in shock, then collapsed. The other cats stood staring at their crumpled chief.

"That was not very honorable, my lord," Kirha observed from the sidelines.

"Anything's fair in . . . *shit!*" Hunter exclaimed as the fallen Kilrathi hooked his leg, claws ripping through the thick leather of his boot. Hunter kicked desperately as he fell, then the huge Kilrathi caught him up in a bear hug, slowly squeezing. Hunter gasped, then reached for the only obvious target he could see, the Kilrathi's broad nose. He drove the heel of his hand into it, then grabbed it and twisted it hard. The warrior yelled in pain and let him go. Hunter rolled away, scrambling to his feet in time to duck a sideswipe of claws from his opponent. The second time he wasn't as lucky. Hunter felt the warrior's claws rip through his jacket, tearing into his back. He jumped backward, standing with his back against the wall. He definitely felt the blood running down his back, sticky and hot. *This isn't going too well.* . . .

The Kilrathi touched his nose, which was bleeding profusely, and roared something in his own language. Then he charged.

Hunter slammed against the wall and was pinned there by the full weight of the Kilrathi, the breath knocked right out of him. He fought to get free, but was pinned tight. "Kirha!" he gasped. "Help me!"

"But, my lord, it is not honorable . . ." Kirha objected.

To hell with honor! "Kirha, I *order* you to help me!" he yelled.

A moment later, the Kilrathi's weight lifted right off of him, for no reason that Hunter could see. Then he realized why, as he began drifting away from the wall, floating in mid-air.

The gravity! Something's happened to the gravity!

Then Kirha, drifting close to the other Kilrathi, grabbed one of the assault rifles from a Kilrathi guard, aimed and fired. He tossed the rifle to Hunter a moment later, wading into the mass of Kilrathi with claws and teeth. Hunter froze for a half second in shock, then brought up the gun and started firing before the startled Kilrathi could react. A few seconds later, it was over.

The face Kirha turned toward him was full of indignation. "My lord, I cannot believe that you asked for my assistance in a ritual combat! It goes against all the traditions of —"

"I know, I know," Hunter said, and pushed himself off from the closest wall, drifting past the lifeless Kilrathi bodies to where Kirha clung to the wall. "We'll talk about it later. Can you get the door open?" he asked.

"I think so, my lord," Kirha replied, staring at the door. He scratched against the plastic, a combination of long and short vertical lines. A moment later, the door slid open silently. Hunter pulled himself through the hatchway after Kirha, into a scene of total chaos.

Dozens of tall, feathered Firekkans were gathered in the large room, all staring at him with large, unblinking eyes.

Frightened, shock-filled eyes.

"Come on, everyone, follow me! This is a jailbreak," he yelled, gesturing to them. "Come on, I'm getting you out of here!"

No one moved.

"Doesn't anyone speak English here?" he shouted into the milling mass of Firekkans. "Hell," he muttered. "I wasn't expecting this."

Kirha spoke quietly. "My lord, I believe I have a solution for the problem."

"Yeah, sure, go ahead."

Kirha took a deep breath, and screamed a vicious snarl in his own language. *A battle cry,* Hunter realized a moment later. The Firekkans flapped their wings wildly, rushing into one corner of the room.

"An inferior prey-species," Kirha commented, looking at the agitated Firekkans. He worked his way around the room, and the massed Firekkans backed away from him, until he was between them and most of the room. And they were now quite near the open door.

"No, I think you were speaking in a universal language, mate," Hunter said with a grin. "This way, this way," he said, gesturing at the door. One of the Firekkans edged forward, then another, moving toward the door. A young-looking Firekkan said something shrill in her own language, and the rest of the Firekkans began moving toward the door as well.

"Let's go, let's go!" Hunter shouted, chivvying the mass of Firekkans through the hatch.

Hunter discovered a trait of the Firekkans that no one had warned him about; when stressed, they moulted.

Stray plumes floated in the wake of the fleeing flock, leaving a trail anyone could follow, and making him sneeze. Kirha batted puffs of down away from his face as he moved beside Hunter, pushing off from the walls to gain momentum in the null gravity. Every few seconds, he screamed another battle-cry whenever it looked as if the Firekkans might be slowing down.

At this point it was probably fair to assume that the escape wasn't exactly covert anymore. Hunter hoped that their very disorganization was going to work in their favor; what the Kilrathi couldn't predict, they couldn't deal with.

But he didn't even know whether they were all in the right corridor. Hell of a note, if their headlong stampede ran them into a dead end, or a docking bay that contained, say, a ship full of Kilrathi ground-troops.

"There!" Kirha shouted, pointing past the bobbing crests of the fleeing Firekkans. "Look! Is that not — "

It was — the docks, the *right* docks too, and there were K'Kai and Paladin, K'Kai screeching something in Firekkan and Paladin faced away from them, presumably watching for more Kilrathi fighters. Now the Firekkans slowed, confused —

All but one, who shot out of the flock like a bullet, heading straight for K'Kai.

A little Firekkan, half the size of the others. As this one began a bob-and-weave dance around K'Kai, Hunter realized this must be the niece, Rikik.

K'Kai spread her wings and Rikik huddled under them; K'Kai cuddled her close, like a mother hen with a chick. At this point there was too much noise from the rest of the Firekkans for Hunter to hear anything, as they figured out that they were not being herded into a slaughter, they were being *rescued*.

And, characteristically, they had to stop and *discuss* it.

Hunter swore. *"K'Kai!"* he shouted. "Front and center —"

K'Kai looked up, and took in the situation in a glance. She uttered a shriek in Firekkan, and shoved her niece away, towards the flock, then ran back towards Hunter, still shrieking.

The rest of the Firekkans jumped in startlement, but began moving again. K'Kai came in from the side, her faster niece from the rear, both of them shrieking alarm calls and shooing the other Firekkans towards the ramp, getting them up and through the airlock as fast as they could squeeze.

Hunter took a deep breath of relief — just as the squadron of Kilrathi ground-troops came around the bend of the docking-corridor and hit the floor in firing position.

*   *   *

K'Kai had used up her entire vocabulary of curse words and was starting over. Most of these gently reared flock-leaders had probably never heard anything like it in their lives, but Rikik had already picked up a half-dozen of the choicest bits of invective and was swearing like a stevedore. K'Kai was proud of her, though Rikik's mother (her memory be forever cherished) was probably spinning on her funeral-tree like a navigational gyroscope.

But she was paying far more attention to the disorderly flock than she was to anything behind her, so the first shots took her as much by surprise as the rest of them. Instinctively, she hit the floor, as two of the flock shrieked and fell.

Rikik kept right on shooing the rest into the ship; Hunter beside her. K'Kai took a quick look around; Paladin was nowhere in sight, but the subsonic rumble of a ship's engines warming up told her he had squirmed in among the Firekkans and was at the helm.

That left her and Kirha to play rear-guard.

And for the first time in months, she was facing Kilrathi as an equal — equally armed, and ready to collect some blood-debts.

"Eat fire, featherless scum!" she screamed, and opened up. Beside her, Kirha was firing too, but she noticed that he was *trying* to keep his shots aimed just above the Kilrathi ears.

For a moment, she was outraged. How dared he spare the enemy!

Then she realized what they were to him. His people, his species. Maybe even cats he knew.

Her rage cooled just a little, and out of consideration for his feelings, she tried to follow his lead, in keeping her shots from actually hitting the targets. No, she couldn't blame him — and when one of the cats noticed what they were doing and tried to charge, Kirha's shot hit him in the chest a fraction of a second before hers did. But his heart plainly wasn't in this—

She glanced back for a moment, as Kirha's volley gave her a free second. The last Firekkan plume cleared the airlock even as she turned, and Hunter was gesturing wildly at her for her to run.

"Kirha," she shouted, "They are clear! Get in the ship, I will cover you!"

He glanced back, saw that she was right, and turned to run; she gave him a volley of covering fire and half-rose for her own sprint —

Pain!

Her leg buckled and she fell to the floor; as if in slow-motion, she saw Hunter tense, tried to stand and felt her leg give again, and knew she wasn't going to make it to the airlock —

Then, something grabbed her. She squawked in mingled surprise and pain as she was hoisted into the air; her breath exploded from her in a *whuff* as her chest hit a furry shoulder. She looked up, seeing the Kilrathi rising to their feet and running towards them —

But Kirha put on a burst of speed that would have been impossible even for a Firekkan, ducked under the oncoming shots as if he knew where they were, and dashed up the ramp just as the airlock door closed behind them.

He dropped her on the floor; growled "Brace yourself," as he dropped down beside her. That was all the time they had; she slid sideways into the rear corner as Paladin blew the docking hatch and accelerated out of the station at max. K'Kai grabbed onto whatever she could, as the ship pulled gees and made some evasive maneuvers that threw both of them all over the lock.

That didn't matter; the pain of her leg didn't matter. Whether or not they survived this escape was out of their hands and in Paladin's. Only one thing did matter at the moment; a Kilrathi had stopped in making his own escape to save *her.*

She caught Kirha's eye where he hung on grimly to handholds on the bulkhead. "Why?" she mouthed.

He stared at her for a moment with round, unblinking eyes, then hunched his head, as if he wasn't sure either. Then he shouted, over the roar of the overstressed engines.

"Perhaps because you are a friend of my liege lord. Perhaps because you are a comrade-in-arms, and an honorable warrior."

Then he twitched his lips in what she had come to recognize as a gesture of feral amusement. "Or, just perhaps, because I wanted to save you for my lunch."

Well, through the haze of pain that was coming between her and the rest of the world, that seemed perfectly logical.

"Oh," she replied vaguely. "Of course."

And she ungracefully passed out, still clinging to the handholds.

Hunter slid into the co-pilot's seat next to Paladin, who was already working fast to bring the freighter up to launch speed. He glanced around curiously. "Where's Gwen? I didn't see her — " He stopped in mid-sentence at the look on Paladin's face. "Oh, no . . ."

"I shouldn't hae let her come on this misadventure," Paladin said, quickly working the controls to lift the freighter off the deck. "I shouldna done it. I could hae stopped this before it began, but I didn't . . ."

"Don't go into a funk on me now, mate," Hunter said. "We can still end up dead, despite our luck so far. What's on the sensors?"

"Several fighters out there, no larger ships yet. We've got a chance of getting out. Maybe. But there'll be more ships along shortly," Paladin said. "We've had the luck of the angels with us so far, but I dinna know how long that'll continue. The *Heather* is a fine ship, but she's only a freighter, not very fast. And we have a long way to go to the jump point."

"What kind of guns does this ship have?" Hunter asked, looking around the cockpit.

"Not much," Paladin admitted. "But there are two Rapiers in the hold, fully fueled and armed."

"K'Kai can fly this ship, no problem," Hunter said. "James, I think we'd better get outside in those Rapiers."

"Agreed. K'Kai!" Paladin called.

The Firekkan woman limped into the cockpit, assisted — and that looked odd! — by Kirha. "Yes?"

"You've got the helm, lady. Course is set for the jump point. Hunter and I are going out there to fly interception. Warn us when you're nearly ready to jump, we'll get back onboard. If we can't, jump without us."

K'Kai's alien eyes were emotionless as she listened intently. "Understood."

Hunter and Paladin ran through the huddled groups of Firekkans in the hallway, down to the cargo hold. Paladin tossed a flight suit and helmet to Hunter, who quickly donned the suit. A few seconds later, Hunter was in the cockpit of the Rapier.

He fired the Rapier's engines as the atmospheric gauge showed the air levels decreasing in the *Heather*'s hold. *I've never launched from a cargo hold before,* he thought, glancing across the deck to where Paladin's fighter was waiting, engines already ignited. *But I've been doing a lot of things lately that I've never done before . . . like falling for a lovely lady who's dead before I even had a chance to tell her what I felt about her. . . .*

Paladin signalled him with a thumbs-up, and the cargo bay door slid open silently a moment later. Hunter shoved the throttle and was out of the hold a moment later, pulling back to spin up and over the bulk of the freighter, turning back toward the station and the five Jalthi fighters that were pursuing them. Far beyond the station, he could see three Kilrathi Kamekh corvettes and a huge cruiser slowly starting in their direction. *We'd better be out of here before they're in range,* Hunter thought.

"Five Jalthi coming in fast, Paladin," he called. "And in a tight formation."

"We don't want to fight those Jalthi head-on," the Scotsman observed. "I'll take the . . . Hunter! What are you doing?"

"Cover me, mate!" Hunter hit the afterburner, heading straight for the Jalthi fighters. He switched to dumb-fire missiles, flying toward the wing of

Kilrathi on a collision course with full afterburners, too fast for their missiles or guns to track. The Kilrathi broke formation in a panic at the last moment, just as Hunter fired the first of his two dumb-fires. He was past them a split-second later, his Rapier rattling from the proximity of the massive explosions. He punched the reverse brakes and brought the fighter around, and was pleased to see that there were only three Jalthis reconverging on the *Heather*. Debris was scattering from the remains of two of the fighters.

"Now we only have three to fight," he said with a grin. "Keep them busy for a moment, all right, mate?"

"You idiot!" Paladin shouted over the vid. "You could have been killed!"

"I'm going to make sure they can't launch any other fighters," Hunter said, ignoring Paladin's outburst. "Hold them off me for a minute, okay?"

He only had one dumb-fire missile left, but it was enough. Skimming the surface of the huge station, he fired it directly into the station's Flight Deck aperture, turning away a moment before the brilliant explosion.

Hunter banked over the station and back into the dogfight, just in time to see a full gun burst from Paladin's fighter blast into one of the Jalthis, sending it spinning out of control. The other two fighters were maneuvering to get onto Paladin for the kill. Paladin's fighter was rocking from the repeated bursts of cannon fire from the heavily armed Jalthis.

"Get them off your tail, James!" Hunter called, punching the afterburners to close the distance between himself and the dogfight.

"I'm trying, lad!" Paladin's voice was strained. "Get over here and help me!"

"Bring 'em closer to me, mate!" Hunter said, switching to Friend-or-Foe missiles. The targeting computer began to beep in an increasing rhythm, searching for a missile lock. "Come on, come on," he whispered, as Paladin banked hard, the Jalthis struggling to stay on their target.

The targeting computer suddenly wailed with a solid missile lock tone. "Got you, bastard!" Hunter shouted, and fired the missile. The lead Jalthi exploded on the missile's impact, and the second Kilrathi fighter veered sharply to avoid the debris. Hunter was on the Jalthi a moment later, firing all cannons at point-blank range. The Jalthi disintegrated, and Hunter pulled up hard. He brought his speed back down, circling around to spot Paladin.

There was no sign of the other Rapier. Hunter scanned the area desperately, carefully flying to avoid the scattering debris.

No! Not James, too . . .

Then he saw the other Rapier a short distance away, lifeless and adrift. "James! Are you all right?"

The vid was silent for a long moment, then Paladin's wavering image appeared. "I'm still here, lad, but this Rapier's in bad shape. I'm trying to get the engines restarted." Hunter watched as the Rapier lurched, then accelerated unevenly.

"Get back to the *Heather* as fast as you can, James," Hunter said. "Those big ships are getting too damn close for comfort. I think it's time we hit the road from here." He glanced at his sensor screen to confirm that, and reacted instantly, punching full afterburners a split-second later. The burst of Jalthi cannon fire raked where his Rapier had just been, close enough to rock the fighter as Hunter desperately dodged the deadly attack.

The last Jalthi, which he'd thought had been incapacitated, came after him at top speed, trying to stay on Hunter's tail for a killing shot. "James! Get out of here, I'll handle this guy!" Hunter called.

The other Rapier accelerated toward the distant freighter, and Hunter followed, the Jalthi close on him. *And those other ships aren't far behind him,* Hunter thought, glancing back. *Hell, I always wanted to go out in a blaze of glory. This could be my big chance.*

At least I won't have to worry about being taken prisoner if that cruiser gets a cannon shot on this little Rapier, there won't be enough of me left for them to capture with a spoon!

The Heather *has to be close to the jump point by now, if I can just shake this one fighter and land, maybe I'll survive this.*

He watched as Paladin's Rapier slowed to dock in the *Heather*'s cargo hold, and glanced back again at the Jalthi on his tail. *All right, mate, now we'll see which of us is the better pilot* . . .

The Rapier was faster and more maneuverable than the Jalthi, but the Jalthi had heavier firepower and armor. If the Kilrathi caught Hunter in his target sights for full burst, that would probably ice Hunter's Rapier on the spot. So the tactic would be to outfly the Kilrathi pilot until he could get a clear missile lock.

Hunter rolled the Rapier to the right, and the Jalthi awkwardly followed. Hunter followed the roll with an Immelmann followed by another diving roll. "Follow that, furball!" he yelled, smiling grimly.

The Jalthi pilot tried hard to recover his original firing solution, maneuvering as tightly as he could to regain his position on Hunter's tail, but Hunter knew he had the upper hand now, all he had to do was force the Jalthi into his targeting sights.

Another tight turn with full brakes, and then the Jalthi was directly ahead of him, overshadowed by the bulk of the *Bonnie Heather.*

You're history, mate. Hunter grinned, and held onto his position on the Jalthi's tail for the kill. *I should get missile tone any second now. . . .*

With a start, Hunter realized that the Jalthi wasn't trying any more evasives, but holding to a single course — directly for the *Bonnie Heather.*

Hell! He's going for a collision course! If he hits the Heather, *it'll go up like a tinderbox!*

"K'Kai, full evasive!" he shouted into the vid. "Do it now, he's trying to ram the ship!"

Hunter forced every last iota of speed out of the Rapier's engines that he could, bringing the fighter up directly behind the plummeting Jalthi and firing all guns. At the last instant, he heard the tone of a missile lock, and fired the missile as well.

Oh God, he's going to hit the freighter . . .

The *Heather* suddenly twisted away in a tighter roll than any civilian freighter had ever done before, just as the Jalthi was about to impact. The Jalthi missed the ship by a handful of meters, and Hunter's missile arced into it a split-second later. The Jalthi disintegrated into a million pieces . . .

. . . but there was no way he could avoid the cloud of deadly debris directly ahead of him.

The Rapier plunged through the remnants of the Jalthi, and Hunter instinctively ducked back in his pilot's chair, even though he knew it wouldn't make any difference. Debris screamed and clanged against the hull of the Rapier as Hunter fought to keep control of the craft. Just as quickly as it had begun, the metal hailstorm was over, and he was in open space again, in a ship that had more holes in it than swiss cheese.

Hold together, lady, just a little bit more. He felt the engines spluttering and dying as he brought the Rapier around, heading directly for the *Heather's* cargo hold. The cargo hold door was already sliding shut. *They're getting ready to jump, I've got to get aboard now. Come on, lady, come on . . .*

The Rapier's engines died as he dived into the hold, sliding across the deck toward the opposite wall. Hunter braced for impact, even as he felt the familiar dizzying twinge of Jump.

With an awful crunching noise, the Rapier slammed into the wall, coming to a complete stop in that moment. Hunter sat in the cockpit for a moment, shaking his head, then yanked off his helmet and clambered out, staggering slightly as his feet landed on the deck.

He glanced back at the Rapier, and winced at the sight of the two silver wings crumpled like tinfoil, the nose of the fighter bent at a ninety-degree angle toward the deck. *Poor old girl. They just don't make fighters tough enough to withstand what I can put them through, I guess.*

The airlock opened, and several Firekkans ran out to greet him, surrounding him and grooming his hair with their beaks. He laughed and tried to duck out from beneath their welcoming ritual.

Amazing. We're alive and on our way out of Kilrathi

territory. We survived it, we succeeded, against all the odds.

All except for Gwen . . .

"Good work, Hunter!" Paladin called, striding in through the airlock. "Though if you ever break from my wing like that again, I'll kill you before the Kilrathi can!"

"You're just getting old, James." Hunter grinned. "Leave the fighting to young turks like myself, mate!"

"Hah!" Paladin clapped him on the shoulder. "Not a chance, laddie!"

K'Kai emerged from the airlock, her eyes bright as she limped toward Hunter and Paladin. Kirha walked beside her into the hold. "We are now in human space, and are progressing toward the next jump coordinates," K'Kai said. "The sensors say there are no Kilrathi in this system, so I have placed the ship on AutoNav."

"You handled the ship beautifully, K'Kai," Hunter said. "That last maneuver to avoid the Jalthi, that was amazing! I told you that you'd be an awesome combat pilot!"

K'Kai ducked her head in embarrassment. "Thank you, Hun-ter."

"And you, Kirha . . ." Hunter searched for the right words to say. "You've served me well, sworn warrior. You've, ah, brought honor to me and my *hrai*."

"I am pleased that I have served my lord well," the young Kilrathi said, straightening to stand tall and proud.

"Hmmph," Paladin said, giving Hunter an odd look. He turned to K'Kai. "It *was* a good trick,

K'Kai, but it's going to take weeks to repair the internal damage. Freighters aren't supposed to roll at high gees, ye know!"

"Quit hassling her, mate!" Hunter protested. "She did a terrific job!"

"I know, but — " Paladin paused, looking back toward the airlock. "What's that?"

Hunter turned; there was a line of Firekkans, carrying improvised torches made of fabric and pipes. Even at this distance, he could smell the engine fuel that they'd used to saturate the cloth. The torches burned smokily, the light reflecting off the metal of the deck.

"It is a fire ceremony," K'Kai explained. "To honor our dead, and Lieutenant Gwen Lar-son."

The Firekkans carrying the torches took flight a moment later, circling near the ceiling of the cargo hold. Then, with graceful, studied movements, they began a series of flying maneuvers, using the torches to create a brilliant pattern of burning fire between them. Hunter watched in awe as the pattern became more and more complex, the Firekkans weaving and gliding into their ritual movements.

K'Kai spoke in the Firekkan language, ceremonial words that matched the rhythm of the flight, then spoke in English. "And so we honor our dead, and remember their glorious last flight."

Their glorious last flight . . . Hunter thought of Gwen, the laughter in her eyes, the way she'd blushed at his teasing. And his last sight of her, in the landing bay of an alien space station. *Goodbye, sweetheart,* he thought, as the Firekkans glided down to land on the deck.

Standing next to him, Paladin wiped his eyes. "She was a good lass, Hunter," he said. "I'll miss her."

"I know, James," Hunter said. *I'll miss her, too.*

● CHAPTER THIRTEEN

It seemed to Hunter that he hadn't looked this —
military — since he'd graduated. Certainly this was
the stiffest he'd stood at attention since that time.

Beside him, Paladin looked much more relaxed
— although, if you knew the subtle signs, his grief
for Gwen was plain for anyone to read.

Hunter's own grief had been buried, with the rest
of his losses. Later, he would mourn her properly
— but the Commodore's office was no place for
mourning, and he was damned if he was going to
let anyone see his grieving. When this was all over
— then, maybe.

And he wasn't going to let anything show to the
brass.

Commodore Steward watched them both from
behind the bulwark of his desk, his face as impassive
as the metal of the wall behind him. Plain metal
desk, plain, bare-walled room, nothing to indicate
the man's personality. Hunter had no idea what to
expect from him. He'd heard that Steward was a
fair man, but a hard one. For Paladin there might
have been some excuses — but Hunter had gone
AWOL into enemy territory, and he was going to
have to talk fast to get himself out of this one.

For a moment, he wondered wearily if it was
worth it — would it be so bad, to be sent out of the

combat zone in disgrace? No more fighting . . . no more deaths on his conscience. . . .

Then he straightened his shoulders, giving himself a mental shake. What was he thinking of? He must have gotten a hit on the head he hadn't noticed, to be thinking like that!

"I brought you two runaways here to see if you have any *reasonable* explanations for your actions," Commodore Steward said, after a long silence. "If you can satisfy me, you just might manage to avoid a court-martial." He looked them both over for another long moment. "Well?"

"Permission t' explain, sir," Paladin spoke up, before Hunter could say anything. Steward nodded his approval.

"Hunter here is good friends with both the Firekkan K'Kai and with Kirha, the Kilrathi lad," Paladin said smoothly. "Actually, he is considerably more than 'friends' with Kirha; he is able to personally command the lad's loyalty, and it is absolute. As a result of that rather odd friendship, the two aliens began talkin' to each other, while Kirha was in detention. As you know, sir, K'Kai has been here at Confed High Command for some time, pressurin' Confed to do something about the hostage situation with her people."

"We lacked manpower to do anything about that," the Commodore reminded him.

"We lacked *conventional* manpower," Paladin corrected. "Sir. And I'm aware ye had other plans for me, but technically, I wasna yet on assignment. Now, even unconventional means would hae been impossible to put into action, except for the one thing no one had forseen — the cooperation of

Kirha. He felt very strongly that takin' those hostages was so dishonorable that it tarnished the entire race, and he was willing to go in there personally to release them in order to remove some of that dishonor. Well — with a Kilrathi *cooperating,* a covert operation suddenly became not only possible, but had a high degree of success. Or so I judged, sir."

Hunter couldn't help but notice that Paladin had omitted being held at gunpoint, and then being kidnapped. He relaxed, just a trifle. Maybe Paladin was going to get them all out of this. . . .

"So you judged." The Commodore seemed a little less than amused. "And why didn't you mention this to High Command? You should have presented this possibility and waited for formal orders."

"Because the situation was time-critical, sir," Paladin replied promptly. "Kirha was goin' to be sent to a detention camp at any moment. The hostage situation itself was precarious. The Kilrathi could hae decided to terminate them at any time. And my standing orders from Vice Admiral Tolwyn are to preserve the treaty between Firekka and Terra at any cost. In fact, if you don't mind my pointing this out, sir, the hostage rescue has not only done that, it has given us a distinct advantage in our dealings with Firekka."

Hunter would have stared open-mouthed if he hadn't been trying to keep his military poker-face on. Where was Paladin getting this stuff? No wonder he was in covert operations — he could probably talk his way out of almost anything!

"At the cost of one of our own."

Paladin flinched, but continued to look the Commodore in the eyes. "Aye, sir. An' that was as much my fault as anythin'. I take full responsibility."

"And what about you?" the Commodore said, turning to Hunter. "How do you explain *your* involvement in this?"

"Well, Kirha wouldn't go without my being along," he lied, thinking quickly. "It's kind of complicated, sir, but Kirha kind of got sworn to me as a sort of personal knight, and I had to be there with him — it's a Kilrathi honor thing." He shrugged. "Paladin — ah, Major Taggart here also figured he might need a fighter covering his tail when we peeled on out of there, and I'm a fighter-pilot, so that kind of settled that."

He couldn't tell if the Commodore believed him or not — but it didn't really matter. After a moment, the gray-haired man nodded, as if he had.

"I'll accept that," he said, shortly. "Dismissed, both of you."

With that, he turned back to the work on his desk — and both of them made their escape before he could change his mind.

Once the door to the office was closed and they were safely out in the hallway where they wouldn't be overheard, Hunter grabbed Paladin's sleeve before he could get away. "How come you didn't mention those orders from the Vice Admiral before?" he asked suspiciously, wondering if Paladin hadn't somehow maneuvered him into this escapade.

"Because I didna have them before," Paladin replied, grinning. "But I will by the time the Commodore checks the files for them — if you'll let go of my arm, that is, laddie! The Vice Admiral is a —

flexible sort of man, where success is concerned."

Hunter dropped his hand, quickly. Paladin turned to go — then turned back, as if something had suddenly occurred to him. "Hunter," he said, "I know this sounds odd — but did you *really* trust Kirha? Right from the beginnin' of this?"

Hunter grimaced. "Well," he said reluctantly, "it may sound crazy, but yes. I did. It's — that honor thing. I don't think he'd turn on me even to save his own life. And this is even crazier — but I kind of like the guy. He has his moments. Why do you ask?"

"Because I'd like to get Ralgha released from detention to work with me on contacting those rebels of his on Ghorah Khar; once he's cleared from interrogation, I'd like to see Confed throw in full support for that rebellion. I think it's the best way we've got of stoppin' this war." His eyes darkened with more pain than just Gwen's death. "That is what it's all about, isn't it? Stoppin' the war? Sometimes we forget that, lad. It's mortal easy t' do, when we've lost so many friends."

Slowly, Hunter nodded. "Sometimes we do," he replied. "Sometimes it's — easier that way."

Paladin nodded, then turned to half-run, heading for his little meeting with Vice Admiral Tolwyn.

Hunter tracked down Paladin later that afternoon, in the mess hall near the flight deck. Over sandwiches and beer, Paladin explained that he had managed to get those orders . . . retroactively . . . from the Vice Admiral, and that a court-martial was looking less likely by the minute.

"So now you're heading off to the Enigma Sector to rejoin the *Tiger's Claw*, Ian?" Paladin asked.

Hunter shook his head. "Not just yet. There are a few things that I have to do first. Do you know where Kirha is?"

"Detention, probably." Paladin sighed. "I thought maybe what we did would help that lad, but it looks like all we've done is cement his fate. The Vice Admiral's belief is that because Kirha didna come over to the Confederation of his own accord, he can't be trusted, even though he's oath-sworn to you, Ian. Their theory is that if anything happened to you, Kirha would revert back to his original loyalties. Ralgha's a different matter. But they'll probably ship Kirha off to a prisoner camp on the next available transport."

"I'd better hurry, then." Hunter held out his hand to Paladin; the older man clasped it firmly. "It's been a hell of a lot of fun, James. Until next time?"

"You bet, laddie!" The Scotsman grinned. "It was insane and nearly suicidal, but I wouldn't hae missed it for the world. We singlehandedly kept the Firekkans in the Confederation, do ye realize that? Without us, their leaders would still be locked up on Ghorah Khar, and they'd probably hae ended up a Kilrathi planet eventually." His face clouded. "All I wish is that Gwen could be here right now to share the victory with us."

Hunter sighed. "I know, mate. Take care of your-self, old man."

"I will. Good luck to ye, Hunter." Paladin made the conventional phrase sound as if he meant it.

"You too, James." Hunter meant it, too.

He walked quickly toward the Detention areas, hoping that he wasn't too late. Striding down the main corridor, he saw two guards escorting Kirha from his cell. The tall Kilrathi was shuffling awkwardly; Hunter saw why a moment later. Kirha wearing a pair of wrist and ankle binders, in addition to the bandages for his wounds . . . standard for prisoners about to be transported, Hunter remembered. "Wait!" he called.

"Sir?" one of the guards asked.

"I need to talk to Kirha," Hunter explained.

The guards were not pleased — but he outranked them. "But this prisoner has to be on a transport in twenty minutes, sir!"

"Just a few minutes," he said stubbornly. "That's all I'm asking."

"Very well, sir." The guard palmed open Kirha's old cell. "You can talk in here."

"Thanks, mate." Hunter followed Kirha into the cell. The Kilrathi stood silently near the open door. "So, uh, have they told you where you're going?" Hunter asked.

The Kilrathi shrugged. "A prisoner camp. It does not matter where." He looked at Hunter, then lowered his eyes. "I thought I would never see you again, my lord Hunter."

He flushed under the embarassment of realizing how he had failed to live up to Kirha's expectations. "Kirha, I'm sorry. I know how much this liege lord business means to you. I wish there was something I could do . . ." An odd thought occurred to Hunter. "Maybe . . . maybe there is. Kirha, is it possible for a Kilrathi liege lord to release someone from their oath?"

"It is possible," Kirha said. "But it is rarely done."

"What would happen if I did that?"

Kirha was silent for a long moment before speaking. "Then I would be sworn to no one. I would have no lord, no master."

All things considered, that only seemed fair. "I think I'd like to do that. You've been through so much for me and the others, it doesn't seem fair *not* to do this. How do I do it?"

"There is a ritual formula for releasing a sworn warrior from his oath, but it happens so rarely, I cannot remember the ceremony," he admitted, after a moment of thought.

All right, this wasn't the first time he'd had to improvise. Seemed like his whole life had been one long improvisation, sometimes. "How 'bout this instead, mate? Kirha *hrai* Hunter nar Aussie, I, Captain Ian St. John, release you from your oath to me. You're a free man . . . I mean, Kilrathi . . . sworn to no one. You are your own master now. You're free."

"Freedom." Kirha said the word slowly, as if savoring the word. "I am free?"

"That you are, mate. Kirha, I was just wondering . . . what's your name now? It wouldn't be Kirha *hrai* Hunter nar Aussie anymore, would it?"

"No," the young Kilrathi warrior said. "My name is only Kirha now. Just Kirha." He smiled, showing his sharp teeth. "Thank you, my lord."

"Don't call me that, Kirha. You're your own lord now. Hell, find yourself a Kilrathi lady an' start your own *hrai,* some day when this is all over." Hunter glanced through the open cell door. "I'd better let the guards take you to the transport. They're starting to look impatient."

"One moment, please." Kirha stepped forward

awkwardly in his bindings, dropping to one knee in front of Hunter. "You are no longer my liege lord, Captain Ian St. John, also known as Hunter. But in my heart, I will always be sworn to you, to fight for you and your honor. To know that you, a human, have given me the freedom to begin my own *hrai* . . . that is a debt I can never repay. My only fear is that someday I will face you in combat, as an Imperial Kilrathi against a Confederation human. I hope that day will never come."

Hunter shook his head. "I doubt it will, Kirha. You're going to be locked up in a prisoner camp, remember?"

Kirha smiled. "I would not wager on that, my lord." He held out his furry, clawed paw for a human handshake.

Surprised, Hunter clasped it. "Goodbye, Kirha."

"Farewell, my lord Hunter," the Kilrathi said.

Hunter stood in the corridor, watching as the guards escorted Kirha away. *I never thought I'd see the day that I'd feel sad to say goodbye to a Kilrathi. But I do. He may be one of them, the enemy, but he's been a good comrade, and a good friend.* He stood there for a long moment, long after the guards and Kirha had gone.

"Hun-ter?"

He turned and saw K'Kai, hurrying down the corridor toward him. "K'Kai! What are you doing here?"

"I wanted to talk to Kir-ha," the Firekkan said. "Is he gone?"

"You just missed him," Hunter said.

"That is sad," she said, looking as if she meant it. "I wanted to say goodbye to him. Even though he is

Kilrathi, I now think of him as a comrade and a friend." She cocked her head to one side. "It is something I never dreamed, as a hatchling in my nest . . . that I would fly among the stars, and meet beings from other worlds. It has not been so difficult to befriend you, Hun-ter, a human . . ." she said, leaning close to Hunter to groom through his hair. "Except that there are never any tasty bugs in human hair!"

"Sorry, I'm not going to put any there for you, lady!" Hunter said, ducking out of reach and laughing.

"I wish I could have said goodbye to Kir-ha," she said. "And given him this gift as well. I suppose we will have to drink it instead."

For the first time, Hunter noticed the large clay bottle in K'Kai's claws. "Firekka's Finest?" he asked.

"Of course," she said, opening her beak in a silent Firekkan laugh. "What else would we drink to celebrate our success? Come come, we will go the Rec Room and drink to our victory!"

And I'll drink a toast to departed friends, Hunter thought. *To Gwen, who died to save the Firekkan hostages and her comrades. And to Kirha, who was brave and honorable enough to fight for his enemies against his own people.*

And to our success. Against all the odds, we did it. Amazing.

"You're on, lady," Hunter said, linking his arm under K'Kai's wing. "We'll drink to the future, and whatever it may bring!"

Chapter Three

Ruberta the housekeeper helped Fiametta lift and slide the heavy red velvet gown over her head, and smooth it down over her fine linen underdress. Fiametta brushed at the folds of its wide-cut skirt, so profligate of cloth, and sighed pure satisfaction. The dress was far finer than anything she'd dared hope for. Master Beneforte had produced it, quite unexpectedly, from an old chest when Fiametta had complained of the sad figure she would cut at the Duke's banquet in plain gray wool. The dress had once belonged to Fiametta's mother; Fiametta and Ruberta had spent a week cutting it down and resewing it. Judging from the measurements, Fiametta was now nearly as tall as her mother had been, though more slender. Strange. She remembered her mother as tall, not short: tall and dark and warm.

Fiametta held out her arms, and Ruberta pulled on the sleeves and tied them to the dress at the shoulders, and fluffed out puffs of the underdress for contrast at the elbows. The red velvet sleeves were embroidered with silver thread, echoed by a silver band running all around that wonderful hem.

"Don't bounce so, girl," Ruberta complained mildly, and pinched her lower lip with her teeth in concentration as she knotted the bows just so. She stepped back and regarded Fiametta with judicious pride. "Now for your hair."

"Oh, yes, please." Fiametta plunked down obediently on the stool. No little girl's cap today, nor hair in a mere simple braid down her back. The dress had come with a matching hair net of silver thread and pearls, magically untarnished with age. Ruberta parted Fiametta's hair in neat, if wavy, wings, wound it up on the back of her head, and fastened the net over the mass of it, except for two dark ringlets she made to bounce artfully in front of Fiametta's ears. Fiametta stared greedily into her little mirror, delighted, turning her head back and forth to make the ringlets jump. "Thank you, Ruberta!" She flung her arms around the housekeeper's aproned waist and hugged her. "You're so clever."

"Oh, your slippers—they're still in the kitchen. I'll go get them." Ruberta hurried out. Fiametta tried the mirror at various angles, and ran her hands again over the soft sumptuous cloth. She sucked on her lower lip and, on impulse, rose and went to the chest at the end of her bed.

She pushed aside linens and found a flat oaken casket. She opened it to reveal her mother's death mask. Many people kept death masks of wax; Prospero Beneforte had recast Fiametta's mother's in bronze, darkened by his art to a rich brown close to her original skin tones. The alert dark eyes were closed, now, like sleep, but a strangely sad sleep, above the soft curves of her nose and wide mouth. Fiametta held the mask up to her dress and peeked over it into her mirror, held out at arm's length. She squinted, in an effort to weld face and dress in the blur. Then she lowered the mask to her chin, and compared the two faces. How much of the paler one was Prospero Beneforte, how much this lost woman? Fiametta's nose had a definite bridge, and her jaw was more sharp cut than this dark visage, but otherwise ... *Who am I? And whose am I? Where do I belong, Mother?*

Ruberta's step sounded on the gallery, and Fiametta hastily replaced the mask in its casket and locked it away again. Ruberta handed the polished shoes in through the door. "Hurry, now. Your Papa's waiting downstairs."

Fiametta jammed her feet into the shoes, and skipped out of her bedroom and around the upper gallery overlooking the courtyard. She took up her skirts to descend the stairs, then shook them out and walked more sedately, as befit her lady's hairstyle. No slave's gown, this, nor mere servant's, but obvious proof that her mother had been the true Christian wife of a great artisan. Fiametta held her chin up firmly.

Master Beneforte was standing in the stone-paved hallway. He looked splendid too, Fiametta decided. He wore a cloak of black velvet that swung to his knees, and a big hat of the same fabric, wound round like a turban with a jaunty fall of cloth to the side. His tunic was of honey-brown cut velvet, high to his neck where a bright white line of linen showed, with a pleated skirt to his knees and black hose. Despite his graying hairs Master Beneforte still resisted the long gowns of the aged, though the sober colors he'd chosen suggested a suitably powerful maturity. He'd set off the tunic with a gold chain of his own workmanship, displaying his art.

He turned at Fiametta's step. "Ah, there you are." He looked her up and down, eyes going strangely distant, muttered "*Huh,*" and shook his head as if to clear his vision.

"Do I look well, Papa?" asked Fiametta, alarmed.

"You look well. Here." He thrust out his hand to her.

Draped over his palm was a silver belt of cunning workmanship. Fiametta took it up, surprised. It was in the form of a silver snake, round and flexible as a rope. The gleaming scales were as fine as a real snake's, their overlapping plates concealing whatever linked its skeleton. Its head was solid silver, modeled as in life, with green chips—emerald? glass?—glittering for eyes.

"Put it on," said Master Beneforte.

"How? I see no clasp."

"Just loop it. It will stay."

"It's enchanted, isn't it?"

"Just a little spell for your protection."

"Thank you, Papa." She fitted it around her waist, curling the tail around behind the head, and indeed it held fast. Only then did she think to ask, "Does it come off?"

"Whenever you wish."

She tried it, and looped it back on. "Did you just make this?" She thought he'd been working night and day to finish the saltcellar.

"No, I've had it for some time. I just cleaned it and renewed the spell."

"Was it Mama's?"

"Yes."

Fiametta stroked it, her fingers sliding over the scales. They emitted a faint musical vibration, almost too thin to hear.

The Duke's saltcellar sat waiting on a bench against the wall. Its new box was satin-lined, ebony to match the base, with gold clasps and gold handles on the ends. Fiametta had helped assemble and polish it. She would not have guessed her father to be nervous, but he opened the box and checked its contents one last time, and rechecked the seating and security of the clasps, then wandered into the workroom and peered out the window.

"Ah. At last." His voice drifted back to her, and he returned to the hall to unbar the door for the Swiss captain and two guards. The guards' breastplates gleamed like mirrors, and Captain Ochs was dressed in his best and cleanest livery, with a new doublet with gold buttons issued in honor of the betrothal.

"All ready, Master Prospero?" the captain smiled. He nodded to the ebony casket. "Shall I have my men carry it?"

"I'll carry it myself, I think," said Master Beneforte, lifting the box. "Have them walk one ahead and one behind."

"Very well." And they started off so ordered, the captain and Fiametta flanking the goldsmith.

"Keep the door barred till my return, Teseo," Master Beneforte called back, and the apprentice bowed awkwardly and closed it behind them. Master Beneforte paused till he heard the bar slide into place, nodded, and marched down the cobbled street.

It was a bright day two weeks after the holy feast of Easter, just barely cool enough for velvets to be comfortable. Trees had budded into new leaf in the weeks since Fiametta had cast her ring. She clutched the lion mask on her left thumb, and let the—sigh—garnet catch and wink back the midday sun. That light glowed, too, off the yellow brick and stones and red tile roofs. Sad dun in winter, Montefoglia almost looked like a city of gold on long summer afternoons. They passed from the street of big houses flanking her father's home and workshop down into older, more crowded construction.

Crossing a side alley leading down to the water, Fiametta glimpsed boats and the docks. A few lazy lake

gulls swooped and squawked. Perhaps when Papa took
her fishing again this summer, he'd finally teach her
the secret spell he used for baiting his hook. The narrow lake extended eleven miles north from Montefoglia, toward the foothills of the Alps beyond which lay
Captain Ochs's home. The first pack train of the season
had come down over Montefoglia Pass a week ago,
Fiametta had heard. Higher and more difficult than
the great Brenner to the east, the route yet served the
needs of the little duchy. Montefoglia was hard hill
country, and would have been poor indeed without the
trickle of trade and the fishing of the lake.

On the east shore, north of town, the monastery of
St. Jerome kept grape vines, spring wheat in terraces,
orchards and sheep. The main road ran up the east
side of the lake past its stone walls, the west side being
too sheer, rocky, and wild for any but goat paths.
Fiametta could see a few figures on horses and a slow
ox cart moving on the dusty white ribbon. St. Jerome's
scriptorium also supplied illuminated books for the
Duke's library, pride of the castle that dominated the
bluff at far end of town. It was the Duke's boast that
his library held none of that cheap modern printed
matter, but only proper calligraphed manuscripts
bound in rich decorated leather—over a hundred vol-
umes. It seemed a constrictive stipulation to Fiametta's
mind, but perhaps it was because Duke Sandrino could
read but not write himself that calligraphy seemed so
significant to him. Old people were ridiculously conser-
vative about the oddest things.

"And how go the betrothal celebrations?" Master
Beneforte inquired of the captain. Fiametta, lagging,
quickened her step and closed the gap to listen.

"Well, the Duchess had an illumination in the garden last night, with a tableau and madrigals. The sing-
ers sounded very pretty."

"I'd have been doing the costuming for that set

piece, but for the Duke's insistence upon this." Master Beneforte lifted the ebony box. "I'm surprised that dolt di Rimini didn't botch the effects. The man couldn't design a doorknob."

The captain smiled dryly at this aspersion upon Master Beneforte's most notable local rival in the decorative arts. "He did all right. For your consolation, there was a bad moment when the candles set fire to a head-dress, but we doused the lady and got it out, with no injury but to her feathers. I knew I was right to insist on having those buckets ready, backstage."

"Ha. I understand the future bridegroom rode in on time this morning, at least."

"Yes." The captain frowned. "I must say, I don't like the retinue he rode in with. A hard-bitten bunch. And fifty men-at-arms seems excessive, for the occasion. I don't know what Duke Sandrino was thinking of, to allow my lord of Losimo to bring so many. The honor due his future son-in-law, he says."

"Well, Uberto Ferrante was a condottiere, before he fell heir to Losimo two years ago," said Master Beneforte judiciously. "He hasn't really been there long enough to establish local loyalty. Presumably these are men he trusts."

"Fell heir, my eye. He bribed the Papal Curia to overturn the other cousin's claim, and again for dispensation to marry the heiress. I suppose Cardinal Borgia wanted to be sure of a Guelf in Losimo, to oppose the ambitions of Venice and the Ghibbellines."

"From my experience of the Curia, I'd say you guess exactly right." Master Beneforte smiled sourly. "I do wonder where Ferrante got the money, though."

"The ambitions of Milan seem a nearer threat, to me. Poor Montefoglia, sitting like an almond between two such pincers."

"Now, Milan's an example of how a soldier may rise. I trust Lord Ferrante has not been studying the life of the late Francesco Sforza too closely. Marry the daughter, then make yourself master of the State. . . . Take note, Uri."

The captain sighed. "I don't know any heiresses, alas." He paused thoughtfully. "Actually, that's exactly what Ferrante did, in Losimo. I trust he does not seek to duplicate the ploy in Montefoglia."

"Our Duke and his son are both healthy enough to prevent that, I think," said Master Beneforte. He patted the ebony box. "And perhaps I can do my little part to help keep them so."

The captain stared down at his boots, pacing over the stones. "I don't know. I do know Duke Sandrino is not altogether happy with this betrothal, and Duchess Letitia even less so. I cannot see what pressure Ferrante can be putting, yet I sense . . . there was hard bargaining, for the dowry."

"Too bad Lord Ferrante is not a younger man, or Lady Julia older."

"Or both. I know the Duchess insisted it be put in the contract that the wedding not take place for at least another year."

"Perhaps Lord Ferrante's horse will dump him on his head and break his neck, betimes."

"I will add that to my prayers," smiled the captain. It almost wasn't a joke.

The conversation lagged as they reserved breath for the final climb to the castle. They passed through a gate flanked by two sturdy square towers of cut stone topped by the same yellow brick common in most of Montefoglia's newer construction. The soldiers escorted them across a stone-paved courtyard and up the new grand staircase the present Duke had installed in hopes of softening the austere and awkward architecture of his ancestors. Master Beneforte sniffed at the stonework in passing, and muttered his habitual judgment. "Should have hired a real sculptor, not a country stonecutter. . . ." They passed through two dark halls and out another door to the walled garden. Here among the flowers and fruit trees the tables were set for the betrothal banquet.

The throng was being seated, just the timing Master Beneforte had hoped for his grand presentation. The ducal family, together with Lord Ferrante and the Abbot of Saint Jerome and Bishop of Montefoglia (two offices, one man) occupied a long table raised on a platform. They were shaded by awnings made of tapestries. Four other tables were arranged at right angles, below and beyond, for the lesser guests.

Duke Sandrino, a pleasantly bulky man of fifty with nose and ears of noble proportions, was washing his hands in a silver basin with rose petals floating in the steaming water, held by his steward Messer Quistelli. His son and heir, the ten-year-old Lord Ascanio, sat on his right. One of Lord Ferrante's liveried retainers was adjusting a footstool with a padded leather top beneath his master's boots, in the shape of a chest carved with Losimo's arms. The portable furniture was evidently for some idiosyncratic comfort, for Lord Ferrante's legs were of normal shape and length. Maybe his silk hose concealed an old war wound that still pained him. Fiametta schooled herself not to gawk, while trying to memorize as many details as possible of the overwhelming display of velvets, silks, hats, badges, arms, jewels, and hairstyles before her.

The Lady Julia, seated between her mother and her bridegroom-to-be, wore spring-green velvet with gold embroidery and—ha!—a girl's cap. Though indeed, the green cap was embroidered with more gold thread and studded with tiny pearls. Her hair was braided with green ribbons in a blonde rope down her back. Did Duchess Letitia deliberately seek to emphasize her daughter's youth? Julia's slight flusterment made a vivid contrast with the Lord of Losimo on her other hand. Dark, mature, powerful, clearly a disciple of Mars: Lord Ferrante's lips smiled without showing his teeth. Perhaps his teeth were bad.

The abbot-and-bishop was seated to Lord Ferrante's left, no doubt both for the honor and to give Ferrante an equal to talk to if Julia's girl chatter or bashful silence grew thin. Abbot Monreale had been a flamboyant knight in his youth, when he'd been severely wounded, and made a deathbed promise to dedicate his life to the Church if God would spare him. He'd kept his promise with flair; gray-haired now, he had a reputation as a scholar and a bit of a mystic. He was dressed today as bishop, not abbot, in the splendid flowing white gown and gold-edged red robe of his office, with a white silk brocade cap over his tonsure. Monreale was also the man who yearly inspected both the workshop and the soul of Prospero Beneforte, and renewed his ecclesiastical license to practice white magic. Master Beneforte, after making his leg to the Duke, his family, and Lord Ferrante, bowed to the abbot with immense and unfeigned deference.

As they'd practiced, Master Beneforte knelt and opened the ebony box, and had Fiametta present the saltcellar to the Duke with a pretty curtsey. The snowy linen of the table set the gleaming gold and brilliant colored enamels off to perfection. Master Beneforte beamed when the occupants of the table broke into spontaneous applause. Duke Sandrino smiled in obvious satisfaction, and asked the abbot himself to bless the first salt, which the steward hurried to pour into the glowing boat-bowl.

Master Beneforte watched in breathless suspense. Now was the time, he'd confided to Fiametta in their private rehersal, when he'd hoped the Duke would fill his hands with ducats in a magnificent gesture of generosity before the assembled guests. He'd hung a large purse, empty, beneath his cloak in anticipation of the golden moment. But the Duke merely, if kindly, waved them to places prepared for them at a lower table. "Well, he has a lot on his mind. Later," Master Beneforte muttered in his beard, concealing his chagrin as they settled themselves.

A servant brought them the silver basin to wash their hands—one of Master Beneforte's own pieces, Fiametta noticed—and the banquet commenced with wine and dishes of fried ravioli stuffed with chopped pork, herbs, and cream cheese rolled in powdered sugar. Baskets of bread made entirely from white flour appeared, and platters of veal, chicken, ham, sausages, and beef. And more wine. Master Beneforte watched the upper table with sharp attention. No blue flames flashed up from anyone's plate, though. Fiametta made polite conversation with the castellan's wife, a plump woman named Lady Pia, on her other side.

When the castellan's wife rose for a moment, beckoned by her husband, Master Beneforte leaned close to his daughter and lowered his voice. Fiametta braced herself for more grumbling about the Duke's ducats, but instead he said, unexpectedly, "Did you notice the little silver ring Lord Ferrante wore on his right hand, child? You stood closer to him than I."

Fiametta blinked. "Yes, now that you mention it."

"What did you think of it?"

"Well . . ." She tried to call it up in her mind's eye. "I thought it extremely ugly."

"What form had it?"

"A mask. An infant, or putti's face, I think. Not ugly, exactly, but . . . I just didn't like it." She laughed a little. "He should commission you, Papa, to make him something prettier."

To her surprise, he crossed himself in a tiny warding gesture. "Say not so. Yet . . . how dare he wear it openly in front of the abbot? Perchance it came to him secondhand, and he doesn't know what it is. Or he's muted it, somehow."

"It was new work, I thought," said Fiametta. "Papa, what bothers you?" He looked disturbed.

"I'm almost certain it's a spirit ring. Yet, if it's active, where can he have put the ..." He trailed off, lips thinned, staring covertly at the upper table.

"Black magic?" Fiametta whispered, shocked.

"Not ... not necessarily. I once, er ... saw such a thing that was no grave sin. And Ferrante is a lord. Such a man should be easy and conversant with forms of power not so appropriate in lesser men, yet proper to a ruler. Like the great Lord Lorenzo in Florence."

"I thought all magic was either white or black."

"When you've grown as old as I have, child, you will learn that nothing in this world is either all white or black."

"Would Abbot Monreale agree with that?" she asked suspiciously.

"Oh, yes," he sighed. His brows rose in a sort of eyebrow-shrug. "Well, Lord Ferrante has a year yet, to reveal his character." His fingers curled, suppressing the topic as Lady Pia returned.

The meats, what little was left of them, were taken away by the servants, and platters of dates, figs, early strawberries, and pastry confections were set before the guests. Fiametta and Lady Pia collaborated on selections and did great damage to the dried cherry tarts. Musicians at the far end of the garden began to play above the chatter and clink of cutlery and plates. The Duke's butler and his assistants poured out sweet wines, in anticipation of closing toasts.

Messer Quistelli hurried out of the castle and stepped under the tapestries shading the high table. He bent his head to whisper in the Duke's ear. Duke Sandrino frowned, and made some query; Messer Quistelli shrugged. The Duke shook his head as if annoyed, but leaned over, spoke to the Duchess, and rose to follow his steward back inside.

The castellan's wife entered into a negotiation, across Fiametta, with Master Beneforte to mend a little silver ewer of hers that had a broken handle. Fiametta could see her father was not flattered to be bothered by such a domestic trifle, apprentice's work, till his eye fell on her.

He smiled slightly. "Fiametta will mend it. It can be your first independent commission, child."

"Oh. Can you do it?" Lady Pia looked at her, both doubtful and impressed.

"I . . . suppose I'd better see it first," Fiametta said cautiously, but inwardly delighted.

Lady Pia glanced at the high table. "They won't start the toasts till the Duke returns. What can be keeping him away so long? Come to my rooms, Fiametta, and you can see it right now."

"Certainly, Lady Pia." As they rose, Messer Quistelli returned, to speak this time to Lord Ferrante. Ferrante grimaced puzzled irritation, but evidently compelled by his host's command got up to follow the steward. With a jerk of his hand Lord Ferrante motioned two of his men to fall in behind him. If she'd seen them on the street, Fiametta would not have hesitated to dub them bravos. The senior of them, a tough-looking bearded fellow missing several front teeth, had been presented as Ferrante's principal lieutenant. Captain Ochs, leaning over to chat with some lady at one of the lower tables, looked up, frowned to himself, and followed. He had to lengthen his stride to catch up.

The two women waited for the men to clear the doorway, then the castellan's wife led Fiametta within. Fiametta glanced aside curiously as they crossed the chamber. Through a door at the far end into a cabinet or study she could see the Duke standing at his desk, with two travel-stained men, one a grave-faced priest, the other a choleric nobleman. Lord Ferrante and the rest of the retinue then blocked her view, and she followed Lady Pia.

The castellan had rooms in one of the square towers. Lady Pia took the ewer from a shelf in her tiny, thick-walled bedroom, crowded with her bit of furniture—a bed and chests—and waited anxiously while Fiametta carried it to a window slit to look it over. Fiametta was secretly pleased to find it not a mere soldering job, but one requiring more expertise; the handle, cast in the form of a sinuous mermaid, was not only loose but cracked. Fiametta assured the castellan's wife of a swift repair, and they wrapped the piece in a bit of old linen and returned with it to the garden.

Passing again through the large chamber, Fiametta was startled by Duke Sandrino's angry shouting, com-ing from the cabinet. He was leaning across his desk on his clenched hands. Lord Ferrante stood facing him with his arms tightly folded, his jaw set and features darkening to a burnt brick red. His voice rumbled in reply in short jerky sentences, pitched too low to be clear to Fiametta's ear. The two dusty strangers looked on. The noble's face was lit with malicious glee. The priest's was white. Captain Ochs leaned with his back to the doorframe, apparently casual, but with his hand resting on the hilt of his sword. Lady Pia's hand tight-ened on Fiametta's shoulder in alarm.

Duke Sandrino's voice rose and fell. ". . . lies and murder . . . black necromancy! Sure proof . . . no child of mine . . . insult to my house! Get you gone at once, or prepare for a war to spin your vile head, condottiere bastard!" Spluttering with fury, Duke Sandrino bit his thumb and shook it in Lord Ferrante's face.

"I need no preparation!" Lord Ferrante raged back, leaning toward him. "Your war can begin right now!" As Fiametta watched open-mouthed, Lord Ferrante snatched his dagger out left-handed. In the same continuing upward arc he slashed it across Duke Sandrino's throat, so powerful a blow it half-severed the neck and bounced off bone. Ferrante struck so hard he unbalanced himself, and he and his victim fell into each other across the desk as if embracing, smeared sudden scarlet.

With a shocked cry that was almost a wail, Captain Ochs ripped his sword from its scabbard and started forward. In the confined space of the cabinet a sword was little more effective than a dagger, though, and both bravos had their daggers out. The gap-toothed lieutenant took the choleric nobleman through the heart with a blow almost as sudden and powerful as his master's first stroke had been. Aged Messer Quistelli, unarmed, ducked, but not fast enough; the second bravo's knife blow knocked him to the floor. Uri, lunging forward, deflected a follow-up blow, then found himself wrestling the man.

As the priest raised his hand, Lord Ferrante gestured toward him with his bunched right fist; the silver ring glared and the priest clutched his eyes and screamed. Lord Ferrante stabbed him through his unguarded chest.

"I must get my husband!" The castellan's wife dropped her ewer, picked up her skirts, and ran for the garden. The lieutenant looked up at the noise, frowned, and started toward Fiametta. His eyes were very cold. Dizzied with shock, her heart hammering, Fiametta whirled and sprinted after Lady Pia.

She was almost blinded by the sunlight. Halfway across the garden, the castellan's wife was hanging on her husband's arm and screaming warnings; he was shaking his head as if he found incoherent the cries that made perfect sense to Fiametta. She looked around frantically in the white afternoon for her father's big black hat. *There*, nodding to some man. The lieutenant turned his head in the doorway, and plunged back inside. Fiametta flung herself onto Master Beneforte's chest, her fingers clutching his tunic.

"Papa," she gasped out, "Lord Ferrante just murdered the Duke!"

Uri Ochs spun backwards through the door. There was blood on his sword. "Treachery!" he shouted. Blood sprayed from his mouth with the words. "Murder and treachery! Montefoglia, to arms!"

Ferrante's men, as surprised as Montefoglia's, began to gather together in knots. Ferrante's lieutenant, pursuing Captain Ochs through the door, cried his comrades to his aid.

"The devil," hissed Master Beneforte through his teeth. "There goes my commission." His hand clamped on her arm, and he wheeled around, staring. "This garden is a death trap. We have to get out of here *now.*"

Men were beginning to draw swords and daggers, and the unarmed to snatch up table knives. Women were screaming.

Master Beneforte started, not for the door, but toward the high table. Captain Ochs and Ferrante's lieutenant were also heading that way at a pell-mell run. Ferrante's lieutenant leaped and aimed a sword swing across the linen at little Lord Ascanio that would have taken off the boy's head if Captain Ochs had not knocked the blade aside with his own. Abbot Monreale started up and dumped the table over on the gaptoothed Losimon as he stumbled and turned for another strike.

With a wild lunge, Master Beneforte caught his saltcellar as it arced glittering through the air, and bundled his cloak about it. "Now, Fiametta! For the door!"

Fiametta yanked convulsively at her skirt, pinned under the edge of the heavy table. "Papa, help!"

Duchess Letitia clutched her daughter and halfjumped, half-fell over the back of the platform into the tapestries. Uri, leaping up, grabbed Ascanio and shoved him toward Abbot Monreale. "Get the boy out!" he gasped. The abbot swirled his red robe around the terrified child, and parried a bravo's sword thrust with his crozier, followed up quite automatically with a powerful and well-aimed kick to the man's crotch.

"Saint Jerome! To me!" Monreale bellowed. His prior and brawny secretary sped to his aid. Another bravo's descent on Ascanio was met with an odd motion of the abbot's staff; the man's face grew abruptly blank, and he wandered off over the side of the dais, sword drooping. He was struck down by one of Montefoglia's guards joining the fray. Master Beneforte, halfway to the door, heard Fiametta's cries and started back.

Uri, guarding the group now growing about the abbot and Ascanio, locked in murderous swordplay with Ferrante's gap-toothed lieutenant. Uri's breath bubbled strangely. In a thrust-and-parry, Uri kicked aside Lord Ferrante's footstool-chest over the edge of the dais. It bounced on its side and spilled open. It was packed with rock salt, which cascaded across Fiametta's feet.

Pickled in the salt curled the shrivelled corpse of a newborn infant. Fiametta screamed, and ripped her caught skirt out from under the table in her recoil. Uri glanced aside, his eyes widening; Ferrante's lieutenant lunged and thrust his sword through Uri's new doublet. Fiametta could see five inches of blade sliding out of the captain's back. The gap-toothed man turned the blade, put his foot to Uri's torso, and yanked it back out with a dreadful sucking sound. Blood gushed from both wounds, front and back. The captain fell. Fiametta wailed, stooped, and flung a heavy platter at the Losimon lieutenant with all her strength. Master

Beneforte grabbed Fiametta's arm and dragged her toward the exit.

The doorway was clotted with struggling men. Master Beneforte fell back, dismayed. He shoved the bundled cloak containing the saltcellar into Fiametta's shaking hands and snarled, "Don't drop it! And stay on my heels this time, damn it!" He snatched up a bottle from one of the tables, and drew his own showy dagger with its jewelled hilt. The mirror-polished blade, never yet used, flashed in the sun.

Master Beneforte tried again to force his way through the garden's only exit. A knot of men exploded outward as more of Montefoglia's guards charged through. Master Beneforte darted forward into the brief breach. Just inside, one of Ferrante's men cut at him. Yelling, he parried, and splashed the contents of the little jug into the man's face. The Losimon yowled and swiped at his eyes with his free hand, Master Beneforte knocked his sword aside, and they were through.

"Magic?" gulped Fiametta.

"Vinegar," snapped Master Beneforte.

There was another vicious struggle going on at the despised marble staircase. Master Beneforte practically tossed Fiametta over the balustrade, and vaulted after her. They pelted across the courtyard toward the tower-flanked gate, now being hotly contested by Ferrante's men and Montefoglia's.

Lord Ferrante was there in person, gesturing with a sword and shouting encouragement. "Hold the gate, and we'll have the rest at our will! Hold!" Almost casually, his sword licked out and tore open the throat of an attacking soldier in Montefoglia's livery. The man had ribbons in Ferrante's colors tied to the flower-and-bee badge of his cap in honor of the day's festivities, and they bounced wildly as he fell.

"Christ Jesus, it's going to be a massacre," Master Beneforte groaned.

Lord Ferrante turned and saw Master Beneforte. He stepped back a pace, his eyes narrowing, then raised his right fist with the silver ring face-out. Master Beneforte growled "Stupid!" in his throat, and raised his own hand in a peculiar rapid wave, fingers moving very precisely. Fiametta's belly wrenched with the tilted gut-feel of clashing magics. There was no subtlety in this. The silver ring began to glow, then suddenly emitted a brilliant flash and an earsplitting crack.

Lord Ferrante, not Master Beneforte, screamed, dropped his sword, and clutched his right hand with his left. A distinct odor of burnt meat wafted beneath another sharp tang Fiametta could not identify.

"Kill them!" Lord Ferrante roared, stamping his boots in agony, but the soldier facing Master Beneforte gave way in confused panic. Master Beneforte skipped backward a few paces, dagger brandished, as Fiametta picked up speed, then they both ran from the castle gate as hard as they could.

At the bottom of the hill Fiametta glanced back. Lord Ferrante was pointing her way, holding up a purse, and yelling something; a pair of bravos sped out the gate. As the houses grew more crowded, Master Beneforte darted between two shops and into an alley, then dodged into another alley. They fought through someone's laundry hung out to dry, and vaulted a sleeping dog. Fiametta was gasping for air; it felt like someone had stuck a dagger into her side, so sharp was the pain of her laboring lungs and banquet-laden stomach.

"Stop, Fiametta. . . ."

They had come to the edge of the buildings, by the shoreline of the lake. Master Beneforte sagged against a wall of dun brick. He, too, was gasping, his head bent to one side. His right hand kneaded his belly, just below his chest, as if to push back pain. When he looked up his face was not flushed, as Fiametta's was, but of a gray pallor, sheened with sweat. "I should not . . . have gorged so well," he blurted. "Even at the Duke's expense." And, after another moment, in a strange, small voice, "I can't run any more." His knees buckled.

MERCEDES LACKEY

The Hottest Fantasy Writer Today!

URBAN FANTASY

Knight of Ghosts and Shadows with Ellen Guon

Elves in L.A.? It would explain a lot, wouldn't it? Eric Banyon is a musician with a lot of talent but very little ambition—and his lady just left him lovelorn in a deserted corner of the Renaissance Fairegrounds, singing the blues and playing his flute. He couldn't have known the desperate sadness of his music would free Korendil, a young elven noble, from the magical prison he has been languishing in for centuries. Eric really needed a good cause to get his life in gear—now he's got one. With Korendil he must raise an army to fight against the evil lord who seeks to conquer all of California. And Eric's music will show the way....

Summoned to Tourney with Ellen Guon

Elves in San Francisco? Where else would an elf go when L.A. got too hot? All is well there with our elf-lord, his human companion and the mage who brought them all together—until it turns out that San Francisco is doomed to fall off the face of the continent. Doomed that is, unless our mage can summon the Nightflyers, the soul-devouring shadow creatures from the dreaming world—creatures no one on Earth could possibly control....

Born to Run with Larry Dixon

There are elves out there. And more are coming. But even elves need money to survive in the "real" world. The good elves in South Carolina, intrigued by the thrills of stock car racing, are manufacturing new, light-weight engines (with, incidentally, very little "cold" iron); the bad elves run a kiddie-porn and snuff-film ring, with occasional forays into drugs. *Children in Peril—Elves to the Rescue.* (Part of the SERRAted Edge series.)

HIGH FANTASY

Bardic Voices: The Lark & The Wren

Rune could be one of the greatest bards of her world, but the daughter of a tavern wench can't get much in the way of formal training. So one night she goes up to play for the Ghost of Skull Hill. She'll either fiddle till dawn to prove her skill as a bard—or die trying. . . .

Also by Mercedes Lackey:

Reap the Whirlwind with C.J. Cherryh
Part of the Sword of Knowledge series.

Castle of Deception with Josepha Sherman
Based on the bestselling computer game, *The Bard's Tale.*

The Ship Who Searched with Anne McCaffrey
The Ship Who Sang is not alone!

Wheels of Fire with Mark Shepherd
Book II of the SERRAted Edge series.

HOW TO IMPROVE
SCIENCE FICTION

Want to improve SF? Want to make sure you always have a good selection of SF to choose from? Then do the thing that has made SF great from the very beginning—talk about SF. Communicate with those who make it happen. Tell your bookstore when you like a book. If you can't find something you want, let the manager know. But money speaks louder than mere words—so *order* the book from the bookstore, special. Tell your friends about good books. Encourage *them* to special order the good ones. A special order is worth a thousand words. If you can prove to your bookstore that there's a market for what you like, they'll probably start to cater to it. And that means better SF in your neighborhood.

Tell 'Em What You Want

We, the publishers, want to know what you want more of—and if you can't get it. But the people who order the books—they need to know first. So, before you buy a book directly from the publisher, talk to your bookstore; don't be shy. It doesn't matter if it's a chain bookstore or a specialty shop, or something in between—all businesses need to know what their customers like. Tell them: and the state of SF in your community is sure to improve.

And Get a Free Poster!

To encourage your feedback: A free poster to the first 100 readers who send us a list of their 5 best SF reads in the last year, and their 5 worst.

Write to: Baen Books, Dept. FP, P.O. Box 1403, Riverdale, NY 10471. And thanks!

Name:_____

Address:_____

Best Reads	Worst Reads
1)	1)
2)	2)
3)	3)
4)	4)
5)	5)